RETURN TO THE CITY OF GHOSTS

JULIAN SEDGWICK

Hodder
Children's
Books

HODDER CHILDREN'S BOOKS

First published in Great Britain in 2018
by Hodder and Stoughton

1 3 5 7 9 10 8 6 4 2

Text copyright © Julian Sedgwick, 2018

The moral right of the author has been asserted.

A CIP catalogue record for this book is available from the British Library.

ISBN 978 1 444 92451 0

Typeset in Garamond by Avon DataSet Ltd, Bidford-on-Avon, Warwickshire

Printed and bound in Great Britain by Clays Ltd, St Ives plc

MIX
Paper from
responsible sources
FSC® C104740

The paper and board used in this book are made from wood from
responsible sources.

Hodder Children's Books
An imprint of Hachette Children's Group
Part of Hodder and Stoughton
Carmelite House,
50 Victorian Embankment,
London, EC4Y 0DZ

An Hachette UK Company
www.hachette.co.uk

www.hachettechildrens.co.uk

RETURN TO THE CITY OF GHOSTS

OR THE PALE REVENANT

For Pam Bradshaw,
a wise woman

Contents

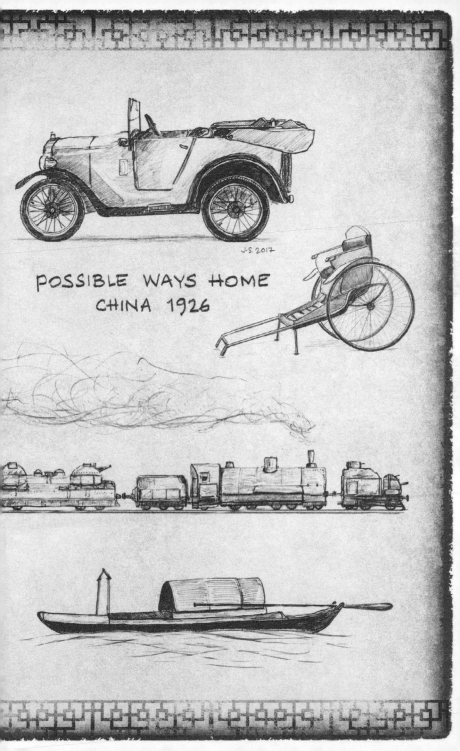

POSSIBLE WAYS HOME
CHINA 1926

J.S. 2017

1926
YANGTZE RIVER

揚子江

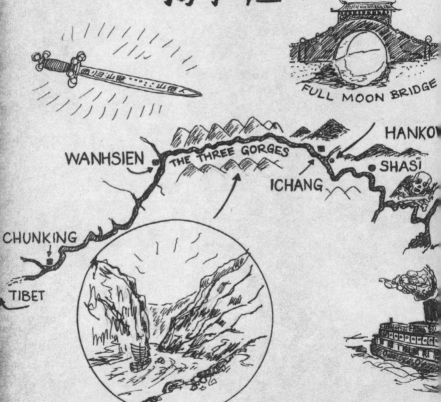

FULL MOON BRIDGE

HANKOW

SHASI

WANHSIEN

THE THREE GORGES

ICHANG

CHUNKING

TIBET

EAST
CHINA
SEA

CHENKIANG

NANKING

SHANGHAI-NANKING LINE

PURPLE
MOUNTAIN

SHANGHAI

PEACH BLOSSOM
VILLAGE

KIUKIANG

PO YANG
LAKE

ANGSHA

HAITVN

0   150   300   450
MILES

1988

At this point, if the ending of Ruby Harkner's adventure is to make any sense, I need to bring myself into the story.

And to leap forward sixty years to a numbingly cold winter day in Shanghai.

I needn't say much about me. This is Ruby's story not mine. But to set the scene, I was still a young student then, and in China to study the language. A year earlier my dad had died unexpectedly, and, rocked by the loss, I had come to Shanghai – in a way – to escape ghosts.

But it's not always that easy . . .

That day I had dodged my language class and drifted to the Bund to stare at the tugs and barges on the river. It seemed like everything was shivering in the cold:

people, birds, boats – even the water. The grand old buildings lining the bank were hazed in mist and pollution, making the whole scene look like a black and white photograph of the city from its glory days of the late 1920s and 30s.

To my left an old lady was leaning against the railing. Apart from us students there were few Westerners in the city then, so I was surprised when she turned and called through the gloom in perfect English.

'Do you believe in ghosts, young man?'

'I'm sorry?'

She approached me, footsteps crisp on the pavement, and as she got closer I saw she was a 'foreign guest' like me.

'Well? Do you?'

'I don't really know,' I stammered. 'I've not really thought about it.'

But I had. Just a month earlier I had seen my supposedly dead father walk past the window of our family home. The experience had shaken me, and I didn't want to get into it with a stranger.

The lady had reached me now, her face pale in the cold afternoon light, hair even whiter where it billowed over arched eyebrows.

'Sometimes it's best not to think *too* much,' she declared firmly.

She held out her hand – slim, ageing – and when I took it in mine I was surprised by the strength in her grip.

'My name's Harkner. Ruby Harkner. I was supposed to be meeting a friend here. Got held up apparently. Fancy sharing dinner with a lonely old lady?'

I hesitated, but she gripped my arm suddenly, and leaned closer: 'I can tell you stories you just wouldn't *believe* about this place! The old days!'

Shanghai's past had always fascinated me, and something in her eyes – determination, vitality – had me hooked already.

'Well, if you're sure,' I said. 'I'm just killing time really.'

'Oh, for heaven's sake don't do *that*, young man. The main thing is to live. Every. Single. Moment.'

She dropped my hand and glanced away at the river.

'Would you like to hear a ghost story? A real one?'

Then looking back at me sharply, she added: 'You've had your own, I can see that.'

Stunned, I nodded, as the cold wind buffeted my skin.

That evening we sat in the restaurant of a once grand hotel. Striplights stuttered over the long bar, reflected in huge mirrors fogged with age. Every now and then a large rat scurried along the half-empty shelves.

Oblivious, my new friend leaned forward. 'Did you know, when they buried coffins here they used to fill them with lead weights so they didn't drift under the earth? Imagine that!'

Her focus shifted, to somewhere just over my left shoulder, as if recognising someone or something. Out of nowhere a shiver jarred my spine, and my head turned to see who or what had drawn her attention.

Nothing but the empty dance floor and an ancient, immobile barman beyond. I shook the sensation away and looked back at her. 'So you used to live here—'

'I was *born* here,' she sighed. 'I saw this city's best. And worst.'

'You mentioned a ghost story?'

She gazed deep into my eyes. Something was changing in her own, as if a younger woman, much younger, was staring out from her lined face. Was that a tear forming in her eye, reflecting the flickering lights?

'It's a ghost story all right. But it's a love story too. It's *my* story. And the little bits I didn't witness directly I heard about later, so I can put it all together now and make it flow. Like a river.' She smiled. 'The thing about ghosts is sometimes we create our own. And sometimes they find us, no matter what we do.'

Another shiver chased through me, but before I could respond the old lady cleared her throat . . .

. . . and began to tell me of a young girl, who loved her city more than anywhere on earth . . .

. . . who grew up acting out brave adventures amongst the gangsters and pleasure palaces . . .

. . . who started to see ghosts when her little brother died, and found an Almanac to help her hunt those ghosts . . .

. . . who fell in love with a Chinese boy.

A story of how that boy's little sister was kidnapped by gangsters and carried into the Interior of China, and of how she and the boy she loved risked everything to travel a thousand miles up the Yangtze river, and fought bandits and rode a steamship into the fearsome rapids of the Three Gorges.

Of how the boat was ripped apart – and overwhelmed, and lost.

I sat there entranced.

At first believing some parts and not believing others – but quickly giving up on any judgement and just letting the current carry me along. The restaurant faded, leaving me with just the old lady's lively eyes, her liver-spotted hands weaving their story.

Three hours passed in a flash.

'And what then?' I whispered as my companion paused after the wrecking of the steamship *Haitun* in the icy water of the Gorges, her near drowning.

'And then I found myself somewhere very strange indeed. I'd heard the stories all my life, read about it in the book – the Almanac – that we found. And now, there I was. In the Otherworld.' She looked up as if seeing it all again. 'Towering black cliffs, a strange green glow hovering over everything, the shadows of shadows . . . I knew I was there as soon as Lao Jin pulled me from the water. And I knew that living people often didn't make it back to what my dad used to call the *Real Blasted World*.'

She glanced at her watch.

'Look. It's past ten. Come back tomorrow night. You might as well hear how my story ends.'

And the next evening, in the same seats, she told me this . . .

第一章

ON THE SHORE
1926

The rapids are thunder in her ears.

Almost lost in the water she can just make out two voices: Lao Jin's, steadily calling her name, and another – a strange, half-choked one – yelling, 'Charlie! Charlieeeee!' over and over again.

It takes a long moment for Ruby to realise that the second is her own. She coughs up a great bubble of water, and sees Jin leaning over her.

Can it *really* be him? He *looks* solid enough, alive, the fabric of his jacket soaked and heavy as she reaches for him. In his eyes that familiar quicksilver is as vital as it ever was. Not dead at all . . .

'Ruby! Ru-by!' he calls again. '*You* did it. You're in the Otherworld.'

She blinks away the cold water, looking around frantically. The cliffs of the Gorge loom on either side, huge walls of vertical rock and shadow. They seem even higher, even more threatening than they did from the boat, and that awful green light is flickering over everything.

'The Otherworld?' she whispers – but she knows at once it's true.

Jin nods. 'You've been at the border for days now. And sometimes you had one foot in the Otherworld. But now you have arrived with both feet! Not many get this far – you did it because you were brave enough, Ruby. And strong enough. I've been with you all along, as best I could. Keeping my eye on you and Charlie.'

Charlie!

Where is he? What's happened to Charlie . . . ?

She staggers to her feet and turns back to the river, hoping against hope to see the *Haitun* still floating there and Charlie standing on deck. Or see him wading out of the shallows, or collapsed on the shore.

But there's no boat, no figures in sight at all. Just the rapids hammering away, the smoke from the trackers' fires, that strange light saturating everything.

'Charlie's in the water!' she gasps. 'We – we've got to save him . . .'

But Jin is already striding away towards the cliff. 'We can't help him,' he growls. 'Not right now.'

'Of course we can,' Ruby shouts, stumbling over the rocks. 'We've got to help him. He can't swim, for God's sake! I'm going to look for him!'

Jin stops, and turns to wave the battered old Fedora hat at her. 'I'll explain later, Ruby. We haven't much time if we want to rescue Fei.'

'But Charlie—'

'. . . was swept away by the river. The *Haitun* – what's left of her at any rate – is wrecked a few hundred paces downstream. And Charlie will have been carried a long way on the current, miles and miles already.'

'Then we've got to look for him—'

Jin grabs her firmly by the arm. 'Ruby, you have to trust me. Charlie is alive and you will find him. But not now. Time here in the Otherworld flows slower than time on the real river. You crossed the Frontier and he's on the other side. Already hours, days have passed there. But we can rescue Fei if we're quick.'

Ruby looks back helplessly to the pounding rapids. In the *Strange Tales* there were all those stories of people walking out of villages, crossing over to other worlds, and then coming back years later, still young. How she loved them – but the reality is far, far scarier. She coughs again, groggy from the half drowning, but determined to focus. 'But how do you know Charlie's alive?'

'I saw some of it from the bank. I was struggling to keep up.'

'But even if you saw him in the water, how do you know he didn't drown in the end?'

'Look down at your hand, my dear girl. Look at it.'

She stares at Jin. His voice sounds weird – maybe it's just the water in her ears, but now his face seems to be doing something odd too. In the blurred light his features look like they're shifting. And as they shift they remind her of someone else, someone familiar.

'Your face . . .' she whispers. 'You—'

'Just look at your hand.'

Confused, she glances down and sees a thin, steady pulse of red snaking round her little finger and away. The thread of destiny! It's visible again, glowing in the half-light, running back towards the water across the rocks and then disappearing from sight downstream. Instinctively she reaches for it – but feels nothing.

'Don't worry,' Jin says. 'It's there. And Charlie's at the other end. And as long as he is alive you'll see the thread now and then. Or feel it.'

'So we should follow it!'

'No,' Jin says, his voice fiercer. 'I told you – Charlie is the other side. And that crossing point has closed now. We'll have to find you another way back.'

She gazes at the thread, biting her lip hard.

'But Fei is here? With Moonface.'

Lao Jin nods. 'And we – you and I – can beat him tonight, while my strength is somewhat refreshed.'

'But how can you be here, Jin?' she splutters. 'You died. Andrei shot you. I saw it. Are you a ghost?'

He waves his hand in the air.

'Not dead,' Jin says. 'And not a ghost.'

In the ghastly light of the Gorge everything is slippery, blurry. Lao Jin keeps looking at her steadily, holding her gaze . . .

. . . and as she watches, his features change, his face sharpening, elongating, ears pointing. The grey stubble on his jaw lengthens, gets thicker, and the pins and needles feeling shoots all over her. Ruby blinks and the vision is gone, and it's just Lao Jin's quizzical face peering at her again.

'You're the fox! The *huli jing*, aren't you?'

Jin smiles.

He rummages in his pocket and pulls out a small blue bottle.

'Remember this?'

Ruby's mouth drops open. 'The spirit bottle. The one we chucked down the well.'

Lao Jin gives her a wink. 'Come on, we've got a thousand steps to climb. A battle to fight.'

Ruby looks back at the river and then plants her

feet. 'No. I can't go on – unless you answer me straight.'

'You can have one more question, Ruby. Just one – and then we've got to go.' Jin glances away at the heights above, as if listening for something. On the breeze comes that faint whistling sound again, the one Marlais said the trackers made to distract dragons in the water.

'One question,' he repeats.

'I know from the Almanac that foxes can shapeshift – but are you a man who changes into a fox. Or a fox who changes into a man. I mean, *what* are you? I need to know.'

'Who do you think I am?'

'At first I thought you were a watchman. Then a Communist. Then a Taoist magician or priest or something. And now . . . some kind of fox spirit.'

The moon crests the opposite cliff, painting Jin's features silver.

'We first met when I was rather poorly and stuck in your world. I was starving and someone laid out some bruised peaches for me. Very kind – but what do you know,' he smiles, 'seems like it was a trap. And they caught me and stuffed me in a bottle and chucked me down the old well . . .'

Everything makes sense now: the way Jin seemed to materialise and disappear, to know what was happening before it happened. The way he fought in Shanghai. All that business with the bottle and how he'd laughed at them.

'It was you all along,' she sighs. 'Scaring us, you were *playing* with us—'

'Not playing, Ruby. Keeping watch, helping you. My *ch'i* was almost exhausted because I was too far from home. And after I was "killed" it was very hard for me to take any kind of form at all. Just a little chance now and then: through images of foxes it's easier. Maybe a cigarette packet. A picture on a wall . . .'

'. . . the foxhunting pictures at the consulate,' Ruby gasps. 'And on the biscuit van, were you the cartoon fox too?'

Jin nods, and points at her shoulder. 'Show me your bruises.'

She pulls off the wet cardigan, tugs up the right sleeve of her dress to reveal the injury. Three fading purple welts still darken her skin there. Gently, Jin moves his hand to cover them, his fingers exactly matching the wounds.

'That van,' Ruby says. 'It was you who saved me.' Her mind races on, and then a chill flows through her. She takes a deep breath, remembering the terrible image of the huge fox goring the *jiang shi* vampires.

13

'And was it you that night in the graveyard on the hill?'

'I said one question. You've had more than that!'

Jin gazes at her. Now she looks closer at his face she can see the lines around his eyes are carved deeper, his cheeks hollowed.

'And – are you OK now?' Ruby says. 'You look tired . . .'

Jin cracks a smile. 'I *was* shot you know, Ruby. Tends to age a body.'

The horrible moment plays in her mind again: when Jin seemed to surrender, to drop his hands and stand still as if giving Andrei every chance to hit the target.

'Why did you let him shoot you?'

'Battle strategy. You give ground unexpectedly to the enemy and it wrong-foots them. And it gave me what you might call a short cut home!'

She swallows hard. 'Oh God. My legs are like jelly.'

'I'm on home soil now, I can spare some *ch'i.*'

Jin raises his hands and turns the palms to face each other. It only takes a few deep breaths and already a fuzzy light is building as he pulses them together, apart, together, apart. The light strengthens, thickening around his powerful fingers, and Ruby watches spellbound as he builds the energy for two more long breaths. Then he reaches towards her. Again the image

14

comes of the fully transformed fox on the bone hill, the wild fury in his eyes, and instinctively she shrinks back from his touch.

'I'm just the same old Jin,' he laughs, and the familiar sound reassures her. He places his hands on her shoulders and she feels the *ch'i* wash down her arms, up into her head through her chest.

Warmth and energy spread throughout her body. Her shoulders ease and a tingling starts to build in her fingers and hands and legs. The strength seems to well back up from there, clearing her vision so that the Gorge walls become pin sharp, unblocking her ears so that she can hear each individual rock as it moves restlessly on the riverbed.

'Better?' Jin murmurs as he lowers his arms.

Ruby nods. 'Better.'

'I hope so. I need your help as much as Fei does. Moonface has been after one piece of prey more important to him than your friend, or you – or even your foolish old dad.'

She remembers how Charlie said Moonface's men took real delight in mocking Jin's 'dead' body. 'He's after you, isn't he?'

'He's been trying to defeat *me* for years and years, that old fox.'

'So he's a *huli jing* too.'

'The very worst kind.'

Ruby gazes up at the cliffs. 'And, after that – after we beat him – we'll look for Charlie. Promise.'

'I like your optimism,' Jin laughs, and then takes the battered old Fedora and plonks it firmly on top of Ruby's damp hair. 'It's a promise. I found the hat – but I'm giving it to you for good. It suits you.'

She glances down again at her hands. The thinnest, faintest trace of the red thread is still just visible.

'So. Are you ready, Shanghai Ruby?'

'I'm ready.'

第二章

FOX MUSIC

They start to climb the rocky stairway.

And climb.

And climb.

Steps are cut roughly into the walls of the Gorge, steep flights of twenty, thirty or more, zigzagging far above them into the night. Every now and then a ledge is hacked perilously from the rock, and after half an hour of hard going Ruby pauses on one of them briefly to get her breath. The voice of the rapids still reaches up to her, funnelled by the walls, but when she glances down again the river looks very small already. Even from this lofty vantage point there's no sign of the *Haitun* or its wreckage. She scans her little finger again. Is that the thread still there – a faintest hint of red tied at its base?

It's faded to almost nothing. Maybe Charlie's in

trouble? Worse.

She glances at Jin, but as if reading her mind he shakes his head. 'It's like a radio signal,' he murmurs. 'Sometimes you're in range, and sometimes reception is bad. As long as you see it now and then he's there. Somewhere. Now let's move.'

The drop grows bigger and bigger beneath her feet, the stairs more treacherous, some of them no more than a few inches wide, hard-won from the rock face. Ruby peers downriver one more time. It feels like she's walking away from Charlie, abandoning him. She reaches out to grab a handhold, steadying herself over the void. But I've got to trust Jin, she thinks. What else can I do?

He's waiting for her on the next shelf, his eyes searching hers.

'Still OK?'

She nods.

'Listen then, Ruby! Listen!'

Again his features seem to shift in the murky green light. It's as though his form isn't fixed properly, and bits of fox keep coming in and out of focus.

'Can you hear?'

Ruby closes her eyes and tries to shut out the torrent boiling below, her hammering heartbeat.

Something else just audible on the edge of her

hearing now: thin notes of Chinese music – flutes and two-stringed fiddles – and the crashing of a cymbal beaten hard. It's coming from far above, drifting down to them on the rocky stair. The tune is wild, as wild as the water below.

'What is it?'

'A hired band, playing for a special event,' Jin whispers.

'What kind of event?'

'You'll see. Can you hear a voice, amongst all the racket?'

She cups her ear with her hand. 'No. Not really . . . '

Jin smiles. 'Well, a fox's hearing is always better than a human's! I'll tell you what I can hear: a high voice, shouting, *Take your stupid, filthy hands away . . . don't you dare, you stinking baboon . . .*'

'It sounds like Fei! What's happening, Jin?'

'Moonface has spirited her across the Frontier for two reasons. First he wants to drain her of her youth and vitality and take it all for himself. She's so young and full of unused *ch'i*—'

'And secondly?'

'And secondly she's the bait to lure *me* here, Ruby. Moonface plans to defeat me for good, boost his power, and then return to Shanghai and lord it over the whole city – stronger than ever!'

'But then we're walking into a trap.'

'I think we can beat him tonight.'

'You *think* we can? What will happen to Fei if we don't?'

'She'll be trapped here for ever. A husk of her former self.'

'Then we have to attack now,' Ruby says, 'whatever the risk.'

'That's the spirit.'

Ruby bites her lip. 'I just *wish* I had the sword.'

'You don't need it,' Jin growls, his voice like he has gravel in his throat. 'It was just a prop really. Let your *ch'i* flow and trust your body completely. And keep hold of this.'

He thrusts the spirit bottle into her hands. Two very complex Chinese characters have been brushed onto yellow paper and glued to the glass since she last held it all those weeks ago in the temple.

'But if the bottle didn't hold *you* then—' She turns back to Jin and her words stop in her mouth.

Her friend is transforming before her eyes, shifting into that half fox, half man she first saw in White Cloud, his arms lengthening from the sleeves of his jacket, fur growing on his face. Still, bizarrely, she can see the resemblance to Jin, even as he becomes more *huli jing* than human, his teeth sharpening in the elongating snout, a wild light growing in his eyes. It should be terrifying, it *would* be terrifying, if somehow that same quicksilver wasn't still shining there.

Ruby's heart is thumping madly now, and Fox Jin holds her gaze, and then – strangely, wonderfully – he winks at her. Despite the weirdness of the moment Ruby feels herself smiling back – and then Jin's away, turning and bounding up the moonlit stairway, taking the steps three at a time.

She grips the bottle and hurries after him as fast as she can, the river dropping further and further below her soft Chinese shoes.

Nothing has prepared her for the awful vertigo that the top of the stairway brings, not even poor old Marlais' words about the horrifying climb. She keeps her eyes focused upwards now, watching Jin as he bounds on ahead.

On the last narrow ledge, just a few dozen yards before the top, Ruby pauses. She glances down at her hand clutching the bottle, and – yes, it's there again! – the faintest hint of red coiled at the base of her finger, tumbling off the rocky ledge and looping away downriver.

The vast rapid of the Grinder is just a trembling white line now.

I'm coming, Charlie, she whispers to the darkness. Hold on, I'm coming as soon as we've rescued Fei.

The last flight of steps is so steep, so narrow, that she has to use her hands to climb. A small sapling growing out of a cleft gives a good hold and she grips it, looking up again. Even the fox spirit is struggling, hands and feet scrabbling, spinning loose grit that rains down on her hat. The eerie music from above is distinctly louder now, with laughter and shouting merged into it. Desperately hoping it won't give, Ruby pulls on the sapling, and as she does so a scream comes ripping across the Gorge. It's high-pitched, but definitely human.

Oh God, maybe we're too late, she thinks, climbing faster, maybe something awful is happening already.

The final stretch of rock is skin-smooth – no more stairs now, just a dodgy-looking bamboo ladder lashed to invisible anchors, and the fox already rattling up it.

Mei wenti, mei wenti, she whispers to herself. No problem.

She tucks the bottle carefully into her cardigan pocket, grips the bamboo with both hands and climbs, focusing on each hold, the rock inches in front of her nose.

Her gooseflesh is prickling even harder now.

Something's coming, something awful. She glances up, and there's nobody to be seen, not a trace of Jin. Just emptiness and pale wild cloud whisking over the peak. A brief panic grabs at her – has he fallen? Breathlessly she scrambles the last few rungs, and clambers up and onto a kind of platform hacked from the summit of the cliff.

With relief she sees Fox Jin stalking away to the far side of the lookout post or whatever it is. His tail has grown out from his baggy black trousers, and it's beating the ground impatiently as he strides to a slope of scree and broken rock that climbs a few dozen paces further into the night. Ruby follows, scrabbling on hands and knees to the very crest of the ridge. Jin turns to look at her as she joins him, big red tongue flicking his sharp teeth, and nods down into the shallow valley ahead of them.

An ugly fortress crouches there, crudely built from boulders and rammed earth. Two watchtowers guard a gate on the nearside, another high tower on the far looking out across the rolling, wild landscape beyond. Along the torch-lit wall, you can make out thin, wraith-like sentries. Shadow Warriors, they must be! Two – no, three – of them patrolling the parapet, rifles slung over their shoulders. Even at this distance you can make out the glow of their eyes as they turn to scour the land. Ruby's heart is still banging away from the climb, but it pumps yet harder at the sight.

I've beaten them before, she thinks. But there'll be more than those few inside presumably, and – whatever Jin said – I had the spirit sword to help me last time.

She pulls her gaze from the figures on the wall. To the left of the main compound a cluster of stone buildings face a cleared area where a huge bonfire is blazing, chucking thick smoke up into the night. Two dozen or more dark figures – stockier than the Warriors – are milling around the flames casting long shadows. Green Hand men. Flesh and blood? Or spirits? It's hard to tell from here. Some are wearing traditional gowns, some in Western suits and hats, all of them drinking, laughing, slapping each other on the backs. Every now and then a string of firecrackers detonates, echoing off the rocks like machine gunfire. And still the wild music plays and plays.

Fox Jin taps her arm and points, and Ruby edges further forward to get a better view. The crowd is turning towards the door of the main building. Still she can't see who's making the music, but suddenly it gets louder still, and five musicians emerge, their cymbals and drum and two-stringed fiddles reaching a caterwauling crescendo. The band moves fast, walking slightly stooped, their heads twitching this way and that – and in the flickering bonfire light she sees the red swish of a tail behind one of them. Then another. And another . . .

They're all fox spirits! A *huli jing* band playing a familiar tune, but in a wild and foxy way, like something from straight out of the *Strange Tales* . . .

. . . and following the band comes an elaborate sedan chair carried by four more menacing black fox spirits. The chair's canopy is draped in white cloth, bells jingling and mirrors flashing shards of firelight across the compound.

And now at last Ruby recognises the tune. It's a wedding song: the whole thing is just like the marriage processions she's seen in the old Chinese City – young girls on their way to be married, often against their will, the sedan covered in crimson cloth, the red bride a hidden jewel inside.

But this one is draped with white.

White is the colour of death and funerals. And this chair must be carrying Fei to be married to Moonface. That's what Jin meant about a special event.

As the sedan sways into the shuffling crowd the bonfire flares, and Ruby sees that each and every one of them is a *huli jing*.

第三章

THE BATTLE OF HELL'S THROAT

Fox Jin gives a loud, sharp bark. And then he's away, bounding full speed down the scree towards Moonface's fortress, a silvery-red streak in the pale moonlight. For a half second Ruby watches him go, thrilled – despite everything – by his speed and power. In this moment it looks like nothing can stop him, and none of the guards on the wall have seen his attack yet. Another firecracker volley rips the night air – and Ruby takes off after him, spirit bottle clamped in her right hand, holding the Fedora with the left, her soft shoes pounding the loose ground.

Mei wenti, mei—

A detonation cuts her words of self-encouragement in half. Not a firework this time, but a gunshot. She sees the muzzle flash on the wall ahead, a puff of dust where the bullet strikes the earth halfway between her and Jin.

No going back now, she thinks. They've seen us. And Jin needs me. As she runs she tries desperately to recall what the Almanac said about the levels of fox spirit and revenants. There was talk of silver foxes – that *must* be Jin and he must be stronger than most of the wedding-guest foxes. But was that the strongest type? What about the Green Hand boss, maybe he's something worse? Maybe he's a pale revenant? They sounded very powerful – and his moony face fits the name.

There's a bell clanging in the compound now, and the music stumbles to a halt as shouts ring out across the desolate landscape. Another salvo of gunfire fizzes the ground at Jin's paws. She keeps her eyes fixed on him, terrified he will fall, mortally wounded for real this time, leaving her all alone. But Andrei's bullet didn't kill him, she thinks, so how can these? Maybe it's different here in the Otherworld . . .

As she runs down towards the gate the fortress wall looms higher, about to block her view of the courtyard. But at the last moment she sees the sedan chair lurch as one of the bearers loses his grip, and suddenly it's down. A small figure rolls from the canopy, ripping a white bridal hat from her head and sending black pigtails flying.

'Fei!' Ruby screams. 'Fei, it's me!'

But in the growing din her friend can't hear. Fei staggers to her feet and goes racing away to the far side of the courtyard – and is then lost to sight. More gunfire blasts from the wall, but Jin doesn't even seem to notice. With a roar he covers the remaining ground in four huge strides and kicks right through the heavy gate, splintering it to pieces.

'Wait! Wait for me!' Ruby screams.

By the time she has clambered through the remains of the gateway, Jin is already wading into a gaggle of fox spirits, batting one away with the flick of a hand, sending another flying through the air with a powerful swish of his tail. The fox musicians, seeing Jin's furious assault, drop their instruments and flee for a door in the far side of the compound.

Ruby catches sight of Fei again, still running hard – but away from her, pursued by two of the larger black foxes.

'Fei!' she yells again at the top of her lungs. 'This way!'

From the corner of her eye she spots something coming at her from the right: a spectral figure, almost the same shade and colour as the night air itself, eyes glowing in its head. A Warrior. Its pistol swings to point at her heart.

'Die,' it hisses. 'Die, filthy human.'

But there is no fear now, just a sudden surge of strength from Ruby's core. Time seems to slow around her – just like that day at the Café Renard when she saw Dad with the Green Hand and fought with the French woman – her mind working so fast she sees and hears every moment . . .

. . . she sees the long, bony finger of the Warrior squeeze the trigger . . .

. . . hears the flare of the cartridge and the whoosh as it accelerates down the barrel . . .

. . . and *watches* the bullet's spin as it emerges from the snout of the gun towards her.

So much time to watch the stupid thing coming, and lean back out of the way. The *ch'i* burns in her belly and then moves swiftly up through her right arm, making her wrist and hand feel strong.

. . . and as the bullet comes past, the energy flares on her right hand, and she gives it a swat.

Nothing more to feel than the sting you'd get from a firmly struck tennis ball, and then just a dull metallic sound as the spent cartridge drops to the rocky floor. It rolls to a stop, and the world is silent for a long moment – and then with a rush everything comes back up to speed. The Warrior howls and launches at her, its thin hands grabbing for her throat. She dodges under the creature's grasp, and with every bit of strength in her body shoves it full force in the back, propelling it into the bonfire, its arms flailing. The thing shrieks horribly – and is lost in the billowing black smoke.

'Ruby! Ruby! Help me!'

Fei's voice cuts through the confusion. She's seen Ruby, and is ducking and weaving frantically as her pursuers try to grab her. Blinking in the smoke, Ruby looks round for Jin and sees him battling two more Warriors, his snout turning this way and that, biting furiously. And then, through the blur of the flame, she sees another figure: a heavy, burly shape stalking towards them, his large round head glowing in the light, pockmarked features creasing in rage. He shrugs the old fur coat from his shoulders, and roars a single word.

'JIN!'

Silence descends instantly. The remaining Shadow Warriors and fox spirits melt back into the shadows, leaving the silver fox standing alone, breathing hard.

Moonface plants his feet. Is it a trick of the light or does he seem to be growing, his heavy shoulders swelling?

Fei shrieks again. 'Ruby! Ruby, he's a horrible fox thing, I—'

One of the foxes wraps a paw around her mouth.

Ruby edges a little closer, transfixed by the sight of the Green Hand boss – but Moonface has eyes for no one else but Jin. Laughter – quiet at first, then louder – bubbles up from inside him, and as that horrible, gurgling sound swells, Moonface swells with it, definitely getting taller, broader, on the verge of some transformation of his own as he takes another step towards Jin.

Do something, Ruby murmurs to herself. Come on, Jin, attack before he changes.

But for the moment all the fight seems to have gone out of her transformed friend. He just stands his ground, tongue lolling from his mouth, looking calm, but exhausted. Maybe it's going to be like with Andrei all over again.

Moonface clears his throat with a growl. 'Jin, you old rascal. I knew you'd come!' He laughs again and throws back his head letting the moon tumble across it. And when his voice comes again it's even louder: 'And you thought you could save this little girl? Defeat me? Well, maybe in Shanghai you might have had a chance, but not here, my old friend. Not here in *my* lair. Not by moonlight.'

And Moonface is really shapeshifting now, his features blurring, changing towards half fox, pure white fur sprouting on his fat face, his long unkempt brush suddenly visible as it sweeps the ground like moonlight.

A pale revenant?

Ruby starts to back away as Moonface advances, his words breaking down into growl and bark, a row of sharp teeth flashing.

He is bigger than Fox Jin now – his face more terrifying, even wilder – and as he suddenly charges forward Jin retreats, taking one, two, three quick steps, his own brush whipping the ground.

What if Jin's beaten? Ruby thinks, desperately. That will be the end of everything. He looks vulnerable now pitted against Moonface . . .

In her sweaty left hand, almost forgotten, she feels the spirit bottle start to tremble and hum. Like it's waking up, charging with some inner energy of its own. Gingerly she takes hold of the stopper with her other hand, takes a breath – and then wills herself forward again.

And as she takes the step, Moonface hurls himself at Jin, mouth snapping for his throat. With a heavy thump the two go sprawling across the floor, locked together, sending the spectators diving for cover. Silver and bright white sparks flash from the fox spirits' tails as they roll close to the fire – and, yes!, somehow Jin comes out on top and takes a heavy swipe at Moonface's hideous head. The transformed gangster blocks, and then strikes upwards, sending Jin sailing a clear ten paces through the air to where he lands heavily on his back. Dark blood is running from a gash on his head, and for an awful moment Ruby thinks he's out cold, or worse. But then he shakes his head slightly, and struggles uncertainly back to his feet. The two remaining Shadow Warriors are advancing on him, but Moonface barks fiercely.

'He's mine!'

The bottle's really buzzing in Ruby's hand, so hard it's difficult to keep a grip. Should I uncork it now? she wonders. Or maybe I've got to wait for the blow, like we did in White Cloud.

Moonface is about to strike again at Jin, whose guard is still down. Ruby steps forward, clutching the stopper, and shouts as loud as she can. 'Hey! You stupid old fat fox. Hey!'

The white *huli jing* hesitates a fraction of a second, eyes blazing in her direction, and then Jin suddenly erupts back into action. He beats down with his tail and leaps high into the air, blocking the moon, his shadow falling across his foe.

Now! Ruby hears Jin's voice in her head. *Now, Ruby!*

She runs forward, stumbling the first step, but then

charging faster, holding up the blue spirit bottle and yelling at the top of her voice.

'Hey, Moonface!'

The spirit turns his head again for a split second – and sees what she's holding. His eyes widen, as if recognising the thing in her hands, and at that precise moment Jin plummets, one paw striking Moonface hard on the head. There's a bang and a flash – like a brilliant bolt of lightning has struck feet away – and Ruby is thrown to the ground. Her vision whites out, but still she keeps hold of the bottle, and as she falls she tugs the stopper free. The thunder rolls and she feels a rush of air over her right hand that gets stronger and stronger until she can actually hear it, like water gushing. In her left, the bottle is getting cold now, rapidly, the whole thing shaking furiously. Got to hold on, she thinks, desperately trying to clear her vision from the flash. The bottle is already so much colder than when they trapped Jin inside it, and still it keeps shaking and shaking, setting her teeth chattering in her head.

Lying on her side, she can think of nothing but the swirl of cold and noise, the deafening roar in her ears that gets louder and louder . . . There's a horrible drawn-out screaming, and then that's cut short and everything is silent save for the ringing in her ears—

And she feels a strong hand take hold of her fingers and guide the stopper firmly down into the bottle's neck.

At last her eyes begin to make out shapes, and she looks up to see Jin – transformed back to the Lao Jin she knows and loves – crouching over her. Blood is trickling from the wound on his temple, and his cheeks look even more hollowed by the effort and pain. But he's smiling. And Fei is standing beside him, hugging herself with both arms, crying and laughing at the same time.

'We got him, Ruby. You got him. Look!'

She taps the spirit bottle. The blue glass is thickly crusted in ice.

'Did you see it? Moonface got sucked into the bottle – and the rest of his foxes legged it. Our fox won!!'

'Fei, thank God you're all right,' Ruby stammers, getting to her feet, still clutching the burning-cold bottle.

'I think I'm all right . . .' Fei says, gazing round her, then uncertainly back at Jin. Her usually bright eyes are red, and she sniffs hard. 'But it's been so awful, Ruby! Just awful! I kept hoping you'd come, but I thought he'd kill me before you got here. And then he said he was going to *marry me*!'

'Here, let me take that before your fingers freeze,'

Jin mutters. He takes the bottle from Ruby's shaking hand and sets it down on the ground, propping it carefully between two rocks. Fei runs to Ruby and hugs her.

'So Mister Jin's a fox?' she whispers fiercely. 'I thought there was something weird about him, right from the start.'

'It's OK, he's on our side.'

Fei holds tight for a moment and then glances up sharply. 'But *where's* Charlie?'

Ruby looks to Jin, hoping he will help her explain – but as she does so she sees him walking slowly away from them. He comes to a standstill, looks up at the faint stars, and then staggers a pace to his left.

And collapses in a heap.

第四章

THE RIVER AGAIN

The moon inches across the Otherworldy sky. Now and then torn clouds block its light and the darkness thickens around them.

No way of knowing how long Jin has been out cold, but it feels like absolutely hours and hours. Ruby leans to his chest now and then to check his heart is still beating, willing him to come back to consciousness, and sit up again. How long does a night last in this place? A day? A month? Maybe the sun doesn't ever rise here. She wracks her brain, trying to pull back details again from the *Strange Tales* or their lost *Almanac of the Other World*, but nothing will come.

Fei is pressing a piece of cloth tight to the wound. She glances over her shoulder at the deserted compound, fighting the shivers that still keep rattling through her.

'I thought I was going mad,' she whispers. 'Fox musicians! And those horrible shadowy things. And Moonface Fox! Jin! It's all real, Ruby. Just like we used to play at – it's *real*. And this place just feels so weird . . .'

'It's because we've crossed the Frontier, Fei, like I told you. The *Haitun* was wrecked, and then I was here. In the Otherworld.'

Fei puffs out her cheeks. 'I just want to go home.' She looks at Ruby intently. 'And wherever we are we've got to find Charlie.'

'I know. We will.' Ruby forces her voice as bright as she can, for Fei's benefit.

'But you didn't see him get out of the river?'

'No. Just briefly when we were under water—'

Fei groans. 'But you know Charlie can't swim! Neither of us can. He'll have drowned for sure.'

'Jin says we'll find him, Fei. He says Charlie is miles away, across the Frontier.'

'Yeah, well now look at him!'

Ruby's gaze slips to Jin, then to the spirit bottle. Every now and then it gives off a strange low hum, as if whatever's inside is straining to force itself back out. If Jin doesn't recover, what then? she thinks. What do we do with it to make it safe? And more importantly how *will* we get back? If we can't we'll have lost Charlie.

Maybe we'll be kind of alive but dead at the same time . . . for ever and ever. Amen.

Fei sits back on her haunches. 'It's been *soooo* awful. Moonface kept leering at me and licking his lips and muttering about my lovely *ch'i*, and I just wanted to run . . . and now you're telling me you've lost Charlie.'

'He's still alive,' Ruby says. 'I can feel it. And I've seen something—'

Jin suddenly gives a mighty gasp and sits upright, one hand clawing at the air and nearly swiping Fei, his eyes blinking for focus.

The relief rushes through Ruby. 'Lao Jin!'

'I'm . . . I'm OK. Just . . . give me . . . a moment.'

'I thought we'd lost you—'

He takes a big gulp of air and winces. 'I think I . . . overdid it a bit. Or Moonface hit me harder than I thought.' His eyes open wider as they seek out the spirit bottle.

'Is he really trapped, Jin?' Ruby says, after a long half minute has passed. 'I mean *you* got out when we caught you.'

Lao Jin clears his throat. 'Beginners make mistakes! I told you that almanac is powerful, but you've got to . . . know what you're doing. I've put the correct characters on the bottle.' He coughs again, then gets unsteadily to his feet. 'It'll hold him for now. A good long *now* I hope. Especially where I'm going to put it. This is his side of the river, his land. On the other side of the Gorge is mine, my birthplace – and I'll put it under a pile of stones there, and write a magic character on each of them. He won't get out for a hundred years. Ow, my head hurts . . .'

'What did Moonface mean about fighting you for centuries?'

'Years ago we were almost friends.' Jin shakes his head. 'But we chose different paths. We've fought each other up and down this old river for years. He got so powerful he could work in the real world, not just making raids from here like most spirits do. And when the times are bad, it's easier for the border to become thin—'

'What about the rest of the Green Hand? Are they all spirits?'

'No. Just Moonface and a dozen or so Warriors who guarded him. Most of them are just stupid blood and bone. Only a handful know Moonface's secret. One Ball Lu for example—'

'You need to get us out of here,' Fei says abruptly. 'We've got to find Charlie—'

Lao Jin holds up his hand. 'I am sure we – or rather you – will find him again. But you're going to have to help him more than that. He's still recovering from the wound he got fighting the hopping vampires—'

'*Jiang shi?*' Fei moans. 'Hopping vampires as well? It just gets worse and worse. I told you they were real, I told you I saw one on the Creek that time.'

Ruby holds up a hand and turns to face Jin. 'What do you mean?'

'Did Charlie look *very* pale after the fight?'

She nods, heart bumping harder. 'Very.'

'And tired?'

'Exhausted—'

'One of them must have touched him. He'll be all right if you find him in time. There's magic to sort that out – characters you will have to draw around the injury.'

'But can't *you* do it? You'll come with us, won't you?'

But Jin just shakes his head. 'I'll come as far as I can. My *ch'i* is weak again as you've just seen – the fight, the binding spell. I'll get you to a place where you can cross the Frontier again. Then I'll have to come back here – to my mountain – and rest for a good long time . . .'

Fei is looking away towards the Gorge, but then turns and tugs Jin's sleeve. 'How do you know Charlie's alive, Mister Jin?'

'Ask Ruby.'

Fei turns to Ruby. 'Well, come on. What's the big secret? He's *my* brother, dammit!'

Ruby glances down at her hand.

'Charlie's alive. I've seen a sign.'

'A sign?'

'I've seen the red thread – the red thread of destiny. It's linking us.'

'The red thread?' Fei gasps.

'Charlie told me he thought he saw it too, before – before I lost him.'

'So why haven't I ever seen it?'

'It's not visible right now.'

Lao Jin rests his scarred hand lightly on top of theirs. 'Ruby can see it, Fei, because Ruby's the one whose destiny is tied to your brother. They're the ones in love.'

'But *I* love him!'

'Of course you do. But in a different way. Trust me, Fei, Charlie's alive. But now we must move. You two don't want to be stranded too long in the Otherworld. There comes a point when you can't get out again, no matter how hard you try.' He fixes his gaze on Ruby. 'Or how far you go.'

The climb back down the Gorge wall is, if anything, far worse than the climb up. Even though she tries to keep her eyes from it, the dreadful, darkened drop pulls at Ruby hypnotically – just one slip will mean certain death on the rocks far below. Within a few yards the moon is blocked out, and they are plunged into deep shadow again. Jin leads the way, the spirit bottle tucked in a pocket, working his way nimbly down the rickety ladder and then descending the steep rocky flight below. It feels like he's in a hurry now, quickly putting distance between him and Ruby. Fei is still clinging to the rungs of the bamboo above, loudly muttering every Chinese and Pidgin swear word she knows.

'Come on, Fei,' Ruby calls. 'You can do it.'

'I know I can. I'll just do it at my own pace, thank you!'

Ruby turns back to the steep flight, torn between hurrying after Jin and waiting for her friend. Every now and then she checks her hand. If only the thread would just appear for a moment, then she could show Fei and raise both their spirits. After the initial relief of rescue, she's been irritable, argumentative even. There's still that irrepressible spirit burning in her eyes, but the events of the last few weeks have clearly shaken her to the core. And she's still so young. Ruby checks on her progress again, then launches down the next near-vertical stairway. If I can deflect a bullet, she thinks, then I can can climb down this, and keep Fei safe too. *Mei wenti.*

Halfway to the bottom, Jin waits for them on a ledge.

'Feeling good?'

She nods.

'Remember what they say – the journey of a thousand *li* starts with the step you're taking right now.'

He flicks her an encouraging smile and then jogs on down the next flight. The voice of the rapids is growing louder, the sky around them darker as they drop deeper. Fei has fallen a long way behind, and as Ruby waits for her again, her eyes fall on a tiny snail clinging to the rock wall by her hand, inching across the dark surface, its trail a pale glistening green. A ghost too? she wonders. Can you get ghost snails—? And then that thought is cut as the red thread appears again, glowing a loop around the base of the little finger and then falling like a plumb line into the void below.

'Fei!' she calls, keeping her eyes glued to the thread, and willing it to stay visible. 'Fei. I can see it!'

'See what?'

'The thread. Hurry!'

It flares brighter for a second or two, but even

before Fei has closed half the distance it starts to fade again, dimming quickly – paler than the snail's trail and then gone.

As Fei scrambles to join her Ruby waves her hand apologetically. 'It went again.'

'But you really saw it? You're not just making it up?'

'Why would I do that?'

'To cheer me up.'

Ruby puts a hand on her shoulder. 'I'm not making it up. I promise.'

Fei wipes her nose, looks Ruby in the eye for a long moment, and then nods. 'OK. Good.'

She gazes back down into the canyon. 'Bloody hell. I was blindfolded when they carried me up here. I wish I was now!'

Jin is waiting for them by the river, silhouetted against the tumultuous white water. As they approach he points to the far bank. 'OK, you two wait here, while I deal with this. No point risking a crossing if you don't have to.'

'Where are you taking it?'

'To my den. I'll get a lift across at the tracker village. If I'm not back by dawn start without me.'

'Why? Is it still dangerous round here?' Fei asks,

glancing over both shoulders, setting her pigtails dancing again.

'My dear young friend,' Jin says, 'we're in the Otherworld. I'd say that's fairly dangerous, for you at least. But we'll have scared anything nasty away for a while with the show we made up at Hell's Throat. Keep each other company. Be kind to each other, that's the main thing. *Zai jian.*'

'Why might you not be back by morning?' Ruby asks, anxiously seeking out his eyes.

Lao Jin looks away across the water. 'Handling powerful magic like this is even more dangerous than making fireworks! Volatile . . . Take care, friends.'

And without another word he lopes away up the boulder-strewn track and is lost in the all-pervading gloom.

Fei slumps down hugging her knees – and a moment later her shoulders start to shake silently. Ruby puts both arms around her, holding tightly, watching the water pouring into the rapid below.

'So what was it like?' she asks after a long ten minutes have slipped by.

'At first it was almost exciting,' Fei gasps. 'I mean being kidnapped by the Green Hand. I was pretty sure they wouldn't hurt me – but I was really worried that Dad or Charlie would get lured out of hiding.'

She sniffs up the tears. 'But then it just got weirder and weirder. And when we were on Moonface's boat, he – he came to see me in the cabin and he changed, right in front of me, into that disgusting thing. If we find Charlie he's *never* going to believe me—'

'*When* we find him,' Ruby says firmly.

Fei throws her hands up in despair. 'But it's worse than that, Ruby. I trusted your dad and didn't do what Charlie said, and that's why we're all in the mess we're in . . .'

Her voice trails off, and she looks Ruby in the eye, anger replacing the fear and bewilderment. 'How could he do it? How could *your* blasted dad betray all of us? My dad, Charlie, me!'

'I don't think he meant any of this to happen—'

'Great! But it did!'

'I think the Green Hand have him in their power. At least he tried to rescue you in the end . . .'

Fei picks up a stone and flings it into the dark water.

'Fat load of good that did. Typical foreign devil if you ask me. He dumped us all in it, Ruby. And now look at the mess we're in. What's a Chinese life or two when it comes to feathering your own nest?'

'It's not *my* fault,' Ruby fires back. 'I didn't know

what he was up to. *I'm* not a typical foreign devil.'

'I know, Ruby. I know you're not. But . . . oh, forget it.'

Silence settles awkwardly between them again for a moment. Fei looks back at Ruby, frowning.

'So, are you and Charlie in love then? That would be – I don't know – really weird.'

Ruby lets out a long breath. A question like that would have made her blush like crazy just a few weeks ago. But not now.

'I don't know. I think so.'

'You *think* so?!'

'The only thing that matters now is finding him.'

'He's *my* brother, Ruby. I love him as much as you do.'

'I know. But it's different. You'll understand when you get a bit older like me.'

'You're not that much older,' Fei says. 'And I know about that stuff. I've seen it in the movies.'

She glances away at the pressing darkness and shivers again. And after a moment puts an arm back around Ruby.

'We've got to be best friends to each other,' Ruby whispers and puts her arm around Fei pulling her closer. 'It's our best hope.'

'I'm sorry,' Fei murmurs, her voice twisted with

the river's noise. 'You're not a typical foreigner. And I believe *you*, Ruby. You never told me a lie.'

Slowly – slower than the snail on the rock wall – the night thins. Fei has fallen fast asleep, huddled close to her friend. There's still no sign of Jin returning, but at least a vague dawn is gathering itself in the mouth of the Gorges – as if a distant lamp has been lit hundreds of miles away beyond a vast doorway. Can't afford to fall asleep, Ruby thinks. I've got to keep a lookout for trouble or Jin coming back. Where's he got to? It's been ages, but then he's got to cross the river, and do whatever magic he said he had to do. *Volatile*, he said. Does that mean it could all go horribly wrong?

She looks downriver again. Home lies through that doorway. And Dad and Mother, the *Real Blasted World* as Dad always calls it. And more importantly, more importantly by far, somewhere between here and there is Charlie. But is he ill, or dying? Or washed up somewhere half drowned?

Damp and cold seep through her clothes into her bones, setting her teeth chattering. That ethereal whistling sound has started up again, and a faint drumming, but miles and miles away. Some boat tackling a rapid already? And is it real or a ghost ship?

She leans back, gazing up at the paler night between

the cliffs, struggling to fight off sleep herself. Her eyes flutter open, shut, open, shut . . .

A vague white cloud of mist or spray seems to be hovering about a hundred or more feet above. She concentrates on it for a while, imagining it as an airship, smooth and elliptical – but then it seems to become more like the hull of a huge boat, powering overhead, streaming a wake behind it . . .

Her head jerks back to wakefulness. Someone's shouting, the voice blurred by the river's roar. She gets quickly to her feet, senses alert for any trouble, and then with relief sees a small, red boat gliding into view on the smooth water above the Grinder, Jin standing tall in its prow.

He jumps into the shallows, wading ashore, beckoning Ruby over.

'It's done,' he calls. 'And I feel better for being in my own den even if just a little while.'

'Did it go all right?'

Jin nods. 'Anything happen here?'

'No. Nothing. I dreamed there was a boat, overhead.'

Jin raises his eyebrows. 'Maybe one day if they dam this place!' He points downriver. 'I just heard we can hitch a ride on a junk if we go right now. Come on, wake Fei.'

'Lao Jin, *how* far can you come with us?'

'I don't know yet. We might be very close to getting you firmly back in the real world – I think it's overlapping with the Otherworld even now,' Jin mutters. He laughs suddenly: 'I'll have to be careful! I don't want to get stuck in your world for good, low on *ch'i* and having to peer out of cigarette packets and biscuit lorries for ever!'

The dawn is growing in the cleft of the Gorges, its light filtering into the steam and spray, washing away the deathly green glow.

'How will we know when we're out of the Otherworld for good?' Ruby asks as they pick their way back to the sleeping Fei.

'We'll know. The main thing is there's a boat going downriver and we need to get on board before it sails. The rest we can sort later!'

第五章

BICYCLE TUBES AND MOONCAKES

Together they pick their way along the tracker path downriver towards the next set of rapids. Fei leads the way, scrambling over the bigger boulders, the return of day lifting her spirits. 'Come on, you two,' she calls. 'I don't want to miss our boat!'

In the half-light the Mincer – though smaller – looks much fiercer than Ruby remembers, all spray and rolling thunder. For a moment she's back on the bridge of the *Haitun*: she and Charlie urging it up that first hurdle, their hands reaching out for each other, so close, so very close—

She cuts the thought.

If I think about it too much I'll go mad, she thinks. Like Mother.

Her eyes scan the rocky shoreline for signs of the wreck, but there's nothing to be seen. No bodies, no stranded sailor huddled over a fire drying out Robinson Crusoe style. Nothing. Poor Old Lee, poor Captain Marlais – she thinks of the walnuts cracking in the Captain's hand, then the moment when the Grinder caught them, churning under the water, the sword lost, Charlie glimpsed and gone in the fury of the water—

No, stop it!

Jin points ahead. 'Here's our transport, Ruby.'

Sun breaks free of the jagged valley wall sending shafts of light spiralling down into the Gorges – one of them picking out a heavy black junk moored to the shore ahead. A figure is leaning on the rail of the flying rear deck, sending wisps of smoke from a pipe into the morning.

Jin waves his hand back and forth, and the man raises a hand in greeting. 'They'll take us as far as they can. Good people apparently.'

'How far?'

'They weren't sure yet, but they said a very long way at least.'

'Is it a real boat? Or a ghost one?'

'Looks real enough, don't you think, Ruby? But like I say, I think both rivers – the real Yangtze and the shadow version – must be following the same course. At least for now. So we need to keep our wits about us.'

Fei has stopped on the path ahead, and is beckoning them on. 'Is this ours, Mister Fox?' she calls. 'It's a beauty!'

'Run on and tell them we're coming, there's a good girl. You're faster than us this morning.'

'I am!'

Ruby looks up at Jin. 'We can ask them if they saw the wreck, or heard anything about survivors. And how far they're going and—'

'Not too many questions – or demands,' Jin whispers. 'From what I hear they've fallen on hard times. Let's not embarrass them. They may have their own problems.'

When they reach it, the junk towers over them. Fei is already halfway up the gangway, waving them on frantically. 'We're just in time – they were going to cast off in a few minutes,' she calls, and then hurries on up. A painted white eye stares down at Ruby unblinking from under the prow. In the junk's shadow the chill of the night still lingers, a touch of frost even on the rocks at their feet. She pulls the cardigan around her tighter and then strides behind Jin up the long, wobbly plank that leads to the deck. An old woman greets them at the top, silvered hair knotted on her head, her face ploughed deep with years of worry and weather.

'You are welcome,' she murmurs. 'Please make yourself at home. And excuse the rest of the family. They are ashamed to be seen in the poor state we have fallen into . . .'

Her voice dies against the wash of the river, then she points amidships. 'Best to sit dead centre, and hold on.' She looks at Fei. 'Especially you, little girl. We're going to run the last rapid and we might hit a dragon pool.'

'I'm not little any more,' Fei chirps back, raising herself to her full height. 'I've nearly been married I'll have you know!'

Ruby gazes around her, the old curiosity stirring and shoving away all worries for a moment. She's never set foot on one of these larger river junks before, not even back home. They always seemed to hold the heart of old China under their creaking sails, moving in and out of port, the crews living their whole lives afloat. Up on the raised deck she catches a glimpse of three young children peering at her from behind a large bundle of cargo covered with oil cloth. When they see Ruby look their way they giggle and duck down out of sight. The sound of their playful laughter lifts her spirits a touch more. With that – and the return of the sun – the task ahead feels that bit more possible. Behind them the man on the raised deck is signalling to a gaggle of stick-thin trackers who have materialised from out of the shadows, and they shove on the spar moor to push the junk out into the current.

'We don't have much to offer in the way of food,' the old lady is saying, 'but you are welcome to what we have. The Wu family have crewed this river for generations. And we are always good hosts.' She nods to where a younger woman and a man are coiling ropes at the prow.

'My daughter,' she says proudly. 'And her husband.'

'We thank you,' Jin says, bowing formally. 'And we will let you get to your work.'

'I bags the best spot,' Fei says, darting away through the crates of cargo lashed to the deck. Ruby follows, peering into the open ones: bottles of dark wood oil in one; pumpkins in another like fat orange heads; a crate of what for a second she takes to be dead black snakes like in the Chinese pharmacies back home – and then realises are nothing more than the deflated inner tubes for bicycles. There's a creak overhead and she looks up to see the junk's brown sail snapping full as it catches the downriver breeze.

'What if we hit a rock or something?' Fei says, her excitement wavering as she wraps an arm around the mast. 'I don't want to fall in the river like—'

'We won't,' Ruby says, quickly.

Jin nods. 'Don't worry. This crew are meant to be one of the best on the river.'

Wind and current combine to propel the junk into the morning. The cliff walls dash past – as fast as if seen from a train, then faster still – and the boat starts to pitch and roll.

Ruby taps Jin's arm. 'Maybe we should be looking out for the *Haitun*? For Charlie? Maybe he's not gone very far.'

'We were one night fully immersed in the Otherworld when we were at Hell's Throat,' Jin growls softly. 'Have you any idea how many days that is on the real river?'

'Much longer?'

'A month, give or take. Maybe more. The survivors have long been picked up, or taken to a doctor to have their bones fixed. And the drowned? Well, they have been drowned for a good, long while now, I'm afraid.'

'Marlais? Old Lee?'

Jin shakes his head. 'I don't know. My eyes were only for you, Ruby. I couldn't look out for anyone else. I'm sorry.'

The river has them in its grip now, and with it comes again the ethereal whistling sound – but this time from very close by, just behind Ruby. High above on the flying rear deck the steersman is leaning into his great rudder, squinting into the spray, and the children stand braced in front of him – two girls and a little boy – whirling bird whistles around their heads for all they're worth, their faces bright with excitement and sun.

'Hold tight, passengers!' the old lady shouts. 'Both hands.'

Ruby looks forward again just in time to see the prow lurch over the Mincer's lip. A groan runs the length of the ship's timbers and her stomach leaps – and then with a mighty *sploofff* the junk ploughs down into the white race of the water. Seconds later it rears again, swinging to port and skirting a huge revolving vortex of water.

Ruby glances at the whirlpool's hollowed out heart as they dash past. Marlais said those things can keep stuff submerged for days and days, she thinks. Weeks. Maybe my sword's down there. Maybe Charlie, his body—

No. Shut up.

On the prow the young husband and wife are keeping lookout to either side, sending hand signals to the steersman as they scan the river for danger. The old lady makes her way back towards the passengers, her steps safe and sure on the heaving deck – as if strolling a garden path.

'That's the last nasty one,' she calls. 'But the river's running much fuller than usual so we'll have to keep an eye. Round the next bend you'll see the Yangtze Rapid boat that got wrecked a few weeks ago.'

Ruby looks at her sharply. 'The *Lu Haitun*?'

The woman nods. 'Not even steam can beat the Gorges some days—'

'Were there any survivors?'

'A handful,' the woman says, a look of pain deepening the lines around her eyes.

'Do you know who?' Ruby asks urgently. 'Do you know if a young boy made it? Chinese, from Shanghai?'

The woman shakes her head. 'No idea. We were a long way further up the Gorges that night. The *Haitun* and two junks were lost. But I heard the pilot washed up half drowned four *li* downriver!'

If Old Lee made it, Ruby thinks, heart beating faster, then maybe Charlie did too.

As they swing around the next tight bend, she sees what at first she mistakes for a ruined building by the water's edge, shadowed by a colossal boulder towering over it. But within seconds the gap closes and the object resolves into the shattered form of the *Haitun*, rolled right over onto her starboard side, the wheelhouse ripped away, railing and upper deck and canopy all smashed or gone. Pointing back upriver the funnel is cracked in half, sticking up into the sunshine like a shark's fin. Their junk is veering closer and closer, and it seems for all the world they will join the *Haitun* on the rocky shore, but at the last second the boat heaves to starboard and whisks past, missing by no more than a half-dozen paces. Ruby's eyes race over the damaged hull, the shoreline and raised ground above. Already it's passing, passing . . .

She grabs the old lady's sleeve. 'We've got to stop! I've got to have a look!'

But the woman just furrows her brow. 'We're riding the rapid, girl! We're wind and current now.'

'But my friend—'

'Might as well try and stop time,' the boatwoman snorts. 'That's the trouble with you foreigners: think you can control everything!'

Jin puts a hand on her shoulder, whispering just above the river. 'Let's pay our respects instead.'

He makes a silent bow to the departing shell of the *Haitun*, its stern wedged above the Yangtze, propeller screws high and dry. Four cormorants sit black and motionless on the blades. Desperately Ruby scans the shore again. Surely there still must be surviving crew nearby? But the whole scene looks like a wreck from years ago, not hours.

'He's not here, Ruby,' Jin says. 'Surely you can feel that? After everything I've taught you?'

And it's true – she can't. Just an emptiness inside as she watches the wreck sweep from view.

'If Old Lee could make it, then so could Charlie,' she says quietly.

Jin nods. 'Exactly.'

The river is picking up speed again, dropping them through a last narrow V between diving cliffs, barrelling them around one last bend, and then – like a cork from a fizzing lemonade bottle – they pop from the neck of the last Gorge and sunlight falls all around.

Fei turns round, bubbling. 'We've done it, right? We're out of there? Out of the stupid Otherworld or whatever it was?'

Jin looks ahead into the brightening morning, then tilts his head to one side.

'Maybe,' he says. 'At least one foot in your real world.'

第六章

LIFE AND DEATH ON A DARK JUNK

After the blackness of the long, long night in the Otherworld Gorges, the sunlight on deck is dazzling.

Everything around Ruby – the junk's mast, the cargo, the old lady as she passes – casts crisp, neat shadows on the polished boards of the deck. This certainly looks like the real world again, but from what Jin said about the rivers running together, maybe it can't be that easy. She looks to the hills as they roll lower, a village or two passing – and in that middle distance there's a strange haze to the air, as if the sun hasn't been turned up quite as bright as normal. And when you look further – particularly to the northern bank – it's as if night still lingers just a few miles away.

Beside her, Fei flops back onto a folded oilcloth. Ruby follows her gaze into the fathomless sky unfolding above them, but even that has a strange quality to it, as if a layer of darkness covers the blue. Are those even tiny stars pinpricking it faintly?

Jin leans close. 'Can you see them?'

She nods.

'Not completely out of the woods yet,' he whispers. 'Keep your eyes open.'

'What are you two whispering about?' Fei murmurs. 'Heavens, this sun feels good. I haven't seen it for weeks. And I need some sleep.'

'Me too,' Jin says, stretching. 'You're on first watch, Ruby.'

The river's surface smoothes as it carries them on into the morning, the current still quick but the rapids gone now. Ruby keeps her eyes on the shoreline, occasionally glancing back at her left hand, hoping for a glimpse of the thread. But in this sunshine it's hard to believe it will be visible. Leaving the fortune-teller's parlour, the first time she glimpsed it, the rays of the sun on the street obliterated it in a moment.

The rest of the family seem to want to keep themselves to themselves, dropping their eyes when Ruby's reach out for theirs. Only the old lady comes to talk to them, bringing a meagre serving of rice and broth for each.

'I'm sorry we don't have more,' she says. 'But my

grandchildren wanted to share the last of their mooncakes with you – from mid-autumn festival. They're a bit shy . . .' She hands Ruby and Fei a small round cake each, the character for 'longevity' stamped on top like always.

'Great! I love mooncakes.' Fei beams, biting into the pastry hard and unlocking the sweet smell of the bean paste inside.

'Thank you,' Ruby says. 'I'll save mine for later. Please thank them for their generosity.'

She tucks her cake into her cardigan pocket, looking to the rear deck where the children are playing around the humped bundles of cargo – but when she waves to them, they just hide their faces. She glances at the impassive steersman gripping the rudder, his face shadowed by a broad-brimmed straw hat. Maybe he'll know where any survivors were likely to have washed up. She goes to make her way to the foot of the ladder that rises from the main deck, but feels a sharp tap on her shoulder. The silvery-haired lady is shaking her head.

'Not on the bridge, foreigner. Only us family. It's bad luck if other people go up. Particularly people like you.'

'I'm sorry,' Ruby says, biting back her frustration. 'Is that your husband steering?'

The lady nods. 'We have a very valuable cargo for a village beyond Ichang. He's the best on the river, my man. Always was. Always will be.'

'What kind of cargo?'

But the woman is already moving away across the rolling deck.

'The most valuable we've ever carried,' she mutters as she goes.

Ruby looks ahead into the channel. All the green murk and gloom of the ghostly Gorges are gone, at least from the river – and a few other junks and sampans are on the water now. The banks sweep by, tall reeds tumbling in the wind. Villages sit atop high land, safely above any flood, and between them tributary rivers feed down to add their water to the vast volume of the Yangtze. But where the low hills ramp up and down beyond, still there's that strange shade to everything, a dimming to the light on both sides.

Fei has fallen asleep, lulled by food and the rocking boat. Curled up she looks so young. Heaven only knows how she's borne up so well under the kidnap ordeal. Her brow is furrowed even as she sleeps, eyelids flickering as she dreams furiously. Beside her, Jin has stretched out full length. The wound on his head is still oozing slightly and he turns to try and get more comfortable. Not a hint of fox now, just a middle-aged man like the day she first met him, flesh and blood. She goes over and nudges him gently with her soft-shoed foot.

'Lao Jin?'

'Mmm?'

'What if Charlie's up in one of those villages and recovering – and we just sail right past him?'

'I told you, you'd see the thread. Or feel it.'

'Maybe—'

'Of course you would. You'd feel it tug like mad if we were going past. Like you had a huge fish on the end of your fishing line. You must have been fishing?'

Ruby nods. She sees her little brother grinning as he spun his silver foil bait into the vast river, eager for the catch. How much Tom loved to fish . . .

'And sometimes it was like you could feel the hook at the end of yards and yards of line, feel what the bottom felt like, or the nibble of the fish?'

'I suppose so, but—'

'We're all more sensitive than we know. And some more than others. So just relax, Ruby. You need to calm your mind a bit. That's the key . . . to everything.'

She breathes deeply and tries to quieten her thoughts. But it's hard – one fragment after another bobs to the surface.

'Just breathe,' Jin murmurs. 'Breathe and follow it—'

A gunshot sounds from the southern bank, echoing across the water – closely followed by another. Ruby sits up, straining her eyes to try and make out what is happening beyond the reeds, but they're hard over to the north shore now – and whatever's going on is hidden by a fold of land. Puffs of smoke drift up over a row of trees shimmering in the early autumn breeze. Jin is beside her now, shielding his eyes as the smoke starts to thicken and darken into dirty clouds staining the sky. Quickly they fall behind.

'What was it, Jin?'

'Heaven knows. Might be a real battle between warlords or bandits. Or it might be a ghost of a battle. A shadow of the real thing.'

'Perhaps we should help?'

The old lady has approached them silently. 'We're not stopping for anything now,' she says firmly. 'We have suffered enough. The youngsters need to be going home.' She nods at her grandchildren playing on the rear deck. The little boy and one of the girls are kicking a shuttlecock back and forwards, their touch sure on the moving deck. Charlie and Fei introduced her and Andrei to 'kick feather' when they first found the temple – but they were never as good as these two, and Ruby watches them in admiration.

'*Hen hao*, very good,' she says to the old lady, still hoping to win her over.

'It's important to play. Our lives are short enough. Though mine seems longer than most for some reason . . .'

The wind gusts, and it snags the shuttlecock mid-flight, sailing it away from the youngest child and down to the lower deck where it lands at Ruby's feet. She bends to retrieve it from the shadows, and a tiny shiver tingles up her arm. She holds the weighted end for a moment, feels the cold of the night still clinging to the rubber, then the little boy whistles brightly to her and she hurls it back in one big, sure loop.

The boy smiles shyly – and then turns back to their game again.

Jin taps Ruby on the shoulder. 'Have you seen downriver?'

In the bright afternoon light, purple and blue clouds are moving in from the east. Thin veils of rain comb the sky, and curving out of one of them, is a pale rainbow.

'Always good to see,' Jin murmurs. 'Even if it's a bit feeble. And now I'm going to get some proper deep sleep. Moonface left me with a bit of a headache. You keep watch and wake me before it gets dark. Or if anything seems odd.'

* * *

Afternoon shades away to early evening. The river here is wide, the banks' low smudges showing more water beyond as the Yangtze starts to split and divide restlessly into countless channels weaving between marsh and lake.

The junk shows no signs of mooring for the night though, or taking on supplies, and tiredness starts to drag at Ruby's head, pulling it down.

Fei's snooze at least seems to have restored *her*.

'I was thinking about that thread on your finger,' she says brightly.

'What about it?'

'Did Charlie really see it?'

'He thought he did, in Nanking. You know how cautious he is about believing stuff like that. And when we were under' – Ruby takes a breath – 'when we were underwater I thought I saw it joining us up . . .'

Fei takes hold of her hand and stares at the little finger.

'I mean, I'm sorry I was cross. Back at the Gorges. I'd just have to get used to it if you and Charlie were, you know, together. I mean kissing and that stuff.' Her voice quickens, as if she needs to rush across the ground. 'I mean, if you can both see it, then you'll get married for sure and you'll be grown up and wow then you'll be my sister-in-law, and you'll have kids and I'll be Auntie Fei and it's—'

'I can't think that far ahead,' Ruby says quietly. 'And none of it matters if we can't find him, does it? We'll be passing a place called Full Moon Bridge soon. I keep wondering if he'd have gone there.'

'Why?'

'Because – because it was the last place where we stood on real, solid ground together.'

'We could ask them to stop.'

'I don't think they're stopping for anything,' Ruby says. 'And when Charlie had to leave me for a while on the way up, he said if *anything* happened to either of us the other one should head back to Shanghai. We should wake Jin soon.'

Up on the tiller, the older man is still cut in silhouette against the late afternoon sky beyond. His wife comes along the deck carrying a smoky oil lamp, light dancing on her face.

'We're not far from home now,' she whispers. 'I should be able to get this lot there by just after nightfall.'

She smiles a faint smile, then moves away into the gathering gloom.

'You should get forty winks,' Fei says, staring at Ruby's little finger. 'I'll keep watch. You look dog-tired.'

'OK. But just a few minutes. Wake us both before it gets properly dark, Jin said.'

'Ruby?'

'Yes?'

'Will it all be OK?'

'Yes,' Ruby smiles. 'We'll do it. And I bet you'd be a great auntie.'

And sleep does come fast to her. Deeper and stronger than she means . . .

It rolls over her like black smoke, stuffing up her eyes and ears. No dreams, just a sleep that wanders like this stretch of the Yangtze from one wide dark pool to another and another, softening her tension, dragging her under . . .

Fei watches, eyes on Ruby's little finger. A chill sweeps the river and she finds another blanket and pulls it over her sleeping friend, and then settles down beside the hurricane lamp. She looks at Jin, snoring steadily, one arm thrown over his eyes blocking out the light. Let them both sleep a few minutes more, she thinks. They must be exhausted and I'm grown up enough to keep watch. We can't get off until they stop after all, and it's not that dark yet.

She looks back at the flying deck, sees the dim figures of the family gathered there, hunkered down on the boards.

An animal calls somewhere on the north bank, a blunted, dark cry that makes her huddle that bit closer to Ruby . . .

. . . to snuggle cosily under the blanket.

She adjusts the wick on the lamp . . .

. . . and in a few quick minutes Fei has fallen fast asleep again.

And that's why nobody – not she, not Ruby, not Jin – sees the old lady come back and snuff out their light.

Nobody sees the junk veer north onto a narrow, dark channel, or the sail fill with a stiffening wind that seems to spring out of nowhere.

Nobody sees a mist come up and roll thinly over them, or the green haze that seeps from the marshy land around them.

And nobody sees that the deck of the junk is totally deserted.

第七章

STRANGE CARGO

Ruby wakes abruptly, a ragged, flapping sound startling her from the depths.

She sits up, blinking in the darkness, struggling to remember where she is.

That's it, on the junk. Night has fallen and it's bitterly chilly. The sound must be the sail snagging in the wind. She staggers to her feet on the heave of the deck, pulling the blanket closer around her.

She glances down instinctively at her hand, hoping for a glimpse of the thread, but there's no trace, and it's so very dark she can hardly even see her palm. The oil lamp has gone out and feels cold when she bends to touch it. How long have I been asleep? she thinks, anxiety rising. There's no sign of any of the crew on deck – impossible even to see the steersman on the rear deck from here. And that frantic flapping sound isn't the sail overhead, it's coming from something back there. A strange feeling of dread wells up out of the darkness, half throttling her voice when she goes to speak.

'Fei? Wake up!'

A snuffling half snore answers.

Something flashes above and she tips her head back just in time to see the long fizzing trail of a meteor carve the night sky. There's a green tinge to the light as it burns and dims, and the cold is biting harder, the goose pimples bumping all over the skin on her arms.

'Jin? Jiiiin?' she whispers fiercely into the gloom. She can just make out his sleeping form, curled tight like a sleeping dog, his nose under his hand. She gives him a nudge. 'Jin! Wake up!'

But he just rolls over and groans and sighs, lost in some vast and deep slumber.

Find out what's going on first, she thinks. I can do that – and then shake him awake if necessary! He trusted me to keep watch and I've let him down. So I need to sort it.

She makes her way back across the roll of the deck, feeling the strengthening wind that's driving them onwards. You can just make out the sound now of water curling at the junk's prow. Isn't it dangerous to sail this fast at night – to move at all on this confused stretch of river? A three-quarter moon breaks the thin cloud overhead, bringing some illumination, but the colour of it is a sickly lemony-green that reminds her at once of the moss in the tunnel in Shanghai, the glow in the Gorges. Not a single light on either bank – just a huge, dark countryside stretching into the distance.

Panic growing, she grips the ladder to the flying rear deck. Black water churns below, and the flapping sounds gets louder and louder as she climbs. She hasn't spoken to the steersman, but at least he might be able to turn around or something! He must have noticed . . .

Except there's no sign of the man.

The haft of the massive rudder is bare to the moonlight – and there's not a soul on the rear deck anywhere. If there's nobody steering then surely the junk is about to ram the bank or a mudflat any moment? The speed of the vessel is terrifying, and Ruby peers forwards, eyes scanning the dark channel, her hands reaching for the tiller. To her surprise the junk is carving a dead straight course down the middle of the river, and the cold wood shifts in her hands – as if gripped by unseen hands far stronger than hers, correcting course on its own. A sandbank ghosts by in the gloom. Her hands and arms are fizzing like anything, and she lets go of the tiller, turning around, trying to make sense of what is going on.

The wind is blowing a near gale now, almost suffocating when she faces into it, and she sees the oilcloth over the cargo bundles flapping wildly, one corner thrashing loose. *That's* what is making the noise.

'Helloooo?' she calls. 'Anyone? Jin? JIIIN!'

Again the covering flaps angrily, threatening to rip free from the humped shapes beneath. It feels wrong to let that happen, and she bends to try and secure it, fumbling at the knot that obviously needs to be undone and then tied again to snag the corner. Her fingers are shaking from the growing panic as she works and like in a bad dream, the knot just gets worse the more she fiddles at it.

Maybe I need to get some slack, she thinks, undo that other one.

She moves to the other side of the cargo.

Ah, this knot's easier. Just got to loosen that, and then—

Whoooofff. In one violent gust the entire oilcloth rips from her fingers. Horrified, she watches as it balloons skywards and then wraps itself around the mast, beating away there like a demented black bird. I'm making things worse, she thinks – the old lady said this was valuable cargo . . .

Looking back she sees now what the cloth was covering – and her blood runs cold.

Six Chinese style coffins are lined up in a row, each raised on high blocks, their polished wood glimmering in the moonlight. Three are the normal, adult size like she's seen in funeral processions back home. But the other three are much smaller – more like Tom's little casket. And one of them is tiny . . . On top of each sits a heavy, humped lid, sealing in the occupants.

Her mouth is dry. It's like the dream she had, back in the Mansions when the fever had raged: her usual dream of the river from high above had lengthened, and she had floated down and landed on the deck of a junk just like this one. And found a coffin on the deck, approached it . . .

Already her tingling fingers are exploring the wood of the smallest coffin, her curiosity burning to know if she's guessed right. With a deep breath she goes to lift the lid – expecting it to be nailed shut – but it opens easily, almost jumping up with a squeal of a hinge.

The moonlight flickers on her hands, strobing through the flapping oilcloth overhead, and as if projected on the cinema screen she sees the body inside. The youngest of the junk's children is lying there, his face as white as her own, eyes closed, hands folded peacefully on his chest. And gripped tight in his little fingers is the *lieh tzu* shuttlecock from their game.

Ruby looks away, tears forming. And through

those blurred eyes she sees Jin standing not two paces away, watching her silently, the wind tugging at his greying hair.

He holds a finger to his lips. 'Shhh, Ruby. Let's not disturb them. They've had enough to deal with.'

'Is it . . . is it the crew?'

'All but our old lady. The rest of them all died upriver a few weeks ago. Drowned. Come on, let's close it.'

He takes her hands, guiding the lid down gently.

'So that's why they were keeping to themselves. That's why we didn't see them eat?'

Jin nods.

'When did you know?' Ruby whispers.

'I wasn't sure. Whether it was a real ship – or a ghost ship – it was heading the right way. At least to start with—'

'And how is it steering?'

'Ghost ships know their way home, Ruby. And *someone* should have woken me up at dusk before the two rivers diverged!'

Ruby glances up at the moon. 'We're back in the Otherworld, aren't we?'

'We are,' Jin says, urgency in his voice now. 'Considerably off course – the channels must have diverged.' He leads her across the flying deck, down the ladder and across to where Fei is still sleeping. 'My fault really. I shouldn't have dropped off.'

'What about the old lady – where is she?'

'Waking up somewhere in the real world, from a dream about how she took her family to their resting place. We need to get off before we're too deep. Wake Fei.'

'And then what?'

'And then we're going to do a little bit of swimming.'

'Can't we just get the junk to shore? Pull the sail down?'

'You can try. But you won't manage, Ruby. This thing is being steered by forces far stronger than you or even me.'

'Swimming?'

Ruby looks from Jin's bright eyes to the dark water surging past them. Her lungs take in a big, big gulp of air, and she tries to blot out that day at the beach when the darkening blue-black water nearly swallowed her whole.

第八章

SWIMMING THE NIGHT RIVER

Fei stands at the rail of the junk, a bundle of half inflated bicycle tubes lashed around her midriff. She eyes the water uncertainly.

'And now you're telling me we've got to jump into that?! I can't swim, Mister Fox.'

'You don't want to go where those poor souls are going. Not yet anyway. Those tyres have got enough air to help keep you up,' Jin grunts, tying a line to her and attaching the other end to his belt. 'I'll do the rest. Trust me.'

'We don't seem to be doing very well, trusting you. All foxes are tricksters Auntie always says—'

'If someone had woken me up in time we probably wouldn't be in this mess,' Jin mutters. He takes a second rope, swiftly knotting it around Ruby's waist. Her eyes too are on the churning river ten feet below the deck, a finger creeping uncertainly up to her front teeth to tap them.

'Are you OK, Ruby? It'll be fine. But just to be on the safe side, humour me with the safety line – the current's really strong here.'

'I'll be all right,' she says quietly, then lifts her voice for Fei's benefit. 'We'll be fine, won't we, Fei?'

'If you say so.'

'We'll be fine.'

They're not far from the bank, but it's still a long fifty yards or more away – and it'll be a lot further with the drift. The day at the seaside taught her that much. And what if they're snagged by a whirlpool? Or some monster thing in the shadow river?

I've come this far, Ruby thinks. I'm the girl who has *far to go*. If I can fight Shadow Warriors I can swim a stupid couple of lengths of water. Even if it is night. Even if we have slipped back into the Otherworld. She takes a breath, glances back one more time at the coffins – and then edges her toes out over the side of the deck. She plucks the Fedora from her head and tucks it inside her cardigan.

'OK. I'm ready!'

'Wait, what if I—' Fei starts, but her protest is cut short as Jin gives her a quick shove. Her arms flail the dark air, and then she's hit the water in a splash, going under, bobbing up a second later, coughing, choking. Jin jumps after her and Ruby leaps a fraction of a second later, one hand gripping the rope, the other feeling for the cold river.

A rush of air, the smack of cold water closing over her, and then that river noise again – horribly familiar from the wrecking of the *Haitun*. The current grips, surprisingly fierce, and she sees the dim underside of the junk overhead like a black cloud. Oh God, she thinks, I'm not coming up. But she feels the cord tighten at her waist – and maybe that reminds of her of something, because, even as she thrashes the blackness around her, she sees it again: the red thread curled around her hand, looping knots in the water above. The sight gives her extra strength, and she kicks hard – and moments later she finds the surface and pushes up through it, breathing river and cold air. Jin is swimming powerfully away and she feels the line at her waist tighten. She launches into a steady breaststroke, like she learnt at the public baths what seems a lifetime ago, determined now to do it under her own steam and not be towed. Dipping her face she reaches forward as far as she can on each pull, gaining a little on Jin. A bit more. At the beach that day she had tired quickly, panic tying up her limbs, but now – despite the cold, despite their situation – her arms and legs strengthen with each stroke. She lifts her head. Fei is just the other side of Jin, one hand clutching his jacket, and the other clawing at the choppy waves.

'Look, Ruby! I'm swimming! I'm swi—' Her mouth floods, cutting her short.

The thread is still just visible, curling away on the dark green water towards the bank, and the sight spurs her on even harder. Pull, kick, pull, kick – she's gaining even more on Jin, but then the tiredness is reaching out for her, her legs starting to cramp. Her cardigan is heavy and pulling her down – should have taken it off! she thinks. There's even that mooncake still in the pocket, extra weight.

Jin is already rising from the water, half carrying Fei through the squelch of the mud and up onto drier bank. With renewed determination, Ruby kicks and pulls hard again, and suddenly her legs are churning watery silt, and she clambers after her friends onto the mudflat. Fei drops down onto the ground, teeth chattering, as Jin frees her from the inflated sausages of the inner tubes.

'You p-p-pushed me in, Mister Jin!'

'And you did really well, didn't she, Ruby?'

'You were great, Fei. Really g-g-great.'

Ruby's own teeth are castanetting now, the wind making everything colder – but with that chill comes a sense of achievement. I did it, she thinks. First time I've really swum since the day at the beach. I did it on my own!

She glances down at her hand, eager to show the thread, but – of course – it's already gone again, as if washed clean by the water. Hurrying over to Fei, she holds out her hand. 'I saw it again, I saw the thread. Charlie's alive.'

Fei squints at her fingers. 'Are you sure you're not j-j-just imagining it?'

'It *was* there. Honestly.'

'Why d-d-don't I ever get to see it?'

Jin starts gathering together dropped branches and twigs.

'Get busy, you two, and gather some wood. I'll build a fire. Get you warm and dry.'

He makes a little pyramid of dried moss and leaves, then rummages in a pocket. From a small battered tin, he pulls out a piece of gleaming metal and a flint, and starts striking one against the other, raining small sparks down on the pale moss.

'If you're a spirit, c-c-can't you just magic it?' Fei's teeth are chattering even harder. 'I'm damn freezing.'

'I'm a fox spirit. Not a *mao shan* sorcerer!' Jin laughs, striking more tiny stars. At last one catches, flares, and sends up a wisp of smoke. Jin cups the flame in his palms, blows on it, and then places twigs on top. 'Come on, anything you can – let's have a real blaze. Don't want you two to catch your death.'

Fei looks at him in alarm. 'Death?'

'Sorry. Figure of speech.'

Ruby puts her arm on Fei's shoulder. 'Come on, let's find what we can.'

The wind gusts again as they hunt for firewood. Above Ruby's head the leaves on the willows surge like rolling waves, and the memory of the beach plays on – much further than normal, as if something has been released. On the wind-buffeted shore that day Tom had been first astonished, then laughed, then cried a bit as Dad lay exhausted, lips blue from the chill, the stump of his leg milky white where the amputation had happened all those years before.

We'd never really seen the stump, she thinks. Not until then. And later that night, when we were home in Bubbling Well Road sitting by the coal fire and all warming up, he had seemed very quiet, quieter than usual, gazing into the flames.

She dumps her bundle of dead wood next to the growing bonfire and stares into the flames, the conversation coming back.

Dad?

Yes, Ruby?

What's it like?

What's what like?

Your leg. Where it – where it got cut off?

Dad had shifted uncomfortably, and Ruby thought he was going to give her the silent treatment. But instead he looked around, checking they were on their own – and then leaned towards her, as if sharing a great secret.

You really want to know?

Yes. I do.

Well, Ruby, the truth is, sometimes I can still feel it. As if it's still there.

Hurting you mean?

Sometimes, yes. Sometimes it really hurts. Like the day it happened and I got brought back from the front. Like the days in the hospital when I met your mother. But sometimes, I can just feel it. I can feel its ghost if you like, sitting there at the end of my leg, feel the toes wiggling as if they're in the bath, or moving around in the shoe. And sometimes . . .

He looked around quickly, and smiled.

. . . and sometimes I get your mother to stroke it, if it's hurting, and I can feel that too. And do you know what? It helps!

Suddenly Mother had come back in, fussing, and

Dad looked away sharply to the evening-filled window. But then, a moment later – one of those rare glorious moments – he had looked back and winked.

A flame cracks loudly, showering sparks heavenwards, and Fei gives a cheer.

Jin holds a finger up to his lips. 'Not too loud. Heaven only knows what's around us.'

Fei's eyes widen. 'What do you mean?'

'Trouble. As always.'

Ruby looks at him. 'We're going to have to find another way of crossing the Frontier, aren't we?'

Jin nods. 'Let me scout around and find out where we are. You two keep close to the fire, and if you hear anything you don't like the sound of, get down in the reeds and quack like ducks. Got it?'

He flashes a smile, but in the light of the bonfire his face looks careworn, exhausted again.

'Are you all right, Lao Jin?' Ruby whispers. '*Ni hao ma?*'

'I'm fine,' he says, '*hen hao*. Sit tight, you two.' He turns and slips away into the shadows under the line of trees.

Fei is silent for a while, watching him go – then gets to her feet and starts dejectedly lobbing sticks onto the flames. 'What did he mean about being in trouble again?'

'He meant that we're back in the Otherworld,' Ruby says. 'The boat took us right back into it.'

'Are you sure? How can you tell?' Fei grumps. 'You two seem so sure of everything and look, now we're just wet and cold and totally lost. One minute you tell me we're out of the stupid Otherworld and the next we're right back in it.'

'Look at the moon – look at the colour of it,' Ruby says, pointing up. 'You can see it's not right. You don't get green moons in the real world.'

Fei glances at it. 'I dunno, Ruby.'

'It's going to be OK,' Ruby says. 'We've just got to trust Jin for now.'

'Trust a fox spirit! You *can't* trust them—'

'They're not all the same,' Ruby says. 'That's like saying that all Chinese are the same, or all foreigners are the same! He rescued you from Moonface, didn't he? And he rescued me.'

'And let Charlie be washed away!' Fei pulls her face. 'And even if we are in the Otherworld and we somehow find a way out of it, we've still got no idea where Charlie is. And even *then*, what if One Ball Lu's got our dad?' Fei groans. 'Your dad might have told them where he is—'

'No,' Ruby says firmly. 'I don't think he'll do that. Not now. Come on, warm yourself up. Get dry.'

'I'd believe it all a bit more if I saw that thread,' Fei says quietly. She looks at Ruby, weighing up a decision, her arms wrapped tight around her. 'If you say we're in the Otherworld, I'm going to believe you, Ruby. I'm going to trust *you*.'

Ruby holds out her hand. 'I'm glad.'

'And you know why I trust you? Because Charlie always trusted you.'

'He didn't trust me enough to tell me when you two were going into the Chinese City that day on your own, when the student got – you know – beheaded.'

Fei shakes her head. 'That's because he didn't want you getting into trouble!'

'Look how that worked out!' Ruby smiles. 'Still friends? Still *all* for one?'

'All for one,' Fei says, and takes her hand and shakes it hard.

Minutes pass. An hour.

Overhead the greening moon shakes the willows, the first of the autumn fall fluttering down around them. No light or sound from the river, and nothing from inland either – and Ruby chucks more broken branches onto the flames, glad of the warmth and stoking it eagerly, getting as close as she dare to dry herself.

The truth is, the story of the phantom foot has prompted a kind of homesickness. Not just for Shanghai. Beyond the desperate longing to be with Charlie again, there's something else: a desire to see Dad again – even perhaps Mother. The thought of her stroking that non-existent foot is . . . incredible, but nice. A reminder of how things used to be.

Strange how I'd forgotten that, she thinks. Still far to go, but we'll do it. We'll return to Shanghai—

Fei suddenly sits bolt upright. 'What was that?'

'I didn't hear anything.'

'Listen!'

Ruby strains to hear over the rush of the leaves overhead. And, distantly, she can make it out now too: a steady barking, not in anger or alarm, just steadily once, twice, three times. Pausing. Then doing it again.

'Is it Jin, do you think? Gone all foxy?'

'No. It's a dog. We must be near a village.'

'But if we're in the Otherworld, then what sort of people live here,' Fei says, edging closer to the fire. 'It might be ghosts, right? And what kind of dog could it be?'

The wind shakes again, and the barking keeps up its steady insistent call, coming a little closer maybe.

'Maybe it's some kind of hell hound,' Fei adds,

reaching for the end of a branch sticking out of the fire.

'Sounds friendly enough,' Ruby whispers, cocking her head to listen harder. And crazy as it seems, she wonders if she doesn't recognise the bark—

Behind them there's the abrupt sound of something or someone running fast towards them, and Fei pulls her burning brand from the fire and grips it in both hands.

'Keep back,' she shouts. 'Or I'll burn you up, ghost!'

But a moment later it's Jin who appears, his face reflecting the bonfire, bright with excitement.

'We need to move,' he growls. 'We're *way* deeper than I thought. You two won't last long this far into the Otherworld.' He points into the darkness. 'There's some nasty spirits out and about. And I think we've caught their attention. But I have one good bit of news for you!'

The fire flickers brighter, and a moment later another figure bounds into its circle of light: a familiar, pale-coloured dog, barking frantically, leaping up at Jin and licking his face.

'It's Straw!' Ruby shouts in disbelief. And then in joy: 'He's found us! Here, boy!'

The dog turns to Ruby, tail wagging, and stretches out his front legs in a long, respectful bow.

'He's done more than that,' Jin says, glancing back out into the darkness. 'He's found you two the way out of here. But now we've got to run.'

第九章

LEARNER DRIVER

Straw gives one more excited bark, then turns and trots away into the darkness.

Fei watches him go. 'Maybe we're closer to home than we thought. Maybe this isn't the Otherworld after all—'

Jin shakes his head. 'We can argue on the way but right now we need to shift.'

'And how does he know where we need to go?'

Jin smiles. 'That dog's much older and wiser than most. Don't let him out of your sight. I'll bring up the rear.'

But already Ruby is pulling Fei by the hand away from the fire's warmth, following Straw as he lopes into the night. 'He helped me in Shanghai,' she says. 'He never let me down then. Come on.'

Immediately the cold and dark press around them.

For a few hundred yards Straw follows the crumbling dyke top, the willow leaves still thrashing furiously above them.

'But how did Straw find us?' Ruby pants as Jin jogs alongside. 'Charlie lost him at Peach Blossom. We can't be anywhere near that, can we? I mean if we're in the Otherworld?'

Jin grunts. 'Maybe Fei's right. Maybe Peach Blossom's closer than we think.'

The pale dog runs on ahead, climbing away from the river to slightly higher ground, past a ruined house, on up another slope. At the top he pauses and barks frantically again. Two sounds over and over.

Ruby turns to Fei. 'Listen, can you hear? He's talking to us! *Gan kuai. Gan kuai.* Hurry up!'

From the rise you can see a village on the plain beyond. No smoke coming from the chimneys, no light, no sign of life – but a village nonetheless, typical of the middle river. Suddenly everything seems much quieter around them, even though the wind is still sighing across her face. Jin is by her side, Fei struggling a few paces behind. A nagging worry is getting stronger.

'What did you mean by nasty spirits, Jin?'

He ignores her, pointing up as Fei joins them.

'Notice something?'

'The moon's all green again.'

'What about the trees?'

Ruby follows his fingertip. The willows here are suddenly bare, not a leaf to be seen on their tumbling branches. She looks around – and sees that *all* the branches on *all* the trees around the dead village are barren. Weirdly, there's not even a leaf on the ground at their feet either.

'It's famine, isn't it?' Fei whispers.

Jin nods, then crouches suddenly, motioning them all to drop low.

'They're coming,' he growls. 'They're coming from the village.'

'Who?' Ruby hisses back.

'The villagers,' Jin says hoarsely. It should sound reassuring that word – villagers – but his tone makes it sound worse than 'bandits' or 'vampires' even.

'Maybe we can ask them for help?' Ruby says.

'Not these,' Jin whispers. 'These are hungry villagers. Very hungry indeed.'

Fei is looking around, nodding. 'I've heard Dad talk about this. Must be nothing left for them to eat and they've stripped the leaves to try and keep eating. Nothing else left, not even food parcels.'

Jin scowls. 'No famine relief will help these souls. These are hungry ghosts. *Egui.*'

'*Egui?*' Fei echoes with a moan. 'Oh my God.'

Jin points again and now Ruby can see them: a shuffling file of shadows coming up the track from the village, still a couple of hundred yards away but heading directly towards them.

Straw starts to whimper and Jin reaches out a strong hand. 'Easy boy.'

Ruby peers into the gloom, expecting to see the typical swollen bellies she's seen in newspaper photographs of starvation. But the moonlight is now picking out far stranger figures than that: really, *really* fat bodies, but with grotesque, thin necks above that support their bobbing heads. As they come closer those ugly heads are swivelling, as if sniffing for scent, or listening.

Shivers start to shake through Ruby again: nothing more fearsome in all the *Strange Tales* than hungry ghosts.

'These are the spirits of the people who caused the famine,' Jin says quietly. 'They starved as well in the end of course. They'll eat anything they can find now: rubbish, rotting stuff, dead bodies. And even then they'll be hungry. You two must be tasty, lightly toasted as you are! Not much will smell better to them. OK, boy? Which way?'

Straw gives a sharp bark, then sprints away across the desiccated field to their right, barking out two different sounds over and over: *Lai ba, lai ba, lai ba . . . come on, come on, come on.*

Fei looks wildly from the approaching figures to Jin. 'Can't you fight them, Mister Fox?'

'Not enough *ch'i* left to transform. And even then not hungry ghosts. Unless you want to be dinner for them, run as hard as you ever ran in your life.'

Still Fei doesn't move, so Ruby hooks her by the elbow, tugging her into motion, and together they both stumble down the bank.

'Just run, Fei. For Heaven's sake!'

'All right! All right!'

Straw's already fifty paces or more ahead of them. Through the soft shoes Ruby feels the dried, spiky stalks of the failed crops amongst the stones and dried mud. It's hard going, and Fei keeps glancing over her shoulder, her plaits whipping around. Ruby follows her gaze for a split second, and sees the hungry ghosts scrambling down from the levee, hurrying to cut them off before they reach the village.

'They're going to get us!' Fei squeals.

'We can get to the village before them!'

'And then what?'

And then what indeed? Ruby thinks, hurrying them both on. Maybe we can barricade ourselves in a house. And will the things just smash their way in? She remembers the awful strength of the hopping vampires as they broke through the building on top of the bone hill. Some of the *egui* are faster than the others, wobbling along at a bizarre speed – and more and more are emerging from left of the village now, a dozen or so moving along the crumbling shells of the houses, definitely set to block their route.

'We're done for,' Fei pants. 'If only we didn't smell so good!'

Smell so good, Ruby thinks. Something that smells good! Her hand is already reaching into the cardigan pocket – and yes, the mooncake is still there, soggy, crumbling, but warm from the fireside. As she runs she breaks the cake in half and the aroma of the sweet paste rises on the night air.

Jin sees what she's doing and nods. 'Worth a try! Wait until we're close, Ruby! Only one shot at it.'

This close the *egui* are even more horrific to look at, the fastest of them sensing their prey and speeding up even more. No more than thirty yards away now, twenty . . .

'Chuck it!' Jin shouts. 'Now!'

Ruby waits another fraction of a moment and then with all her might hurls the halves of the cake towards them. Immediately the closest two give a shriek of excitement and veer towards the broken sweet as it hits the ground. In a frenzy they dive for the pieces, fighting each other, howling and making grotesque lip-smacking noises, others piling into the scrum.

Already the disappointed ones are looking up and turning back to their quarry, but the distraction has given a tiny chance. Jin grabs Fei's hand and leads them away at a fearsome pace across the next dried-up paddy field.

'I can't run that fast!' Fei squeaks.

'Yes . . . you can,' Ruby pants, struggling to keep pace. 'You're as fast as me . . . now. Faster!'

They make the far edge of the village some good yards ahead of their closest chasers. Straw weaves on between a gap in the buildings, leading them at speed through the dark streets, past houses with no roofs, broken doors – and on into a small square.

In the middle of it a small truck sits splashed in moonlight, a dark tattered cloth arched over its back.

Straw runs to it, wagging his tail furiously. Even as they reach the lorry Ruby feels the skin on her back prickling, and glances back to see the first of the *egui* rounding the corner behind them. The mismatching thin necks and fat, ugly heads are even more awful than she thought.

'Everybody in,' Jin snaps, virtually hurling Fei into the back of the lorry. 'You too, boy!'

Straw gives one more angry snarl at the creatures and then turns and scrabbles up to join Fei.

Jin turns to Ruby. 'Don't suppose you know how to drive one of these?'

'No.'

'I'm not much better. But at least I know how to start it.'

As Ruby clambers onto the bench seat, he fiddles with something on the dashboard – then dashes to the front of the bonnet, reaching down for the crank. There's a little bang and a spark, and the engine chokes into life. Jin darts back round and jumps behind the wheel, stamping hard on the accelerator. The engine screams, every single bit of the truck vibrating, as if about to explode – but the stupid thing doesn't budge an inch. Frowning hard, Jin's gaze darts around the cab. Over the whining engine, Ruby hears a screech behind them – and in the cracked wing mirror she sees the first of the hungry ghosts just yards away, its arms raised, reaching for the tailgate.

'Now, Jin! Now!'

'*Mei wenti, mei wentiiii,*' Lao Jin growls, pulling and pushing at anything and everything on the dash. Suddenly his eyes open wide and he yanks a lever, sending the truck leaping forwards. Gripping the big black steering wheel he pulls it left then right, narrowly missing the village well and bumping over the raised stonework beside it, before slaloming away through the ruins at the corner of the square. Ruby glances in the wing mirror and sees the *egui* sprawled on the ground, the rest still chasing but already falling behind, their lumbering speed no match for the lorry.

'We're doing it,' she shouts.

'We'll put some more space between us and them before I ease off,' Jin mutters, leaning into a corner and nearly clipping a wall. 'They'll be able to smell you for a dozen *li* or more now they've got your scent.'

From the back of the truck Ruby can hear Fei cheering wildly. She turns to Jin, heart still pounding from the chase, from the horror of what she's just seen. 'Lao Jin?'

'Yep?'

'What did you mean about Peach Blossom Village being close? We were hundreds of miles away when we were still on the real river.'

'You'll see,' Jin says. 'I always wondered how Moonface used to outrun me all the time. Now, shhh a minute. I need to concentrate.'

The track gets worse, thumping Ruby up and down on the sprung seat, the engine clattering. There's a churning in her stomach, but it's nothing to do with the movement of the little lorry – or even what they've just seen. It's about something that is approaching fast now. She watches her strange friend peering forward into the gloom, riding the potholes and ridges of the road, the faint moonlight picking out his silver-flecked hair, the lines on his face. If a Frontier crossing is coming then it's nearly time to say goodbye, she realises.

Jin glances at her.

'What is it, Ruby?'

'You do know how to drive.'

'Just about!' Jin snorts. 'I made a real mess of it the only time they asked me to do it in Shanghai! Hit a melon cart. Horrible mess. What was it you really wanted to ask?'

'I don't want to say goodbye to you, Jin.'

'It can't be helped. I am so very tired, Ruby. I need my earth. My den.'

'But we need your help—'

'You'll do fine. It was you who got us out of that last bit of trouble. And we all have to go *home* in the end. Hold tight,' he shouts over the rattling engine, and steers them towards a black gash in the hills ahead.

第十章

TUNNEL OF SIGHS

Ruby glances sideways at Jin as he rubs at the windscreen with the sleeve of his jacket. He whirls the wheel with the other hand, sinews working on his wrist and forearm.

If he can't come with us, we'll just *have* to cope on our own, she thinks, chewing her lip. Even beyond the crossing, whatever that may be, there'll still be hundreds of miles to home. And Charlie to find. And even more to be done when we finally reach Shanghai.

Shanghai. She can feel its pull, a yearning to be home, for everything to be as it was.

But it can't be like that any more, can it? she thinks. Without Tom, with our gang torn apart, Fei growing up, and Charlie and me . . .

She glances at her hand shaking as the lorry bucks. If only the thread would beastly well appear again –

some little bit of extra hope. The engine roars as they almost leave the ground over a bump.

'Jin?'

'No arguing, Ruby. I can't come with you.'

'No. I wanted to ask you something else.'

'What is it?'

The track is cutting into the hill now, diving between narrowing walls covered with ferns and moss picked out by the feeble headlights.

'No, it's about Charlie. Even if I find him, what about his wound? The vampire touch?'

'The Almanac will help you. You'll find instructions there.'

A knot rises in Ruby's throat. There's one big problem with using the ghosthunter's manual.

'The Almanac's lost, Jin. Charlie told me – before we set off from Shanghai.'

'Ahhh.' Jin pulls a face, then smiles reassuringly. 'Well, I will try and work some magic from my side and you just head back for White Cloud with Charlie when you've found him. Help comes from unexpected quarters sometimes – you just believe it will come, and it will. Got that?'

'I don't understand.'

'Just head for home. I'll sort the rest.'

The road bites deep into the shoulder of the hill,

seemingly for a dead end. In the headlights the ground beneath their wheels is dark green now, a carpet of creeping tendrils of ivy.

Jin points dead ahead. 'There it is, Ruby!'

There's a darker patch in the wall of greenery ahead, and as the truck careers towards it, Ruby sees there's a hole or cave of some kind punched into the hillside. Jin slows the truck, and then, switching off the engine, lets it freewheel, bumping to a halt. Ahead of them the rough track runs on into long weed and scrub, and then disappears into the black semi-circle of what looks now like an old tunnel. The pitch darkness cupped inside it is truly forbidding. Jin points at it through the windscreen.

'That's it, Ruby. The way home.'

Ruby stares into the opening. 'If you're sure.'

'Straw seems pretty certain.'

Already the dog has jumped down from the back of the truck and is trotting determinedly towards it. Fei bangs on the window, holding up her thumb and forefinger an inch apart.

'You cut it that fine, Mister Fox,' she squeaks. 'One of those things was this close to getting me! This close!'

Ruby opens the door and clambers down, watching Straw pad through the weeds towards the tunnel. The lights of the truck don't seem to penetrate even a single pace into the darkness.

'What's going on, Ruby? Why have we stopped?'

Ruby points to where Straw is waiting for them. 'We're going in there. Jin says it's a route back across the Green Frontier.'

Fei peers at it, and puffs out her cheeks. 'Really? I don't like the look of it.'

'Straw used it safely enough,' Jin smiles. 'But I think it only opens for a short while. Follow Straw until you see the other end. Then run for it.'

'You go first if you're so sure! What if it doesn't end up where you think?'

'Jin's not going,' Ruby says quickly. 'He can't risk getting stuck in our world.'

'What? Go in there on our own?' Fei groans. 'You've got to be *joking*!'

'It's either that or wait for the *egui* to follow your scent,' Jin says. 'And Straw will lead the way.'

Fei shakes her head, then looks at Ruby. 'What do you think?'

'Even if it only gives us a chance of getting to Charlie quicker I want to try it.' She glances back at Jin. 'It'll be safe, won't it, Jin?'

'Nothing's totally safe. In either world. But you'll probably be fine.'

'Probably?' Fei echoes. 'Very reassuring. But I said I'd trust you, Ruby, so – so let's go.' She lifts her chin and takes a few steps towards the black hole.

Ruby turns back to Jin. There's a knot in her throat, pulsating away.

'Lao Jin, I—'

'It'll be fine. Once you're in keep walking, and don't turn around – and be as quick as you can.'

'It's not that. I . . . I just don't want to lose you, Jin. I don't want to say goodbye.'

'Nor do I. But real friends never part, Ruby. You and I are real friends. But your future – well, that lies with Charlie.'

He gives her a strong one-armed hug, then propels her towards the tunnel, the weeds brushing and prickling her legs. The temperature drops as they get closer to the thin curtain of greenery veiling the opening.

'But what is it, Jin?'

'Just an ill-advised piece of civil engineering.'

On tiptoe Fei peers over Ruby's shoulder. 'Ohhh, you can't see a damn thing.'

'But Straw can. He'll turn back when you can see the other end. Let him guide you.'

'And what about you, Mister Jin? Those hungry ghosts won't get you, will they? I like you – even with you being a fox after all!'

'I'll keep guard a while longer. Then I'll take the lorry, head towards my mountain. Besides,' he grins, 'I don't smell as tasty as you two. *Zai jian*, my friends.'

Straw gives a short, sharp bark and trots away into the dark.

'Don't lose him,' Jin urges. 'Get going.'

Choking back emotion Ruby looks one more time into Jin's eyes, hugs him again with all her might – then turns and strides quickly forward, her feet silent on the carpet of moss reaching like a green tongue from a gaping mouth. On the threshold she hesitates for a second. Is that a soft-moaning sound? The wind funnelling over something deep in the tunnel? Something else?

Fei's eyes reach out for hers. 'I don't like it, Ruby.'

'Let's hold hands. That way we won't lose each other, whatever happens.'

Fei nods, and her small, warm hand reaches out thankfully for Ruby's.

'Let's go.'

As soon as they enter the passage the smell of cold damp is overpowering, and the darkness folds tightly around them. A few yards further a wind rises, channelled into the tunnel, sighing around them.

'Don't look back!' Jin shouts. 'Just keep going. Good luck!'

Ahead of them Straw barks again impatiently, urging them on, the echo racing away and dying in the gloom ahead. Ruby hurries them on. The desire to turn around and run back to Jin's reassuring presence is almost overwhelming, but she knows he's right. They *have* to cross the Frontier now.

'Just keep your eyes on Straw,' she whispers.

For ten, twenty, fifty, a hundred paces they march silently forwards. Any light from the moon and the truck is long gone, and the floor is invisible, soft, silent. With every step, the cold breeze swishes harder and harder around them from behind. And after another hundred yards the darkness is total. Straw trots on, his shape marginally lighter than everything else, as if a faint glow is coming from within him. Or maybe the last rays of the lorry's lights are still helping.

How close are the walls? Ruby thinks. She reaches out tentatively to her right but feels nothing. What if there's a big hole in the ground ahead – you wouldn't see it until you fell. And into what? The breeze is stiffening even more, racing through the tunnel, almost like the brushing of invisible hands now. And with it comes something else: the soft, moaning sound is back, getting louder, and with it – yes – the faintest whispering of voices? Ruby strains to hear, trying to decipher the soft, shushed syllables around them. Too indistinct to make out, but definitely there now, voices to either side in the permanent night of the passageway.

'Ghosts,' Fei hisses, her nails digging hard.

'They won't hurt us,' Ruby says, quickening her stride. 'Most ghosts don't hurt people, do they— Oh!'

Something definitely nudges Ruby in the back, and tingles shoot from the base of her spine. She swings around, sweeping with her free hand to feel for whatever has just touched her. Nothing but cold air.

'What is it?' Fei whispers fiercely.

'False alarm. *Mei wenti.*'

In the distance the tunnel mouth is a remote, pale opening in the blackness now. Like when Dad showed her Saturn floating in his telescope all those long years ago. Squinting she can just make out Jin, a tiny silhouette framed there, waving.

'*Zai jian,*' she whispers.

'Let's go!' Fei hisses. 'I can hardly see Straw.'

It's like walking in a void now. Just the whispering wind, the half heard voices, the brushing sensation from unseen ferns or hands – or goodness knows what.

And still Straw trots on resolutely in front, the palest of spectral shapes.

'Oh God,' Fei groans. 'I *can* hear things.'

'Concentrate on Straw.'

But Ruby can hear them too now. Fragments of

mumbled speech, chopped up like broken words on the radiogram when the reception's gone bad.

. . . come back, come back to me, come back . . .

. . . it was Cousin Zhang who did it. He made me . . .

. . . never, never, never . . .

. . . where are you going? Stay with us. Stay—

Ruby glances to the side as the last voice hisses in her ear. There's nothing there, or rather *nothingness*. Eyes closed, or eyes open, there's no difference, and she lifts her free hand, to see if she can see it. Surely now the thread should guide them – like some mythological story – out of the Otherworld and back into the light.

There's nothing, and her spirits falter – but then, looking ahead again you can just make out a very slight thinning of the darkness ahead, a semi-circle of charcoal grey, that gets a little bigger, a little brighter with each step.

She glues her eyes to it and quickens her pace, spirits lifting again.

'What is it?' Fei hisses. 'Have you seen something? I've got my eyes shut!'

'It's going to be OK,' Ruby murmurs. 'I can see the other end.'

And then Fei must have opened her eyes, because she suddenly gives a yelp of delight and lets go of

Ruby's hand, and darts forward.

'Let's get out of here!'

Ahead, Straw has come to a stop, wagging his tail side to side in the growing light. When they reach him he nuzzles his nose against Ruby's hip, as if nudging a goodbye, or urging her on, then utters two more sharp barks: two gruff syllables that with a little imagination sound like *zai jian*.

Goodbye.

He licks Fei's hand with a big slurp, then pricks his ears as if he's heard something – and bounds away at full speed into the darkness of the tunnel behind, running as fast as Ruby's ever seen him run. Within seconds he's dwindled to almost nothing, and swallowed by the gloom and gone.

'Race you!' Fei shouts. And together they both run for the opening, eyes for nothing now but the semi-circle of light, the ground visible again, a carpet of dark green moss that leads them at last to fresher, less chilly air. They push through a thick, tangled curtain of hanging plant growth and stumble out into the glow of a silvery-grey dawn. Warmth.

After the total darkness, the light is dazzling.

'Thank Heavens!' Fei gasps, plonking herself down amidst the weeds. 'At least we're out of that! Do you think this is the real world?'

Shading her eyes with a hand Ruby gazes at the rolling countryside before them. Early morning sunlight filters down to illuminate a village about half a mile away. It certainly looks real enough, smoke rising from a house or two. Beyond that there are fields, another cluster of buildings and a stubby pagoda silhouetted further off.

And beyond that, gleaming like tinfoil in the morning, is the Yangtze again. Somewhere above in the gauzy clouds you can even hear the drone of an aeroplane, and from somewhere on the river the blast of a ship's hooter.

'I'm sure,' Ruby says. 'And I think I know where we are.'

'I don't really care *where* we are,' Fei sighs. 'As long as we're not *there* any more.'

Ruby gazes back at the opening behind them. This side is a neat bricked archway, covered in moss and ivy and creepers, and the inky blackness inside looks somehow even worse when seen in daylight. And somewhere at the other end, far away in the Otherworld, Jin and Straw must be riding that ghost truck back towards their home.

Ruby swallows hard, and then offers Fei her hand, and together they turn towards the village.

SHANGHAI
1988

'And so – hungry, tired, feeling desperately sad to have left Lao Jin behind – we walked down from the ghostly tunnel towards the village, and the river—'

The old woman looked up at me sharply.

It was late, really late again – and my head was swirling with what she had told me so far. She waved away a waiter who was hovering again at my elbow trying to encourage us to leave.

'Maybe you think I'm just a confused old lady!'

'Heavens, no!' I said. 'Go on. Please.'

In that moment all I wanted was to hear what happened next.

'I saw it with these eyes,' she added. 'That young girl was me – if you can believe it.'

I could. Her face may have been lined and aged, her hair silvery grey, but each time I looked into those eyes that melted away, and all I saw was the determination and vitality of a much younger Ruby Harkner gazing back at me.

'Time is the greatest mystery of all,' she said, peering deep into my eyes. 'May I ask whose ghost it was *you* saw?'

'My father,' I said quietly.

It was the first time I'd told anyone what I had seen. 'He walked past the sitting room window of our cottage in Wales. Just as if nothing was wrong and he'd forgotten he couldn't be there.'

That memory – the rising of the hairs on the back of my neck, the uncanny sense of presence – was still alive in me. But sharing the story felt like it was lifting a burden off my shoulders.

'I was lucky to find someone like you to listen,' the old lady said. 'Someone open to things.'

She looked around suddenly, as if snapping from a dream.

'My God, almost midnight,' she said, getting up abruptly. 'How about meeting me tomorrow one more time? We'll go for a walk and I'll tell you how my story ends. It's not all doom and gloom, I'm glad to say! And I'll show you some things . . . bits of the old "Paradise of the Adventurers"?'

That was easy to answer. 'I'd love to. Thank you.'

'*Hao*. Good. Two o'clock sharp on the Bund where we first met. And I'll tell you about how I found my way home again. We're all looking for home, wouldn't you say? My friend should find me by tomorrow evening, but we can get the rest done in plenty of time. I'll start with what I found about what happened to Charlie . . . *Zai jian*.'

That night I lay awake for hours in my hostel.

My false start into adult life, my confusion over my father's death eased to the side for once. Instead all I could think about were steamboats and snarling rapids, pale dogs and spirit foxes. At about two in the morning – giving up on sleep – I rolled out of bed, went to my desk and started to scribble down as much as I could remember of what the old lady had told me so far, trying to get down every little detail before it slipped from my grasp.

A solid day of classes were scheduled for the next day. I wouldn't be going to a single one of them, I realised.

第十一章

WHAT CHARLIE SAW

For a long time there was a great blank space right where Charlie's head should be. A space which ought to be full of memories and images and sounds and thoughts – and instead contained nothing but emptiness.

At first he had thought he might be dead, but the aches and pains seemed to dismiss that idea.

At least I'm alive, he thinks vaguely now.

Days have gone by, Charlie knows that. Weeks, or even months.

Outside the high window he has seen daylight turn to darkness and back again, but how many times? A very few bits and pieces are starting to come now, fragments of things he used to know, or ought to know. And questions.

Like: *where's Ruby?*

Like: *what's happened to Fei?*

Like: *where am I?*

Some kind of hospital, that much is clear. The first thing he sensed was the sting of iodine and bleach in his nostrils. Now as he struggles to open his eyes again a nurse floats through the ward – one of the American missionary ones, all busy-ness and starched uniform – carrying something under a towel.

'Missee, please?' he calls out, his voice hoarse.

She glances at him. 'Stay in bed, I'll come back later.' Then she adds in basic Chinese: 'You rest. Doctor says not well.'

And with that she's gone.

Charlie groans and rolls under another wave of tiredness, closing his eyes.

He remembers the Gorges – just. Remembers holding Ruby's hands and Marlais swearing, the walnuts cracking. The shock of cold, churning water – a great roar as the boat rolled over him and a tongue of flame fizzing in the water, then extinguished.

A glimpse of Captain Marlais reaching out a big white hand.

Then nothing until, after a long blank, a huddle of worried faces peered at him and firm hands started pushing the water from his lungs. And then nothing more, just blackness and motion, as if he was on another boat again, bobbing with the waves, but everything dark. Hard to tell when he was awake and when he was asleep and dreaming. And sometimes the dreams that did come were nice: he was talking to Ruby, holding her hand again, and everything felt so close . . .

. . . and sometimes they weren't nice at all. A feeling of dread, darkness pressing even closer – and out of nothing the face of a hopping vampire leaning in close with its rank breath fuming, grabbing for his chest.

He would wake with a start – to find nothing but night.

But just once, possibly twice, on that waking moment, he had seen the red twine twisting round the base of his little finger, and felt on it the gentlest of tugs.

He opens his eyes again. Without his glasses everything is blurry. At least the people either side of him seem solid and human – though it's clear neither of them are very well at all. He's tried talking to both, but the woman to his left is barely conscious, and the man to his right just keeps muttering under his breath about the old Empress and doesn't seem to hear Charlie's questions.

He wants to get up now, to find out where he is and start planning how to get out of here, to set about looking for Ruby and Fei. Save Dad too.

But every time he as much as half lifts himself from the mattress, his head goes funny, and he has to lie down quickly again and wait for someone to come and feed him the warming soup that clears the chill inside him for a few minutes.

Yesterday – or was it the day before that? – he awoke to find a gruff-looking Yankee doctor at the foot of his bed.

'What's wrong with me?' he croaked, first in Chinese and then in Pidgin.

The doctor furrowed his forehead, then perched on Charlie's bed for a moment. 'We don't know really. Your temperature's very low and your blood pressure isn't much better.'

'I do not understand,' Charlie said. 'Tem-per-a-ture?'

'You plenty cold,' the doctor had said, rubbing his own torso with his arms and making out he was freezing himself.

And it's true. The cold areas in his body seem to be spreading. And when he focuses on the chill his mind leaps instantly back to the boneyard on the hill and the hopping vampires. That awful feeling when the thing touched him.

The doctor smiled brusquely, then stalked off, leaving the nurse to take his temperature once again.

'They say there's a big storm coming,' she said, glancing at the glass tube, then shaking it out. She frowned. 'Plenty big storm, savvy? Big wind! Typhoon. But you're safe here. Whoever you are.'

Charlie pulls the blankets tighter around him now. In the distance there's the low rumble of something that might be thunder. Or big guns. But he's too tired to care. With the index finger of his right hand he strokes the little one on his left.

If it is a storm, he hopes Ruby has somewhere to shelter.

An hour or so later – it can be no more than that – he wakes again to feel his shoulder being gently shaken. It's the old lady from the next bed, somehow recovered and looking brightly at him. It's dark in the ward, but her face is lit by a lamp somewhere to one side.

'You're better . . .' he mumbles, sleep still heavy on his eyes.

'Yes. I'm leaving now,' she says. 'I just wanted to wish you well. And make sure you knew about this.'

She reaches down and points to his hand on top of the blankets. And there, pulsing gently, is the glowing red thread.

Charlie nods, smiles – and seconds later, is pulled back to sleep again.

第十二章

BLACKTOOTH

At the entrance to the village below the tunnel three old ladies are sitting on a bench enjoying the morning air. They're chattering quietly, a ripple of laughter breaking out as Ruby and Fei approach. Behind them a boy is drawing water from the well whistling a scrap of folk tune. But, seeing them coming, he grabs his bucket and hurries off, slopping the contents and calling out a single word of warning to the women: 'Strangers!'

The ladies look up sharply.

'Where are you from?' one of them shouts, getting to her feet. 'What do you want?'

'I'll handle this,' Fei whispers. 'No point stirring up too much curiosity about you, Ruby. Good idea?'

Ruby nods. Fei's relief at being out of the tunnel and in daylight has obviously put fresh strength in her.

She smiles at Ruby and then strides forward.

'What do you want?' the woman shouts again. The others are also standing now, peering at the newcomers.

'Morning,' Fei says brightly. 'We want breakfast!! And you do not want to know where we've come from, believe me!'

'Have you come from over the hill? Did you see any trouble there? General Ho's lot are being driven back by the Nationalists.'

'Bother that,' Ruby hisses under her breath, 'ask them where we are!'

One of the other women obviously has sharp ears, because she turns to look at Ruby and smiles, revealing a line of stubby black teeth.

'This is Green Earth Village, my girl. Long Ridge County. And where on earth did you get that *horrible* accent?'

But Ruby's eyes have already slipped beyond the women, towards the cluster of buildings just visible in the middle distance. They stand about a mile or so from the wide sweep of the Yangtze, elevated above any flooding. The pagoda really looks familiar now, its position against the river just right.

'What province are we in?'

'Don't even know what province you're in?' the

first woman says. 'This is Hupeh, of course!'

'Are you *sure*?'

'I think I would know where I was born, wouldn't you?' the woman huffs.

Ruby's eyes are still on the distant houses. There's no smoke rising from them, no figures setting out into the fields.

'What's that village over there?'

The old woman turns, following the direction Ruby's pointing.

'Nowhere,' she grunts. 'Nobody lives there any more after what the bandits did years ago—'

'But what's its name?'

'Peach Blossom. Used to be a lovely place, but nothing good about it now.'

'Peach Blossom!' Fei gasps. 'You were right, Ruby! That old Mister Jin was right about the tunnel!'

Ruby's heart soars. It's true, she thinks. That's the pagoda we saw when the *Haitun* moored on the flood. The river's further away now with the water receded – but the shapes of the hills beyond the river are the same. This is where Charlie rowed ashore with Tian Lan. The tunnel out of the Otherworld has lopped off hundreds of miles of journey.

'Where did you say you came from?' the black-toothed woman asks, tapping Ruby on the chest. 'Ah, I see now why you can't talk properly! Are you from France, America?'

'Me? I'm from Shanghai,' Ruby declares, 'and I've got to get back as fast as I can.'

'My family come from Peach Blossom!' Fei adds proudly.

'Really? Give it a wide berth now if I was you,' the first woman says, her face shadowing. 'People see fox spirits all the time around it. Been bad ever since the foreigners drove that tunnel through the hill.' She nods back at the ridge. 'For the railway that never happened. Disturb sleeping dragons for nothing and see what happens!'

Fei glances back. 'Have you ever been through it?'

'Never,' the lady hisses. 'People do go in, my dear. But they *never* come out.'

Blacktooth clucks. 'Superstitious nonsense. Now let me get you something to eat. We do hospitality right in Green Earth. Whatever the state of the world.'

Raised spirits give way now to exhaustion and hunger. When food comes, Ruby takes the bowls of rice and fried vegetable eagerly from Blacktooth. Fei, if anything, wolfs hers down even faster, talking and eating at the same time.

'Apart from that little bit on the junk, I don't know

when I last ate proper food! This is good stuff!'

The woman snorts. 'We've been lucky here. Lots of places have been half-starved or worse. Famine upriver earlier in the year. Flooding. But there's so much superstition about our neighbouring village, bandits and the like tend not to come here much. We just get on with life most of the time. Peach Blossom's bad luck was our good, I suppose . . .'

Fei turns to Ruby, whispering. 'And you last saw Straw when Charlie went ashore? I think I heard all that happening! Moonface had stopped somewhere near here and he and his men hurried me back on the motor launch. There was some shooting and then we were away again. That horrible old pock-features was in a very bad mood.'

The woman looks at her. 'What are you whispering for, girl? No secrets.'

'Nothing,' Ruby says brightly. Probably best not to say too much about Moonface. She smiles at the old lady, and bows, trying to get her onside. 'Thank you so much for this lovely food.'

The woman nods curtly and looks at Fei. 'Not many foreign devils can speak our language. She's a clever one obviously.'

Fei bristles. 'Ruby's really clever – cleverer than anyone I know,' she chirps. 'Well, at least as clever as me and my big brother and my dad.'

Blacktooth looks at her sharply. 'What did you mean about your family coming from here?'

'Dad – and Auntie – grew up around here. My auntie is Ruby's *amah*. They fled after the village was shot up. Ended in Shanghai where Charlie and me were born. Did you know them? The Tangs? Maybe I've still got relatives around here.'

'Not many survived the attack there. A vicious bandit ransacked it, murdered dozens and stuffed them in the well.'

'Oh we know all about stupid old Moonface,' Fei says brightly. 'I've been this close to him!' She holds up her thumb and finger a fraction apart – but Blacktooth doesn't seem to be listening suddenly, and she gets to her feet, reaching out for the empty bowls. 'I'm sorry, young lady, but if you two are mixed up in something to do with that terrible man and his lot I'd rather you left. We don't want trouble here.'

'But he's dead now,' Fei shrugs. 'Or something like it—'

'I don't want to know any more,' the lady says firmly. 'Ignorance is bliss.'

Ruby gives Blacktooth her best smile. 'Please. We need help to try and track down Fei's brother. He's lost – and very ill.'

The lady chews her lip with the blackened teeth.

'Best if you head for your own people, foreigner—'

'They're not *my* people,' Ruby bridles. 'And anyway we must be a hundred or more miles from that kind of help, even if we did want it.'

'There's an Englishman about thirty *li* back towards Hankow. He writes for the foreign newspapers. Maybe he'll help.' She sucks the stubs of her teeth. 'Though the fighting must be pretty close to him. I'll get my nephew to show you the way. And may Heaven take care of you all. General Ho's on the prowl round there and he's worth avoiding.'

'General Ho?' Ruby asks. He's not one of the warlords she's heard Dad banging on about.

'Didn't get enough cuddles when he was little, if you ask me,' the old lady says. 'Now he's vicious. A crackpot. I'll get my nephew.'

A track leads away from Green Earth towards the remains of Peach Blossom Village. It skirts the most outlying buildings, giving a clear view of the well in the middle of the square. Ruby shudders, remembering Amah's horrified tales of bodies stuffed *from the bottom to the very top* . . .

'Couldn't we just have a quick look?' Fei asks the young man who's leading them silently. He's short and stocky, his face as hard as iron. In answer he just shakes his head once.

'And why not?'

'Need to hurry. The frontline's moving about like a snake in a bag right now.'

Ruby looks away from the river, judging the angle of the sun as it climbs towards noon. 'Shouldn't we head west though? To go towards Hankow?'

The nephew grunts. 'Sometimes the longer way is the safer way.' He jerks a thumb inland. 'Communists there, beyond the ridge. Nationalists ahead. All kinds of bad people in between. But this is a forgotten track.'

And with that he stumps off. Fei sticks out her tongue behind his back, and then takes one last look at the ruined village, chewing her lip. 'I wonder if . . .'

'What, Fei?'

'Well, I wonder if my mum's ghost might be here?' she whispers. 'I don't even really remember her though. I was really, really little when she died.'

Ruby looks at her, remembering what Mister Tang said about seeing his wife's ghost one day in the alleyway outside their house. 'You should talk to your dad sometime about that,' she says.

'What do you mean?'

'He – told me he saw her in Shanghai.'

Fei's eyes open wide. 'Dad said that?!'

Ruby nods. 'So I doubt she's here.'

'Blimey, he never told us that—'

'Oi, you two!!' the nephew shouts from the track ahead. 'Get a blasted move on.'

Ruby puts an arm round her young friend's slim shoulders. 'Come on.'

An hour passes. Overhead the sun dances through the leaves of willow and aspen as the path curves away through a tangle of brambles and honeysuckle. Small birds flicker in and out through the shelter. That day outside the Mansions was like this, Ruby thinks. When Charlie and I crouched low in the bushes trying to work out what was going on. It felt warm and safe in that moment. And close. Like we could never be parted, even though all the trouble was getting worse: agent Woods dead, Fei missing, Dad acting so strangely . . . but Charlie and I were together and it felt everything would be OK.

She glances down, but there's still no sign of the thread. Not a hint of it since the swim to shore, she thinks. What does that mean for Charlie? She shoves the thought away as firmly as she can, and hurries to follow the others.

Bramble tendrils snag at them. Not many people come this way, that's clear enough, but it's making this long thirty *li* even longer. And for what? Some silly Englishman who might just lock her up like the consul did in Nanking. Or who will treat her like a child and nothing more.

Fei is trotting along beside the stocky nephew. She may still be young, but you can see she's grown a bit recently. Not just the little sister tagging along in their games – she's only a head shorter than the man leading them along. Ruby catches Fei and taps her on the shoulder.

'Maybe we should go our own way,' she whispers. 'Straight for the river.'

'No. This is better,' Fei says firmly. 'We can get some proper help from this journalist type. He'll know people, right?'

'I think it might be a mistake.'

'Well, I don't. And I should get to make a decision once in a while. Charlie's my . . .'

'. . . brother. I know. Ow!'

A thorn rips into the skin just above Ruby's knee, and she stops to pluck it out, leaving a thick red drop of blood on her white skin.

For two long hours they pick their way through the twisting, sun-warmed corridor. Overripened berries and the drowsy buzz of bees mingle with the chirring of crickets in every bush. Hard to believe now in famine or battling warlords or hungry ghosts. But Blacktooth's nephew doesn't look relaxed: he strides on relentlessly, head twitching this way and that, beckoning them irritably every time they drop too far behind.

Fei stops and puffs out her cheeks.

'I'm done in. Oi!' She raises her voice towards the man. 'Any chance of a rest?'

The man shakes his head. 'Not here. And keep your damn voice down, pipsqueak.'

Fei pulls a face. 'Fathead,' she whispers, then glances at Ruby's hands. 'I keep thinking about all that stuff about Charlie being ill. From the *you-know-whats*?'

'It'll be OK, Fei. We'll find him. We'll make him well again,' Ruby says, putting as much belief as she can into the words. Fei meets her gaze, forces a half smile, then turns slowly to trudge after the nephew.

As Ruby follows, she goes on chewing the thought in silence. How cold Charlie's hand felt when they stood on the *Haitun*'s bridge and braced for the climb up the Grinder, how awfully pale he looked—

'Ruby!' Fei hisses.

Blacktooth's nephew has stopped dead on the path, waving at them to stay where they are, his whole body suddenly alert. He's listening hard to the silence around them.

The crickets have all stopped, and the only birdsong is very distant now. The nephew's shoulders slump, the way you would if you'd dropped a precious cup or something and seen it smash to bits. The damage already done.

A second later a low whistle comes from the undergrowth behind, and then an answering one from ahead – and, materialising from out of the flies and rusty-leaved brambles, a squad of ragged soldiers surrounds them, bayonets sharpened by the bright afternoon sunshine.

第十三章

HEADS MAY ROLL

It only takes a heartbeat to go from freedom to captivity. Ruby's wrists are bound tightly behind her back and a grubby rag pulled around her mouth.

Two of the soldiers have the nephew by the scruff of the neck, his toes barely touching the ground as they shout questions at him in a weird northern dialect.

'I have no idea, no idea,' he keeps repeating. 'Take them. But let me go and look after my family. That one's English. Good money!'

One of the soldiers comes over and tips back Ruby's hat. His eyes widen. 'The General will want to see this.'

Twisting in her captors' grip, Ruby sees Fei try to give the nearest soldier a mighty kick in the shins.

'Dirty monkey,' the soldier shouts, and cuffs her hard around the back of the head. 'You be a good little girl, now.'

The nephew's pockets are being searched, some copper cash and a knife taken from him – and then he's sent on his way with a boot to the backside that brings broken laughter from the soldiers.

'Run, dog! And tell your village General Ho expects total loyalty!' the leader of the men snarls. 'Or heads may roll.'

Ruby shoots Fei a warning look. No point fighting this lot: they look like they'd snuff out your life without so much as a second thought. She searches from one chiselled face to another. As the excitement of capture ebbs away from them, she can see how exhausted they all look. Half-starved by the looks of it. General Ho can't be one of the important warlords – but there are so many of these tinpot leaders it's hard to keep track. Some are powerful like the Shanghai Warlord, but there are dozens of insignificant ones. People laughed about it at Mother's tea gatherings – *all their names are the same and they're all quite simply dreadful* – but this is scary and not funny at all.

The leader of the platoon gives a short barked order and moments later she and Fei are being frogmarched along the track at a ridiculously fast pace – even faster than the nephew. It's all she can do to keep her feet on the uneven track. On either side of her the soldiers are silent, rifles gripped, their eyes searching every shadow, every bend for possible trouble.

As they cut away from the line of the river, she tries to work her hands free, but it's hopeless, and the cord just bites into her wrists. The cloth around her mouth seems to get more stinky by the second. The breakfast they gulped down at Green Earth is turning over and over in her stomach, mixing with frustration that they're losing time, and the rising sense of fear. She remembers what she's heard about captives in the Interior – it takes time, but you tend to come out alive in the end. Just depends what *this* general is like. Some of them are no more than glorified bandits. Some are modern, forward-looking – and some are just fruitcakes, Dad said once.

Over the tramp of the soldiers' boots comes the sound now of distant gunfire. A ripple of tension runs down the line and a couple of men crank the bolts back on their rifles.

Maybe we'll be rescued, Ruby thinks. But who by? Could be out of the frying pan and into the fire, that's the problem. The whispered words of Mother's stupid friends, gossiping about the fate of missionary captives in the Interior, creep back into her ears. Of *fates worse than death*. Of ransoms paid *a day too late*.

Poppycock, Ruby thinks, trying to buoy her sinking

spirits. They just like to make it sound worse than it is. General Ho *might* be a decent man, though the black-toothed lady didn't seem to have a good word for him.

They're climbing towards a cluster of houses on a low ridge. A fence runs along the side of the path, and on each post ahead something has been tied – a round, dark object. From a distance she at first mistakes them for lamps – or maybe pumpkins put out to ripen. But people don't tie them to fences do they? she thinks. Maybe it's some kind of decoration or—

Her legs go watery as she suddenly realises what she's seeing: a row of severed human heads. Five or six, and a few more beyond that, gazing out at the path, each buzzed by its own little cloud of flies.

Oh God! *Heads may roll* . . .

At the last second she pulls her eyes away from the grim objects as she is hurried past. Breakfast churns harder in her stomach, threatening to come back up, and she shuts her eyes for good measure, stopping up every sense until the nightmare is safely passed.

This general isn't one of the good ones then, she thinks, heart pounding. He must be one of the bad. The mad.

The gunfire ahead is intensifying, and the soldiers are jogging now, tugging their captives along with them. The path narrows onto uneven flagstones and then cuts into the corner of a walled compound as sentries wave them hurriedly through, each face creased with fatigue and tension.

The last time Ruby saw troops like these was that stifling day in the old city when the student got pulled from his barrel mid-speech, and that swallow skimmed a streak of blue over his head. The horrible speed of the executioner.

She tries to take a deep breath – but somehow it just won't come, and it's hard to run like this, bound like a chicken.

Stop running around like a headless chicken, Mother always says. Headless . . .

Don't panic, she thinks. It doesn't mean that's what's going to happen to us, does it?

Doing her best not to stumble she follows the soldiers as they hustle across a courtyard, past a stubby field gun pointing towards the river, up a short flight of steps – and into a darkened hall.

The room reeks of tobacco and sweat. As Ruby blinks in the half-light, she sees a cluster of soldiers gathered round a wide table. Light slants through the smoke, and, as the men turn to look at her, they part.

Brilliantly lit in a sunbeam, a tall, heavyset man is leaning over a chart, jabbing at it with his finger.

He's wearing a white, Western military uniform – the kind of thing top Navy men wear when they're doing ceremonial stuff on the Bund. His shoulders are widened by ridiculously huge and tasselled epaulets, a row of medals reflecting light on his breast as he straightens. His mouth sets in a hard line as he peers at his visitors, the toothbrush moustache above that bristling.

He looks preposterous, like someone playing at being a general. But the sight of the heads and the intensity of his gaze leave no doubt that this is no game. The man coughs and takes a few steps towards her, the men around glancing to the captives, and back to him, clearly afraid to move until they get an order. And still the gunfire outside bangs away.

What was that horrible story about one of the mad generals? Something about people pushed into a steam train's boiler? Don't be silly. That's probably just made-up—

The man snaps his fingers, then waves her and Fei forward. He motions for the rags to be taken away from their mouths and leans back against the table. Ruby takes a gulp of air, trying to compose herself.

'And what on *earth* do we have here then?' he asks in perfect, cut-glass English. 'Spies from the Nationalists and Reds in Hankow? Or a Sunday school outing?'

Now it's Ruby's turn to feel her eyes widen. His accent seems so unlikely amongst all these rough and ready Chinese soldiers.

'Well? Enlighten me, young lady?' His eyes narrow. 'And be quick about it. I'm fighting a battle on three fronts, may the good Lord have mercy on me.'

'What's this idiot saying?' Fei squawks as her gag is removed. 'Let us go, you old windbag!'

The man makes a slight movement with his finger and three soldiers grab Fei again.

'My name is General Ho,' he growls in Chinese. 'You address me by my rank or say "sir". Is that clear? The last person who gave me lip, left without a lip. Got it?'

Fei nods quickly. 'Sorry. Sir. General.'

'Check their necks,' Ho barks. 'Maybe they'll have to join the other Reds on the fence posts.'

Fingers tug at Ruby's collar, her neck turned to the light, held there, then released. They're doing the same to Fei, she sees, checking her throat for something.

'Nothing,' one of the men grunts.

The General smiles at Ruby. 'Do excuse the examination. Stupid Communists all wear those rags. Cheap material, cheap dye. Sweat tends to leave an imprint on the skin. So we can tell – and then sort the wheat from the chaff so to speak. Then you pop the old heads on posts and it does wonders for the local morale I can tell you. Wonders.'

His tone is light, as if discussing whether you want milk with your tea.

Ruby nods, but her mind is racing: the image of Charlie winding that red cloth in his fingers the night on the railway – when the armoured train thundered past. What if he's been wearing it, what if he's been caught? What if—

'But I expect you are what we used to call at Oxford a God-fearing Christian soul,' Ho drawls on, his face lightening a bit. 'So we will take good care while we decide what to do with you and your foul-mouthed friend. I keep telling the men that the Christian way is the best way. Forgiveness, where possible. I converted a bunch of them last week, baptised them with a hose in one go! But I don't think they understand really – China's in a mess and look at what I have to help me: riff-raff!'

Ruby takes her chance. 'I – my father works in Maritime Customs in Shanghai. I'm trying to get home.'

'Customs? They're a bad lot. Not much better than smugglers. The whole thing runs on bribery and squeeze—'

A larger explosion shakes the door in its frame. Ho glances out of the window and scowls.

'And what is your name?'

'Ruby. Ruby Harkner. Sir.'

'And this urchin?'

'Tang Fei,' Ruby says. 'We're trying to find her brother. He was swept away when the boat we were on capsized and . . .'

How much should she say? Maybe the General hates foreigners. And Mister Tang seemed to be caught up with the Communists. Maybe better just to keep it simple.

The General is looking hard at her. 'Shanghai is a sinful city. Sodom and Gomorrah if you ask me. The worst excesses of the foreigners, and the basest instincts of our own people. Gambling and dancing and heaven only knows what.'

He rubs his chin. 'But it's good you should drop by. Very good.'

Another huge detonation reverberates close by. Bits of rock and soil patter on the roof. A soldier puts his head in the doorway, beads of sweat on his forehead bright in the light.

'General. The Nationalists are getting very close. We need to get out of here.'

'Maybe not,' Ho says, switching to Chinese. 'Looks like we have something to bargain with now. Send a runner under a truce flag – tell them we have an

English hostage. Our terms: safe passage for us all to the railhead, *with* our weapons. A hundred silver dollars in cash. They get the girl safe and sound to buy favour with the foreigners. If not, we will have – very sadly – to execute her and her companion.'

Ruby's breath lodges in her throat. Presumably he doesn't mean it, though? Just the kind of thing you say in negotiating . . . but the image of the dead student keeps rushing back at her now. The swallow departing over his stricken body – and those heads on the fence posts, buzzed by flies.

Maybe being foreign won't save me, not out here, maybe—

She swallows the plum stone back down.

The General glances at his fob watch. 'Let's say six p.m. sharp, shall we? Tell them they need to decide very quickly.' He switches back to English: 'And while we wait we can have a little civilised conversation.'

Fei struggles a step forward, seething. 'Don't you *dare* touch my friend, you ridiculous turtle's egg!'

Ruby pulls her back. No point antagonising the man.

The General turns away into shadow, ignoring her, sticking to English: 'Now don't worry too much, young lady. I think there's at least a fifty-fifty chance

143

the Nationalists will play ball. They will want to ingratiate themselves with the powers in Shanghai. Reassure them.'

But then he turns to one of his men and growls in Chinese. 'And you, go and see if you can find the executioner.'

Some thirty minutes later the shooting stutters to a halt and an eerie silence descends on the compound. Lowering behind the shuttered windows, the sun sends beams of orange light slanting into the gloomy hall and a fly dances in and out of them, fat and shiny in the autumn light.

General Ho settles into a heavy wooden chair, clears his throat, and starts to talk – and talk – his voice quiet, intense. In his flawless English he lists all the good works he has done, how his new-found Christian faith will reward him in the next life, how he spared at least some of the villagers who had given food to a band of Communists last month.

'We will be a great civilisation again,' he drawls on. 'Blend the best of the old and the best of the new. Ah, but first there will be more bloodshed,' he sighs heavily. 'As my tutor at Oxford used to say, one cannot make omelette without breaking a few eggs. We'll have to crack a few more yet.'

Ruby half listens, nodding when she thinks it best to, trying to shoot Fei a look now and then to make sure she keeps her mouth shut. Gripped in the General's hand, the tick of his fob watch is just audible. Her thoughts stray from his words, her gaze travelling down to her own hands. In the deepening gloom of the hall there's a tiniest, tiniest hint of the thread again.

Isn't there?

Maybe it's just imagination, desperation, conjuring it. No, there's definitely something on her little finger. She watches as it fades, flickers, fades – and the concentration dulls the fear for a moment. If the thread's there, then I *am* fated to be with Charlie, she thinks. That's what the stories say. And if I'm fated to be with him, I can't die here, can I?

Tick-atick-atick-atick . . . the watch keeps counting away the seconds, the minutes.

The General's list of hopes and complaints drags out as the sunbeams shift to horizontal. Six o'clock can't be more than half an hour or so away judging by the angle. His men stand patiently to attention in the shadows. Now and then he pauses, and those pauses get longer each time. When the General's train of thought about damming the Yangtze stumbles to a halt – and that pause drags out to well past a minute – Ruby realises that his eyes have closed. The next second the General snores loudly, setting the medals on his chest rattling.

Fei's voice comes to her in a whisper. 'Psst. Rubbbyyy?'

'What?'

'What's he going on about? Us?'

'No. All kinds of other stuff. Building a dam on the river.'

'Then he's bonkers. What time is it?'

'I don't know.'

'It must be getting on for—'

'Shhh a minute.'

There's another sound now, over the buzz of the trapped fat fly, the General's snore: a rumble of engines approaching at speed.

The General's men stiffen to attention. There seems to be a reluctance to disturb his sleep, but at last – after a lot of nudging – the toughest-looking of them bends close and whispers.

Instantly the General is on his feet, eyes blazing. 'Well, why the hell didn't you tell me sooner!' he roars in Chinese. He glances at his watch and laughs, then turns to Ruby.

'Five past six. By rights we should have dealt with you by now, but my men were too afraid to *wake* me! Ha. Well, are you ready to be a bargaining chip, Miss

Harkner? Try not to look too brave. It's not an empty threat you know. Where's that bloody executioner! Chop, chop. Ha!'

And with that he draws a finger slowly across his throat and glares at Fei.

第十四章

MISTER QUINN

A black, open-topped car comes thumping into the General's compound. The white flag fluttering from the cab is stained by the early evening light, and beside it another flag ripples: the red field, blue sky and white sun of the Nationalist Army. The soldier standing in the back of the car looks better equipped, his uniform cleaner, than the ragged men surrounding the General. But his face is just as hardened, just as fierce.

Ruby watches him as he jumps down and glares at General Ho. Maybe it is out of the frying pan . . . ?

Rumbling behind the car is a beast of a vehicle: a kind of small truck, every inch of its surface plated over with metal shields – like some kind of angular, mechanical rhinoceros. Another Nationalist flag flutters from its gun turret. It clanks across the compound until it's just a handful of paces from the snout of the General's field gun and grinds to a halt.

And nothing happens: just dust settling, a gut-churning sense of tension as the General's troops aim their rifles at the beast, and the little gun turret on top swivels from one to the next.

General Ho holds up his hand. 'Enough. We're under a truce here. Who is your negotiator?'

A hatch on the rhino squeaks open and a white flag pokes out, followed a moment later by a Nationalist officer in a peaked cap. He clambers down, throws Ruby a withering glance, and then rattles a stream of Chinese at Ho.

'After what has happened upriver, who cares about the lives of foreigners?'

Ruby swallows hard, glancing from the man's face to General Ho, then to the men around her. No sign of an executioner still. Maybe it *is* just a bluff. She peers at the dusty windscreen of the little Austin car, trying to make out the face of the driver. He seems to be smiling as he looks her way, but his features are blurred.

'First of all, *that*,' Ho says in a firm voice, 'is *my* armoured car. I had it built for me in Harbin at *considerable* expense—'

'Our National Army will defeat you and the other

warlords,' the officer in the cap cuts across him. 'And then we will defeat the foreigners and unite the country again!'

'Well, I am sorry to say it is you and the filthy Reds who will be annihilated,' the General says. 'It is just a matter of time. And you need to curry favour with the foreigners *just* as much as I do.'

They stare at each other for a long half minute. 'If you want the English girl,' Ho adds calmly, 'you must allow me and my men four hours' head start and free passage out of the valley. With all our weapons. And give my vehicle back. What you do with her and her little friend is up to you. But I imagine you can get a good deal out of the British for her safe return.'

Ruby bites her tongue. It's unnerving to hear yourself being talked about like some kind of token. Currency. She's aware again of those eyes watching her from behind the windscreen of the black Austin, an intense gaze fixed on her.

'You can have *two* hours' start, with light weapons,' the Captain says. 'We take the foreigner. That's the offer. Take it or leave it.'

The General stares at him, then turns and clicks his fingers. It's like the sound of a chicken bone snapping. Immediately a lumbering brute of a man steps from the shadows, a long curved sword gripped in both hands.

The air goes out of Ruby's chest, and she hears Fei groan.

'Four hours. Or we kick you out of the yard now and execute our hostages immediately. We'll start with the younger girl just to make our intent clear.'

'Scumbag!' Fei shouts. 'If you do my brother will kill you!'

'SILENCE!' Ho roars, his face going red. 'Just keep your mouth shut, got it?'

Fei nods, and swallows hard.

In the lull that follows the Austin's door clunks open, and the driver gets out. As he steps into the fading sunlight Ruby sees he is a young Westerner, dressed in a rumpled white shirt and baggy trousers. He sweeps back his hair – almost as blond as her own – and then shoves his hands in his pockets. He looks from one party to the other, flicks a gaze at the executioner and takes a couple more steps forward.

'Now then,' he says in ropey Chinese. 'We can all come to a friendly arrangement I'm sure.' Unconcerned by the bristling weapons being pointed at him, he strolls over to the captives.

'Ruby Harkner, I presume?' he asks in English.

'Y-yes,' Ruby stutters, astonished. 'I am.'

The man glances round the compound again, and then adds out of the corner of his mouth, 'Don't worry, it's all going to be fine. I think.'

What kind of Englishman is riding around the civil war in a Nationalist car? Ruby thinks. And how on earth does he know who I am? Charlie always says the Nationalists aren't to be trusted, that they're more ruthless than the Communists . . .

The young man turns back to her, looking calm and collected, just a few beads of sweat on his forehead. 'Pleased to meet you. My name's Quinn, Arthur Quinn. Doing a spot of reporting for the Manchester *Guardian*. Flying a bit of mail too up and down the river. And who's this young lady with the big mouth?' he continues, keeping his voice bright, throwing a glance at Fei.

'My friend Fei,' Ruby says quietly, her mouth dry. 'Help us. Please.'

'Don't worry,' he whispers, 'I've told them all your dad is really, *really* important in the Council. Not the corrupt little pen-pusher he really is.'

Ruby's heart bumps. 'You know Dad?'

'Silence!' General Ho bellows, and points at Quinn. 'You! Don't interfere with my hostages.'

Quinn holds up his hands, and saunters towards the General, a smile on his face even as the soldiers train their weapons on him.

'Don't be a fool, Ho. You won't get your armoured

car back and you won't get more than two hours. I'd take it if I were you. And I'll put in a good word in my article. And people will say, *oh he's the kind Christian warlord.* Maybe we won't hunt him down for all the crimes he's committed. Savvy?'

The General looks at him, at Ruby.

'Don't teach me to suck eggs—'

'You should see the firepower they've got now, Ho. You'll all be mincemeat the second you kill your hostages. You know that. Now give us the girl and her friend and get out, there's a good chap.'

He goes over to the Captain and says something into his ear – and then with a shrug returns to the driver's seat of the Austin.

Ho looks from the Nationalist officer to Ruby to his executioner and back again. Nothing else moves but the flags rippling on the vehicles. The man with the sword is gently sliding a whetstone along its length, making the blade sing in the deepening silence. Very, very distantly to the east there's a long drawn-out roll of thunder.

Fei moans again. 'Oh God, I think I'm going to wet myself.'

Ruby's eyes are still on Quinn – and he suddenly flashes her a thumbs-up.

'It's going to be all right,' Ruby whispers. 'I think

153

it's going to be all right.'

'You keep saying that,' Fei sniffs back. 'I want to keep my head, Ruby! Go home—'

The blade keens down the stone again, cutting Fei short.

And this time the silence that follows deepens – and deepens – into what seems like an eternity, until again the thunder rumbles again somewhere far away to the east.

The General throws a hand in the air.

'Very well!' he barks, and turns his back on the officer in the peaked cap. 'Deal.'

Quinn dashes back across the compound.

'It's going to be OK,' he mutters. 'But you're now both prisoners of the National Revolutionary Army. Situation: marginally improved, but not much! Get in the car.'

'But how do you know who I am?' Ruby repeats.

'Tell you in a min. Main thing is to get out of here with your head on your shoulders.'

'Both of us?'

'Of course!'

The young man seems likeable, but can they trust him? After all he's knocking about with the Nationalists. He seems calm, in control as he opens the door for them and ushers them into the car. But as he reaches for the starter, Ruby can see that his hands are shaking. Already the armoured car is edging back towards the gate, the fat barrel of Ho's field gun pointing at it all the way.

'Keep an eye on Ho and his men,' Quinn mutters under his breath. 'That man changes his mind more often than you or I change our socks.'

He reverses the Austin at speed through the gates, turns, and then accelerates hard after the armoured car as it trundles down a dirt road towards the setting sun. At the last moment Ruby swivels round and catches sight of the General watching from the steps of the hall. He makes the sign of the cross and then disappears back into the gloom.

On the back seat next to Fei the Nationalist guard spits loudly, and says something indescribably filthy about the General.

'What will happen to him?' Ruby turns to Mr Quinn as he slams the car through the gears and powers them away down the lane.

'They'll give him his two hours. They'll keep their word. No idea after that. Every time I think I've got the hang of this messy war it wrong-foots me. Utter madness.'

'We go where now?' Fei squeaks in Pidgin.

'Well, *you'll* be probably put with some family in

Hankow,' Quinn says, breathing out a long sigh. 'But you, Miss Harkner, may be facing a longish time in a lock-up, I reckon, while they try and negotiate a deal.'

'But I *simply* can't. We need to help Fei's brother. And what do you know about my dad? Is he OK?'

'How should I know?' Quinn blows out the tension through pursed lips, squinting through the dust at the armoured car ahead. 'I'm just along for fair play. Neutral! British Consul in Hankow sent me because they're confined to quarters since the Nationalists took the city. I just happened to be around when the news came in that you were being traded by General Ho and remembered the name from a bulletin that was going up and down the river. Half the foreigners on the river are looking for you, young lady! Your dad's put out some huge reward before he vanished. Thousand dollars.'

So he *is* hiding, Ruby thinks. The Green Hand must want him, or the Settlement authorities, or both. He made a mess of things – a horrible mess – but at least he's trying to get me back. Where on earth would he get a thousand dollars though? Mother's always complaining we don't have two pennies to rub together.

Quinn gives her a grin, as if enjoying a private joke. 'Now do you have any idea where a customs man might get *that* much money? Or why he's gone into hiding?'

The guard jabs the snout of his pistol into Quinn's shoulder. 'Shut up and drive.'

'All right, all right. No need to be rude.'

Ruby looks at him again: there's something of the rogue about Quinn. Like he might tell you a tall story just for the fun of it. But each time he smiles it's genuine, reassuring.

'About to cross the lines,' Quinn murmurs.

Ahead the sun is a big ball of fire now and Ruby has to shield her eyes. They're charging towards a barricade across the road, with field guns positioned to either side. Soldiers salute and a roll of barbed wire is pulled away to allow the armoured car and the little Austin through.

Ruby glances back. Through clouds of dust the eastern horizon is threatening now: towering cumulus walling off the sky, their upper parts lit by the sun, but darkness gathering beneath. Home lies that way, through what looks like a huge storm. It's time to take a chance on their new companion.

'I can't wait around in a cell in Hankow,' she says over the engine's roar. 'It might be too late for my friend. For my dad. Can't you help us? Please?'

Quinn doesn't answer for a moment. He accelerates to the rear of the armoured car, then glances at her.

'Well, obviously I don't intend to let you rot in

some hell-hole. Might be able to get you home faster . . . much faster. Do you think your dad would pay up, by any chance?'

Ruby shakes her head.

'He might . . . he would. If he had it. I just want to find my friend and get us all home.'

'And who is this friend?'

'Fei's brother. He's . . . he's very important. To me.'

'How . . . important?'

She feels herself blush very slightly. 'Very.'

Quinn wrinkles his mouth in thought, then flashes another quick grin.

'Then hold tight.'

'I said shut up!' the guard shouts again, standing up in the open back seat and waving his pistol.

Quinn throws a quick look at the man's reflection in the rear-view mirror.

'Well, that's it then,' he mutters, as if to no one in particular, and takes a very deep breath. He focuses hard on the road ahead, his knuckles whitening as he grips the knobby wheel. 'Hold tight!'

'What are you talking about?' Fei shouts. 'Why can't you both talk in Chin—?'

A violent convulsion seems to shake the little Austin's engine and Ruby is hurled forwards in the seat, her hands reaching out to brace on the dashboard.

She hears a grunt as Fei slithers into the footwell behind, and turns to see the guard slamming into the back of her seat, his arms flailing to try and stop himself being thrown out of the car. Immediately Quinn stamps back down on the accelerator, throwing them all back in their seats. Caught off balance a second time, the Nationalist soldier flies backwards, just managing to catch the crook of his arm on the rear seat, one leg high in the air, the other over the side. His pistol clatters to the floor, as his free hand claws for a hold.

'Give him a shove!' Quinn yells. But there's no need: the car bangs over a pothole and the impact jars the guard straight over the rear seat in a tumble of arms and legs. One hand on her Fedora, Ruby stands and looks back to see him rolling in the dust behind.

Quinn pulls her down. 'Keep low for Heaven's sake.'

Ahead the armoured car is still rolling forwards, but it's already slowing, the Captain in the raised turret silhouetted against the sun, waving at them.

'That's it,' Quinn murmurs. 'In for a penny . . . ' He bites his lip and pushes even harder on the accelerator, a high-pitched whine coming from the engine as they hurtle towards the armoured car. The officer in the peaked cap is raising a pistol, levelling it at them.

'Get right down!'

Ruby dives to the floor just in time to hear a gunshot. She glances up at Quinn, afraid he will have been hit – but he's OK, wrenching the wheel to the right, back to his left, then quickly right again. He ducks and there's another loud bang – and she hears the roar of the armoured car's engine as they pass it, every bump in the road jarring up through the floor of the Austin.

'Passed them!' Quinn shouts again. He's leaning forward over the wheel, weaving long snaky lines down the road. He flicks his gaze to the mirror again. 'Let's just hope they can't get the cannon on that thing working fast enough.'

Ruby eases up from her seat and peers back. Their dust is saturated with orange from the lowering sun, the armoured car a black monster tearing through it. There's a muzzle flash from the stubby cannon, and then a *whoomp* as a big mushroom of dirt detonates a dozen or so yards behind.

'Are we gaining on them?' Quinn says, gritting his teeth.

'I don't know. Yes, I think so.'

As the gun on the armoured car fires again, the road sweeps round a bend and hops over a hump-backed bridge. Ruby feels her stomach lift, her body weightless for a second as it rises off her seat. A row of trees stripe shadow and the orange sun across the road.

'I really would hold tight,' Quinn shouts. 'We need a good head start.'

'For what?'

'My own private world, Ruby. I think you'll like it.'

SHANGHAI
1988

'Like a tiger's stripes, can you imagine?' the old lady said. She was peering into my eyes with her intense grey-blue gaze. Behind us the usual stream of cyclists were rattling over the Garden Bridge, in front a breeze fretting the Huangpu's steely surface. 'Orange sun and and black shadows across the road—'

'I can,' I said, enthralled. I could see the striped light in my mind's eye, sniff the dust, hear the rattle of the car. I had read enough stories of travel in old China to fill in the gaps. And more than that I could *feel* her story building around me. Could feel what it was like to be there with her, tearing along in that little black Austin 7 as a clanking rhino-car took pot shots at them.

'Go on, please. What happened then? What did Mister Quinn mean about his own private world?'

She seemed not to hear me for a moment, and turned the collar of her fur coat up against the breeze. 'Let me show you something. If I can still find it. We have time enough and it will help you really understand the story, young man. I can show you where some of it happened.'

Without waiting for an answer, she turned away from the river, beckoning me to follow.

'I hope it's still there. But the thing is what's real and true today isn't real and true tomorrow. I mean, I could run once and now I can't. I could do handstands – and now I'd break something. I used to think parents were strong and reliable, but I lost that belief the moment my little brother died. We change. And the world changes around us even faster.'

She turned back to me. 'But some things – well, some things take longer to change and fade. Memories, some places.'

I nodded. 'So where are we going?'

'To where the story ends, young man. Of course! If you have time?'

There was no way I was going to abandon the adventure now. 'I've been making a few notes. I hope you don't mind?'

'Not at all. It shows you are a proper listener. I'm glad I met you!'

We had been walking the length of the Bund, under cranes starting tentatively to build the new metropolis. The old lady smiled and looked at the sweeping river again, her face lifting.

'So where was I? Yes! Mister Quinn got us away from the armoured car, through a horribly banged-up town. And beyond that was a long straight road that led to a wide open field. And beyond that – well, beyond that was something ab-sol-utely *wonderful* . . .'

第十五章

CHOCKS AWAY

Quinn wheels the Austin off the road, past a couple of corrugated iron buildings and out onto a wide expanse of patchy grass and bare earth. A little red and white windsock is blowing fitfully in the breeze, and as their new friend brings the car bumping around in a big arc Ruby's jaw goes slack. Parked on a worn-out strip down the middle of the field, washed with the reddening sun, stands a large, modern biplane.

Beside it an Indian man in a yellow turban and overalls is getting up leisurely from a deckchair, watching them race towards him.

'You ready?' Quinn shouts to Ruby. 'Any sign of that blasted armoured car?'

'Ready for what?' Ruby gasps. But her heart is already hammering nineteen to the dozen. 'You mean *fly*?'

'Your choice. You can can stay here with my Sikh friend, Mister Singh. He's very nice. Or come up for a spin. But I for one am not hanging about for those Nationalists. Burnt my bridges there.'

'No, it's fine,' Ruby says, nodding eagerly. 'I'm ready.'

Quinn skids them to a stop by the plane.

The man in the turban is looking at them quizzically as Quinn jumps from the car, and gives him a hearty slap on the back. 'Need to go up, Mister Singh. Right now. You take the car and head home. They won't bother you – it's us they're after.'

Singh rubs his chin. 'She's fuelled, and that strut's fine. But, Arthur, have you seen the weather that's coming?'

'It'll be all right,' Quinn says, throwing him the keys to the Austin. 'Just a bit of a blow.'

'We're going up in that?' Fei asks, eyeing the machine. 'Maybe we'd be better taking the car?'

'It'll be fine,' Ruby says firmly, tugging her over to the plane. 'We can get home faster. Find Charlie.'

'I'm not scared,' Fei says, eyes fierce for a second. 'I just meant maybe we'd miss him – be too high or too fast or something.'

'We'll trust the thread to tell us,' Ruby whispers.

Fei puffs out her cheeks. 'Well, I still haven't seen that blasted thread. And what if we fly straight back into the Otherworld. Look what happened on the junk! We ended up worse than we were before.'

'I saw the thread in General Ho's place,' Ruby whispers. 'Just a glimpse. This has to be the right thing to do.'

Quinn's already pulling on a leather flying helmet, struggling into some baggy overalls. Still Fei looks unsure – then she taps him on the shoulder.

'Excuse me, Mister, but are you real? Are you alive? Or are you a ghost?'

'Very much alive, I hope,' he says, puzzled. 'But we won't be for long if you two don't get on board.'

'You promise you're not a ghost.'

'I absolutely promise.' Quinn puts his hand on his heart and turns back to Ruby. 'It's going to be a squeeze. But you should be OK. Hop up in the gunners' cockpit. Put your feet there, there – not there.'

Ruby's hands are already reaching for the holds. How many times has she watched planes hum over Shanghai and longed for a chance like this? And now it's happening, it's really happening . . .

She grabs a handle, plants a foot where Quinn points, and pulls herself into the open cockpit, plumping down on the seat and gazing in amazement at the wings, the struts and tensioning wires cutting the view to pieces.

In the surge of excitement she's forgotten the chase, but now she hears an engine, growling somewhere behind the broken buildings. She dreads to think what that armoured car's stubby gun could do to the thin skin of this plane. And there it is! As she reaches out to help Fei in, she sees a cloud of dust rising behind the last building . . .

'They're coming,' she shouts. 'Hurry up!'

Quinn vaults up onto the wing and then with one more easy stride into the pilot's cockpit. He cups his mouth, and bellows, 'Contact, Mr Singh!'

The Sikh is already at the nose of the plane, pulling down the propeller hard. The engine coughs and the blades spin once, twice, snorting exhaust in little blue puffs . . . but then grind to a halt.

The sound of the armoured vehicle is louder now, the cloud of dust larger. Ruby's hands grip the cowling tighter.

'Again!' Quinn booms. 'CONTACT!'

Once again the man in the turban pulls the blade down, and this time there's a ripping sound, and a whirr from the exhausts as the propeller spins faster and faster.

Quinn signals with both hands.

'Chocks away!'

The next instant the plane is lurching forward across

the grass, slowly at first, but then quickly gathering speed on the bumpy strip.

'Strap in one of you!' Quinn bellows. 'Other one get down in the footwell.'

Fei looks at Ruby. 'What's he saying?'

'That you should get down in the space there—'

'That's fine by me!'

Ruby struggles with the harness as the biplane rushes across the ground, the wind whipping at her hat. She tugs it off and sits on it – then snaps the buckle shut.

But still they haven't left the ground. Just the rapid *bump*, *bump*, *clump* of the plane's wheels on the rutted grass. A line of fence is approaching, twisted wire and trees beyond, and it looks like they're going to plough straight into it. But at the last, Quinn breaks and slows the plane to a crawl.

'What are you doing?' she shouts, looking round to see the armoured car emerge onto the airfield. 'Can't we take off?'

'Need the full length,' Quinn yells back. 'Here we go.'

He wheels the biplane around in a tight U-turn, then throttles up again, accelerating straight for the armoured car, the gap between them vanishing swiftly.

It's madness surely, Ruby thinks. They'll shoot us

or crash into us and it'll be worse than if we'd just been good prisoners and then—

But the plane surges even faster, throwing her back in her seat and pushing Fei against her legs. Everything's shaking – the plane, her vision, her bones – and then that vibration suddenly stops, and magically the aeroplane lifts from the earth and carves steeply upwards into the streaming evening light.

If there's any shooting from the armoured car, Ruby doesn't notice it.

All she can feel in that second is the elation of speed and lift as she – Shanghai Ruby – finally takes to the sky. Leaning over the side, her eyes watering in the wind, it's as if the airfield is falling away from the plane. Quickly – so much more quickly than she ever imagined – everything shrinks: the buildings, the trees, the armoured car all ridiculously small in a few seconds. Only the puff of smoke from its turret to show it's not something from out of Tom's old toy box. The Austin is just visible on the distant road, like a shiny black beetle scurrying into the lengthening shadows, and then that too is whipped away, as Quinn banks the plane and the earth tips to be replaced by the vastness of the sky.

As he levels the plane off the young man glances back and shouts something at the top of his voice.

'WHAT?' she yells.

Mister Quinn points up into the heavens. The last of the sun is bleeding onto the clouds banked to the east, picking out high cirrus above in orange and pink. With an extra surge the aeroplane lifts even faster, climbing, climbing. She gasps.

'You should look, Fei. It's amazing.'

Fei shakes her head. 'You look for us both . . .'

Ruby grips the cockpit edge with both hands and rises out of her seat a little further. Immediately the wind howls in her ears and mouth as it streams over the cowling, snatching her breath away. The power of the machine, the glorious sky work together . . .

. . . and for a moment she feels nothing but joy surging through her as she revels in the thrum of the propeller, the singing of air over the wings, the opening of the vast, twilit landscape of China below.

Tentatively she lets go her white-knuckle grip of the cockpit rim, and straightens her arms out into the howling gale around them, the wind freezing cold on her hands. Flying like she's always dreamed. I really am the child with *far to go*, she thinks, feeling a huge smile spread across her face.

Ahead Quinn gives a whoop – like a boy watching his model plane catch the wind – and she gives a long cry of delight back, the kind of war cry she always gave when leading an imaginary attack by the Outlaws.

Quinn swivels in the seat and grins.

'Hold tight!' he bellows. 'TURNING!'

She grabs hold again and a fraction later the biplane banks steeply to the left.

Ruby gasps as the sky swings away over her head . . .

. . . and into view, just like the vision that has haunted the edge of her dreams for so many years, she sees the mighty Yangtze again. A vast ribbon of beaten metal, twisting away from them downriver, towards the darkening east.

Shivers and tingles rattle the bones in her back as she drinks in the sight. It's come true, she thinks. I always knew I would see this one day. And now it's happening.

At last her gaze drops to Fei, and her eyes focus on a small maker's plate bolted to the cockpit's front wall.

FAIREY 'FOX' MARK I.

She bangs it with her knuckles. 'Look, Fei! It says the plane's a Fox!'

Of course, she thinks.

Of course. And her eyes fill with the shining Yangtze again.

第十六章

BAD MEDICINE

Dimly, the ward swims back into Charlie's view.

The tiredness seems a little lighter on him, and as long as he keeps right under the covers the sense of cold not so bad. Felt like I slept ages that time, he thinks. Days and days . . . ever since the old lady woke me up. He glances at her empty bed – the sheets stripped away. That glimpse of the thread was good, he thinks. Even if it seems more like a dream now. Outside, the storm is beating harder against the ward's windows, rain washing the glass against darkness and occasional brilliant lightning. The Yankee nurse passes, and he lifts an arm to beckon her over.

'You awake again?' she says, perching on the foot of his bed.

He nods. 'Lady, next bed,' he whispers hoarsely. 'She go home-side now?'

The nurse looks confused. 'Which lady?'

Charlie points to the bed to his left, and a shadow slips across the young woman's face. 'Oh, no. I'm sorry to say she died. Early in the night. She was old and very unwell—'

A fierce shout cuts the nurse short, and she looks away in alarm. It's the kind of shout you get from people used to giving orders and expecting immediate action.

'But I speak to her . . .' Charlie says, confused.

The nurse isn't listening. A moment later the door bangs open and Charlie swivels his gaze to see three blurred figures standing in the doorway, one of the doctors and a Chinese nurse trying to block them. Both are shoved roughly out of the way at gunpoint.

'We represent the Shanghai Warlord. The rightful government. We are searching for Communists infiltrating in advance of the Revolutionary Army scum. Prepare to identify yourselves.'

The American nurse gets to her feet. 'Say nothing,' she whispers fiercely to Charlie. 'Whatever they ask you.'

The men are already moving from bed to bed, snarling questions, pulling off sheets, the doctor protesting until one of the men turns and levels a gun at his temple.

Charlie screws his eyes up, trying to make his

eyes focus. One of the soldiers is shining a torch at the neck of each patient. For what, for heaven's sake?

A patient three beds away, scrawny and half eaten by starvation, is dragged from his bed, and hauled down the corridor. Charlie can just hear the arresting soldier mutter the word 'red' as he bundles the protesting man away.

Red?

The only red thing he can think of is the kerchief – the red strips of cloth Dad's friends use to identify themselves. Tied round the neck.

What happened to mine? Charlie thinks in alarm. Can't remember. Maybe it's jammed in my trouser pocket. Then that will be it. No hope of seeing Dad or Fei again.

No hope of ever telling Ruby how I really feel.

He swallows hard, tries to summon strength to rush from his bed, or to fight.

No chance. His legs feel like watery tofu.

The men are coming closer, getting more impatient as they do, while the American nurse pleads to no avail, and outside the typhoon – it must be as much as that now – keeps battering the darkened glass.

One of the soldiers is at the foot of Charlie's bed now.

He closes his eyes in resignation.

Ruby, he thinks. I hope you are OK. I hope you know I love you.

'And where are this boy's clothes? We need to check papers,' the soldier rasps. 'Or we'll take him anyway.'

第十七章

MOTH TO A FLAME

'LOOK! Hankow!'

Quinn is pointing down at a sprawl of buildings clustered on the north bank of the river. Dusk is advancing, swallowing the city street by street.

Hankow. Somewhere down there is the temporary family house where her little brother died. Ruby gazes down as it passes beneath their wings.

Look, Tom! she thinks. I'm flying. Just like I always said I would.

To the west the sun is already dipping below the horizon.

'Not meant to do night flying!' Quinn shouts, pulling his hands back, and the biplane's nose lifts, climbing quickly. The air brightens around them, like someone's switched on a light – and Ruby sees the orb

of the sun rise again, as they gain altitude, Fei's face –
beaming now – beautifully lit.

'Wow!' she shouts. 'You made the sun come up
again, Mister! Brrr, it's cold though!'

Quinn nods his head, and then banks away from
the city, steering for the river again. Beneath them the
Yangtze's surface holds the last of the light, and you
can make out tiny boats dotting its skin. Ruby peers
over Quinn's shoulder, through the blur of the
propeller, and sees the river stretching far, far ahead
to where it slips under the towering bank of cumulus
into the night.

Fei's right, it *is* cold now. And the sky and the land
ahead look bleak as the last of the sun fades.

Quinn jabs his finger at the night ahead. And as he
does so a huge bolt of lightning goes fizzing across the
sky. Half a minute later, just perceptible over the
thrumming engine and wind, felt more than heard,
comes a prolonged rolling of thunder.

'We'll just do our best!' he yells. 'See how far we
can go.'

As dusk deepens all you can see below is the vague
pathway of the Yangtze, and, as the light ebbs further,
Ruby feels her joy and hope ebbing with it. More
lightning flickers ahead: first every minute or so, then

every few seconds. A huge storm by the looks of it. She glances at her hands in the dark well of the cockpit: it seems ages since she had any sign of the thread on her finger. Just that brief glimpse maybe in the General's hall. Has Charlie seen it, wherever he is? And if he does see it, will he trust it? When he went off with Tian Lan and her comrades, he said that if they got properly separated then the other should head for Shanghai and the safety of the temple again. Maybe he'll just shrug the thread off as imagination . . . superstition.

The Fairey Fox judders on invisible wedges of air, and when Mister Quinn glances back his face looks older, the seemingly perpetual half-smile gone.

Drops of rain needle Ruby's face, and the temperature plummets as they broach the edge of the weather. Below, the river is no more than a smudge now, and Quinn guides them lower, as if to hold on to it for comfort. To either side the lightning and answering thunder keep flashing and banging, and the plane shakes as it fights gusts of wind and rain.

'We'll keep going!' he shouts in a brief, smoother passage of air. 'As long as I can see the water.'

'Where are we?'

'Just past Kiukiang. I think.'

He points down. Beneath and to their right is what looks like a puddle in the gloom, a tiny channel just visible linking it to the Yangtze.

'Po Yang Lake!' he shouts.

Po Yang? Ruby thinks. The one time she saw it, on an excursion from the trip out to Hankow, it had seemed like an inland sea. From up here it feels like you could just step across it in one big stride.

Quinn banks them left and it falls away, leaving nothing but inky, turbulent sky to fill her vision . . .

. . . and suddenly, for no more than three or four heartbeats, she sees the tangled red thread spooling out from her hand, from the cockpit, swirling ahead into the storm. She grabs for it with the other hand, feels it – or imagines she feels it – feathering her palm, and then Fei grips her shoulder tightly.

'No way!' she squeals, the whites of her eyes shining like porcelain. 'I can see it! I can see the thread, Ruby! It's real!'

Instinctively she reaches for it too, but even as she closes her fingers it's gone, blinded by a searing flash of lightning. Almost instantly there's a bang very, very close and the plane drops.

Fei screams.

For a heart-stopping second it seems as if they will just keep dropping and dropping, but then the wings bite the air again and the Fox steadies itself.

Quinn is shouting something.

'I can't HEAR,' Ruby screams into the wind.

'. . . pea . . . OF CAKE . . .' he yells.

Piece of cake. As if!

The thunder roars again. You can hardly make anything out now, but it's clear they're losing height rapidly. The Fox's engine coughs – catches, then coughs again. To Ruby's left the river is a blur, then that too is gone, leaving nothing but darkness. There could be anything below their wheels.

Quinn banks the Fox sharply again, and glances over his shoulder. He's shouting again but the words are ripped apart by the wind.

'. . . minute . . . bit faster . . . tight . . .'

With his right hand he mimes gripping an invisible hold, then jams it back on the controls. More raindrops, bigger and colder, spatter the cowling and smack their faces.

'Hold tight, Fei. Hold tight.'

In the next lightning flare Ruby sees they're very low now, just a few hundred feet over a village straggling out along a track. Quite clearly she sees the roofs, trails of wispy smoke. In the next flash a white horse startles in a field and gallops away into the oncoming gale. Then it's dark again.

The engine splutters badly – stops.

In the sudden lull Quinn shouts: 'Brace! Br—'

Bang! Bang! All the smooth power of flight is gone in a shuddering impact. The wind is knocked from Ruby, and then everything's quieter for another second or two as the plane surges back into the air, before banging down again. A wild vibration seizes the the Fox as the undercarriage scores into the ground, the wings twitching violently like a candle-singed moth. It ploughs on through bushes into a field, the crop swishing against the underside, snagging the wheels – and then they hit something. The plane's nose dives into the earth and Ruby is thrown forwards violently. The harness snags hard and she hears Fei yelp as she is ripped from her grasp. A second later the tail of the Fox rears up, leaving Ruby tangled in the harness, dangling in the cockpit like a discarded puppet.

The engine has cut, leaving nothing but the wild voice of the storm around them. And when she calls out Fei's name – and Mister Quinn's too – she hears no reply.

Confused, tipped half upside down, she struggles to free herself from the straps. Her head is hurting a bit – and there's a smell of something burning, and a strong whiff of petrol too. She fumbles harder with the harness, half remembering a story about a pilot burnt to a crisp on the Shanghai airfield.

Thunder crackles overhead.

'Fei? Fei!' she calls again, but still there's no reply, just the wind rushing over darkened trees nearby like water over a sluice, rain pock-pocking the wings and fuselage.

So this is what it comes to, she thinks: crash-landed in some sodden field in the middle of nowhere. And all the effort of fighting Shadow Warriors, Moonface, of evading vampires and foxes and crackpot warlords will go no further than a remote village and a plane crash that ends in a ball of flame.

第十八章

RED OUT OF THE BED

Charlie's been lying down so long it's strange to be vertical again.

At least the men gripping him are real flesh and blood and not those horrible things from the bone hill that haunt most of his dreams. That's about the only good thing you can say for the situation though.

'Move it,' one of the Warlord's men snarls.

Stuffed back into his jacket and trousers he's being marched out of the hospital, the staff watching quietly, protests silenced by a single, echoing gunshot into the ceiling. No arguing with the Warlord's soldiers, not since the damp, red kerchief was pulled from his pocket.

'Red scum,' the commanding officer hisses in his ear. 'You will be taken to Shanghai. We'll make an example of you there.'

Together with a young woman, and the other patient from his ward, he's bundled down the rain-lashed front steps towards a covered lorry.

'I'm not a Communist,' he manages to whisper hoarsely to the man who has him gripped under the armpit. His feet stumble. 'I'm ill. I . . .'

'Doesn't matter,' the guard grunts. 'Walk. Or you'll be finished here.'

'He's just a boy!' the American nurse shouts as Charlie is dumped into the back of the lorry like a sack of coal. The canvas back is pulled down and the lorry lurches away into the night.

The rain and wind have sent fresh shivers shaking through him. Not fear though, strangely enough. He feels disembodied, like he's watching a film, curious to see what will happen next. Shanghai is home ground, and the thought of being there is reassuring. Maybe Ruby will find me there, he thinks. That's what I told her when I went off with the Red Lanterns.

It suddenly strikes him that he hasn't for one minute doubted she is alive. She's Shanghai Ruby again, after all. He glances at his hand. There's nothing to see when he raises it, shaking in front of his face.

The young woman, her hands bound behind her back, looks at him with pity.

'How old are you?'

'Nearly fifteen,' he says, trying to sound strong. 'What do you think's going to happen to us?'

'Train to Shanghai. Then . . .'

Her voice trails off. She lifts her head, and forces a smile.

'It will be all right,' she murmurs. 'You don't need to worry.'

Charlie nods, closes his eyes, feels his body getting heavier again.

Behind him the other prisoner groans as the lorry jars down the road and squalls of rain and wind buffet the canvas. But Charlie's last thought, as he drops off the edge of awareness, is of miles away: it's of Ruby, and that wonderful, glorious, sun-warmed moment at Full Moon Bridge.

第十九章

TYPHOON TAIL

Ruby's fingers fumble with the buckle. The stink of petrol seems no worse, but there's still that whiff of burning. She goes to call Fei's name again, but just then the heavens open, as if buckets of water are being chucked at her.

'Fei!' she splutters. 'Help!'

And then, over the downpour she hears – incredibly – laughter, and torchlight splashes her face.

'Just when you think it can't get worse,' Quinn shouts from where he's standing by the fuselage. 'Are you two all right?'

'I can't find Fei!'

'I'll look.'

She pushes against the cockpit wall, and at last the harness pings loose and she eases herself out. Quinn's torch is already swishing this way and that across the beaten-down corn – and, thank God! – there's Fei, holding her head with both hands as if worried it'll fall off if she lets go. She looks OK though, apart from the blanket of mud down one side.

'Are you hurt?' Ruby yells, clambering down and sprinting towards her friend.

But Fei ignores the question, her eyes bright. 'I saw your thread, Ruby,' she gasps. 'We're going the right way!!' She looks around, mouth open. 'And then I think I flew right out of the plane. When we crashed!'

'It wasn't a crash,' Quinn says, flicking the beam over the fuselage. 'It was an emergency landing.'

'I could smell burning,' Ruby says.

Quinn shines his torch around the nose, the engine. 'Looks all right. Maybe rain put out whatever there was. Reserve tank ruptured – we're not going anywhere for a while.'

He moves the beam on down to the undercarriage to show the Fox's wheels buried to the axles in mud.

'But we can't wait,' Ruby says firmly, as the rain thickens around them.

'Can't be helped. Let's see if this is friendly territory. And keep our wits about us until we find who's in control.'

Somewhere close by in the darkness the horse whinnies loud and shrill.

An hour later it's as if the stupid clouds are trying to drown the village.

At least that's how it feels to Ruby as the night deepens. Just when you think the rain can fall no harder, it does just that, pounding on the tin roof where they've been sheltered for the night. In an oil lamp's flicker all you can see from the windows is a curtain of water pouring from overloaded gutters. The village headman joins her, stroking his sparse white beard. He frowns and points at the torrent of muddy water flowing left to right, away from the maize field where they crashed, past the house and away into the night.

'Will the village flood?' she asks him.

The man tilts his head, considering. 'Who knows? Seen it worse, but these days everything's topsy-turvy. When the country is in turmoil, the rivers are too. This can be a beautiful place you know. Our village in springtime is like heaven when the weather and the soldiers allow.'

'We need to get to the river, head for Shanghai.'

'You'd be crazy to go out in this, young lady. There's a good bit of the typhoon's tail left yet.'

He stalks away to move a bucket to catch a fresh leak that's started drip, drip, dripping in the middle of the room.

Quinn is sitting near the door, scribbling in a pocketbook, and Ruby goes over to him impatiently.

Without lifting his head he checks her before she has time to speak. 'I said no arguing, Ruby. I can't abandon the plane here, and I am not letting you out of my sight now I've found you—'

'So you can get your beastly reward?' The words come more abruptly than she means.

'Don't care about rewards,' Quinn sighs, closing his pocketbook. 'Well, not much. I am *responsible* for you now.'

'But we can't hang about here!'

Her eyes slip to the door. Lodged in the corner is a furled, black umbrella with a bamboo handle. It looks as though it's seen better days. Quinn follows Ruby's gaze, and he laughs. 'You'd need a bit more than that,' he says, raising his voice over the storm. 'Count yourself lucky you're not rotting in a Nationalist cell. And you might be a bit grateful to your pilot for that skilful emergency landing.' He looks up, the smile back on his face. 'We'll move as soon as we can work out the situation, and we can assess the damage to the Fox.'

'I . . . I'm sorry,' Ruby says, biting her lip, reining in her frustration as best she can. 'I am grateful.'

The biplane's name echoes in her head. Strange the way Quinn materialised to rescue us, she thinks.

Fairey Fox . . . too much of a coincidence maybe?

Lightning flickers, and as if in reply the unseen horse shrieks again.

'Mister Quinn?'

'Fire away.'

'Are you a friend of Lao Jin's or something?'

He looks genuinely puzzled. 'Lao *who*?'

'Jin. He's from up near the Gorges, but he's been living in Shanghai. Normally wears a hat like this . . .' What more to say? He's a caretaker? A Taoist priest? A fox spirit?!

'Don't think I know him.'

She takes a deep breath. 'Do you believe in ghosts, that kind of thing?'

Quinn wavers his hand, palm flat. 'What is it with you two and ghosts? Who's this Lao Jin chap then?'

'Doesn't matter.' Ruby's fingernail finds its way to her front teeth, tapping away at them like Mother does. She pulls it away.

'You called my dad a corrupt pen-pusher—'

'That's what people are saying.'

She shakes her head. 'Do you know what's happened to him?'

'A friend in Customs said that if your dad's got any sense he'll be keeping his head down for a year or more.' He glances up at the leaky roof. 'Until the whole mess has blown over . . . Now get some rest.'

'How soon can we move?'

Quinn shrugs. 'Who knows? Storm could last another couple of days, and it'll take a team of oxen to pull the Fox out of the mud. Then we need to check her over. I'd love to file a story for the paper. But I'll need to get to Nanking at least.'

'Then just take us to somewhere on the river so we can get a boat—'

'Sorry. No dice, Ruby. We're staying put until the weather and the picture are much clearer. Got it? And in case you get tempted to do anything stupid I'm going to sit right here in the doorway like a guard dog. Look . . .'

He pulls a rumpled map from his overall pocket, spreads it out and stabs his finger at the snaking line of the Yangtze. 'We're about here. Close to the river, about forty miles short of Nanking I think. Roads will be rivers now. Bandits and pockets of warlord troops anywhere and everywhere. And the Nationalists will be moving fast and they'll have my guts for garters if they find us. Probably literally.'

Ruby's eyes fall on the date at the top of Quinn's notebook entry.

October the 12th, 1926.

A shiver runs the length of her back. So it's true

what Jin said. Weeks *have* passed. In that time Charlie could have made it back to Shanghai. He might be waiting for me there right now! She gets to her feet, but Quinn catches her arm. 'This brother of Fei's you're so keen to find. Is he that special kind of important?'

Warmth spreads to her cheeks again – a hint of the old beetroot face. But who cares what people think?

'Yes,' she says, feeling a kind of relief to say it out loud. 'He is.'

Quinn smiles. 'If you feel close to him then hold on to that. It's a big country in a terrible mess. But some links are hard to shake, that's been my experience . . . and I experienced some amazing things in the war. Amazing things happen in amazing times.'

'Like what?' Ruby whispers back.

'You asked me about ghosts,' Quinn sighs, the smile slipping from his face. 'A *really* good friend of mine – James Belden, eighteen and a half like I was then – got shot down over no man's land. Plane caught fire. That was it. I saw him spiral down and crash.' He pauses, and looks away into the gloom.

'And?' Ruby prompts.

'And, the next evening, I was flying through some awful weather – really awful stuff like tonight – and I thought I was going down, and all of a sudden I just felt incredibly safe. Like nothing could happen to me. And I looked to my right – and there was James, flying along beside me, almost wingtip to wingtip.'

Another shiver darts through Ruby. 'Go on . . .'

'Couldn't believe my eyes, but James waved – and moved ahead of me, and guided me during the next fifteen minutes through the worst of it, and then – *poof* – well, he just vanished. Now let me write my story – in case I do get to file it.'

'Did you ever see him again? Your friend?'

'Every day, Ruby. But only in here, you know.' Quinn taps his head lightly. 'Or here.' He rests his hand on his heart. 'Now be a good girl for me. And trust my judgement. Fei needs a rest even if you don't – she's dead to the world. And you'd be absolutely mad to go out in this.'

The rain comes harder again, almost drowning his voice.

An hour or so later Ruby is still awake, her ears still full of the storm. If we wait for the Fox to be pulled out and repaired that could easily take a week, she thinks. And what else could we do? On foot to Nanking might take two or three days and the Nationalists could arrest us anywhere along the route. Or the Warlord's men as they retreat. It has to be the river. No other way.

She glances back to the door. Quinn's still awake, sitting in a pool of light, his head bent to his notebook. Rolling onto her back she holds her hand up against the darkened ceiling, willing the red thread to reappear. But there's nothing, and she rolls back over onto her side, hugging herself, thinking of Charlie, of him holding her hand, and bit by bit that calms her choppy mind.

The rain keeps steadily falling, and firelight flickers and the stream outside gurgles louder and louder and louder in her ears . . .

. . . and she dreams of a fox – a female *huli jing* – walking along in the night-time downpour, a black umbrella held nonchalantly over her head. She's much younger than Jin, a beautiful shade of russet red, and she's moving nimbly along a saturated path, jumping the bigger puddles, towards a cluster of houses crouched in the darkness ahead.

And in the dream Ruby's jogging along just behind her. The fox lifts her head, peers into the rain, then hurries on past the tumbling willow trees. When the lightning flashes, her red fur lights up like neon, and white characters are picked out on the umbrella's skin. 'GOOD WIND'.

Wait, Ruby calls, but the fox spirit is too swift for

her and slowly she's left behind on the track. Already the *huli jing* has reached the village, a small red figure burning under her black brolly. At the first big house she reaches she suddenly takes the umbrella, shakes off the water and furls it, and then lifts it high in her two front paws and bangs the tip of it on the front door twice. The fox looks back at her.

GO NOW!

The words seem to come from inside Ruby's dreaming head, spoken slowly in a soft, foxy voice – and she's about to run forward, when she hears the *huli jing* again.

GO RIGHT NOW!

The fox looks back to the door, then lifts the umbrella and rams the wooden panels with incredible force—

BANG!

Ruby wakes abruptly, sitting bolt upright as the sound echoes on the edge of her dream. Thunder is rolling away, the after shocks still shaking the house on its posts. She half expects to see the door burst to pieces, or the beautiful fox standing there, but everything is quiet and ordered in the headman's house. All the lamps but the one by the door are out. Quinn has finally succumbed to sleep, slumped at his guard post there. She listens hard: it sounds like the rain has eased quite a bit. Just a gentle pattering on the roof now. But the urgency of the fox's words – the power of the knock – are still loud in her mind. Just a dream, Ruby thinks, but maybe Jin sent it to me somehow. Whether this is just a lull, the eye of the storm or something, we need to act now, she thinks. I'm sure of it.

She shakes Fei with her foot, one finger to her lips.

'Whattt?'

'Shhh. We're going, Fei. We're going now.'

'Where?'

'To find Charlie of course. The rain's stopped.'

Fei looks over at Quinn, blinking. She's not going to want to go out in this, Ruby thinks – especially not after I forced her to go up in a plane that ended up crash-landing.

'We have to go, Fei,' she whispers intently. 'I had a dream. There was a fox outside the door and she told me we had to go to Charlie right now.'

'A dream fox?'

Fei looks down at Ruby's hand, thinking hard.

'If you don't want to come, then that's fine, Fei. But I really *want* you to come and—'

'No. It's fine, Ruby. If you say we're going, we're going. You're attached to Charlie, just like you told me. By the thread. So let's go!'

'As long as you're sure.'

'Totally sure.'

Ruby gives her a swift hug, then tiptoes across to Quinn's sleeping form. She takes his pocketbook from the floor where it's tumbled from his hand. The last lines of his entry read: *Get R to tell her story, spin it up for a piece for the Illus. London News or similar.*

She turns to the next blank page, takes the pencil from the spine and scribbles:

THANK YOU SO MUCH. SORRY FOR ANY TROUBLE. WE'LL BE OK. Ruby H.

She sets the paper gently on his lap, and as she does so her eyes fall on the furled umbrella by the door. It'll be better than nothing . . . Fei has come to join her, pulling the blanket around her shoulders.

'I'm ready.'

Ruby holds her finger to her lips, grabs the brolly by its bone-dry handle and gives it to Fei, then eases back the bolt and opens the door. She has almost expected to see the neon fox staring up at her, hoping even that it might lead them away from the village – but outside there's nothing but water and darkness.

As a fresh squall of rain blows down the street she latches the door shut and Fei releases the catch on the umbrella, blooming it into shape.

'Which way then?' Fei says looking up at it.

There are a few small holes, but otherwise it seems sound enough.

'I suppose if we follow the water it'll take us the right way,' Ruby says.

'It's not all that bad now really,' Fei says, trying to sound a bit brighter as they splash down the village street. 'We've seen far worse than this in Shanghai. We have proper typhoons! They don't know what they're talking about, right?'

'Right!'

Ruby glances up at the sky above: a great mess of pale cloud, and darkness – like someone's poured a bit of milk into a bucket of ink and given it a stir. It looks threatening despite what Fei says, but away to the east there's the very first hint of dawn, faint light staining the horizon. And is that a star or two? A hint of moon on the cloud edge? The rain raps harder on the umbrella and she feels Fei's hand on hers.

'What if the thread doesn't show again?'

'Charlie said whatever happened we'd meet back at that cross we made on the ground at White Cloud. He'll do everything he can to get there. So we should too.'

The two of them squelch on through the last of the storm, two tiny figures huddled under an umbrella under an enormous sky – away from the village, from

Quinn, from warmth, from safety.

And in the shadow of a willow tree a beautiful fox – in animal form – watches them go, and then glides off into the rainy dark. She looks like she's smiling.

第二十章

THE RIVER GODDESS

Storms in Shanghai were always some of the best moments, Ruby thinks as they splosh down the meandering track that leads from the village: maybe it would be Tom and her sprinting for home as the thunderheads rolled in from the sea and the city crackled with energy. Or maybe the whole gang crouched in White Cloud as curtains of water fell from the roof, daring each other to dash across the courtyard and back as the lightning forked down. But always home had been close by, the cosiness of the house on Bubbling Well Road waiting for them to dry out and warm up. Even if this isn't as fierce as some of the coastal typhoons, the vast, dark clouds churning above are daunting.

The water flows around them, a black skin on the paved sections, cutting grooves in the soft track in others. Round each corner there's a sense of the land opening up, the great river approaching – and the water hurrying towards it. But there's still no view of the Yangtze, and the huddles of trees and scrub are thick with menacing shadows.

'At least there won't be bandits out in filthy weather like this,' Fei grunts. 'Even hopping vampires probably keep tucked up in rain like this. Don't you think?'

'I reckon so,' Ruby says, and links her arm into Fei's, as the rain comes harder and harder again.

After another soggy half hour the path climbs a short rise, then dives round a broken-down hut, dropping sharply to their left. As if a tap has been turned the rain suddenly stops, and, glancing up, Ruby sees the clouds teasing apart, the moon gliding through their glowing edges.

She breaks into a half run, and rounding the building sees the land drop away to reveal the Yangtze once again: even wider now, curving into the distance, a huge pathway of reflected shimmery moon. The sight puts fresh belief into her and she runs on down the path.

'And now what?' Fei calls, struggling to close the umbrella.

'We hitch a ride on a junk or something. Hurry up!'
'I can't see any boats,' Fei shouts.

'There'll be something.'

But when at a tight bend she stops to take a good look at the sweep of river, Ruby sees it's true: not a single vessel in sight. She hesitates, breathing hard – and then for a split second, perhaps the briefest glimpse so far – sees the red thread curl away from her hand, arc through the predawn air below her and dive towards the reed beds lining the shore.

'I've seen the thread!' Ruby shouts, and charges away full speed down the steep track leading to the river.

Thirty minutes later, as dawn spreads into the frayed clouds to the east, the renewed urgency is waning though. Nothing but reeds, reeds, more reeds along the river path they're exploring. Not a house or port village in sight – and still no boats on the river. Fei swishes the brolly through the wet rushes.

'You definitely saw it, Ruby?'

'Yes. It went in somewhere about here. Let's keep looking. Maybe we're not trying to find a boat.'

'Then what?'

'I don't know. Let me concentrate.'

She glances hard at her hand again. No sign of the thread reappearing, but she walks on determinedly, looking back up to the building on the ridge, trying to judge where the red trail disappeared into the reeds. About a hundred paces further on she sees the vaguest of paths veering off from the main track, not much more than a wider gap between the stalks.

'Hold on a minute.'

'But what's the point. There's nothing out there.'

'The thread went in somewhere near here. Just let me look!'

The reeds close, pressing tightly around her. The path – such as it is – twists and turns, almost doubling back on itself after a few dozen paces as if it's lost its way, then veers away diagonally back upriver. Ruby's just starting to wonder if there even is a path to follow, when it suddenly widens and becomes more definite. There's an old piece of cloth tied to a stick – a kind of marker – and then another, and she starts to jog, pushing through the wet stalks. Rounding a bend the track suddenly breaks from the reeds and runs straight, out onto a rickety jetty perched over the lip of the river's mile-wide course. The boards are wet and rotten in places, but the moonlight beyond pulls her on, and she picks her way onto the shaky ramp. Even now, the scale of the Yangtze takes her breath away: thousands of tons of water drifting past in near total silence. And she edges on, stepping over a gap, to the very end.

And now what?

She hears Fei rustling behind. 'Ruby? Where are you?'

Her eyes scour the jetty. From the last pole a dark, mouldy rope drops to the downriver side. Holding to one wobbling upright she leans out to peer into the shadows beneath, and her heart thuds harder. An old sampan is lurking there, most of it tucked tight under the platform: you can just make out its curved canopy in the gloom. It looks as though the thing hasn't been used for ages, though, maybe years. But in the last half hour they've seen nothing else on the water and surely it's better to get moving – even in something like this – than wait around any longer? She leans further, her hands grasping for the mooring rope and pulls with all her weight. Slowly the sampan rotates from under the jetty. Its canopy is half rotted away, and the deck is precariously close to the water. But it's floating – just.

Fei runs to join her on the landing stage, following her gaze.

'That old thing,' she pants. 'It doesn't look in good nick to me . . .'

But Ruby is already scrambling over the side, lowering her legs, then swinging by her hands for a moment as she eyes up the drop.

'Ruby—'

She lets go and falls to the open front of the boat, landing in a heap and setting the vessel bucking wildly, sending ripples into the reeds. Her momentum swings the sampan further out into the pale light. Quickly she crawls under the canopy.

'Well?' Fei shouts. 'Is it leaking?'

'Don't think so.'

'We'll need the oar to scull with.'

There's a half sack of rice that stinks like anything, a tin cup, nothing else . . . and then she sees it: a long-bladed *yuloh* oar lying snug to the side of the deck.

She clambers to the stern, hands fumbling at the mooring rope.

'Got it, Fei! Jump! I'm casting off . . .'

The knot is more slime than rope, and as she pulls at it, thick gloop smudges her fingers. She hears a sharp intake of breath behind her, and then feels the impact as Fei lands in the bow. With one more tug the knot disintegrates and she leans to the jetty and gives it the hardest shove she can manage, spinning them out nose first into the slow current at the river's edge.

'Auntie's cousin's uncle has one on Suzhou Creek,' Fei says breathlessly, crawling back to join her. 'They're always having to patch it up. But I've rowed it a few times. We need to get the oar in the little cutaway thingy at the back. You'll have to help me lift it.'

Together they manoeuvre the long blade from under the shelter, the sampan wobbling like mad, and heave it upright before dropping it into a worn notch in the stern.

'Is that right?' Ruby pants.

'Yep. Think so.'

Fei looks tiny as she grapples the huge oar and leans into it with all her weight. The blade bites the water, for half a stroke – then suddenly rips clear, nearly toppling her straight over the side.

'Perhaps I should do it?'

'No, I can do it!' Fei says. And setting her mouth in a determined line, she heaves again, sweeping a long figure-of-eight in the river. The sampan shudders forwards.

'I'm getting it,' she shouts. 'We just have to get to the channel and then I can steer with the current. But you keep an eye and see if it leaks. And watch out for sandbanks and stuff!'

She flashes Ruby a grin, and untidily – but steadily – nudges them further out towards the middle of the river.

Ruby crawls back to the prow, eyes raking the river ahead. It *does* look like the water is very close to the deck. If Fei misses a stroke out here, she'll be in the drink and under in seconds. No way to rescue her.

'Be careful!'

'No kidding,' Fei says through gritted teeth as she heaves the blade again. Again.

'That's it, you're doing it!'

A couple of dozen twists of the blade later, the current grips the sampan and they are away, slipping eastwards, towards the dawn.

'Look at me!' Fei calls proudly. 'Must be in the blood!'

Sleeping villages pass as the dawn grows ahead.

As they round the next sweeping bend a junk comes into view. Moored on the far side of the river it looks dwarfed by the water. On the warship going home from Hankow – on the *Haitun* and even on the ghostly junk – Ruby has only ever seen the Yangtze from high above the water. Now it feels like they're part of it, tiny, like insects on a huge pond.

Ahead there's a flicker on the water's skin, the kind of thing that poor Captain Marlais said showed a submerged sandbank. She calls it out to Fei and with a bit of trial and error the sampan jags to port and swings round it with distance to spare.

'How long do you think it will take us to reach Nanking?' Fei calls.

'I don't know.'

She tries to do the mathematics. The river's flowing at what she guesses is a bit faster than walking pace. So what's that? About four miles an hour. Maybe five if we're lucky. Times that by twenty-four hours, that means we might get almost a hundred miles by this time tomorrow. That's not bad. Nanking was only forty miles or so according to Quinn. And from there to Shanghai, how much is that? Something like three hundred miles by river didn't Dad say?

She puffs out her cheeks. If we've got to go all the way there that's going to take a week or something. And deep down she knows that will be way, way too long for Charlie. Isn't that what the dream fox was trying to say? Maybe we should go ashore at the first big river port and try and hitch a ride on something faster? But what if we're nabbed by the authorities or the Nationalists? Well, at least we're moving now.

And every now and then she feels – or thinks she can feel – a tiny pull at the base of her little finger. As if a fish is tugging at bait on the end of a really long fishing line. Jin said she'd feel it, and now it seems to be happening.

Gradually more boats appear on the water and Ruby takes a go at the oar, Fei proudly showing the blisters welling on her hands as she slumps to the matting. It's a bit like having the rudder on a rowboat at the recreation ground, and you put a bit of extra oomph into the forward movement by swishing the long blade back and forwards. But mostly now it's just a matter of steering.

Blustery showers pucker the water's surface as, carefully, Ruby gives an upriver junk a wide berth. Not long after, a smaller one overtakes them, a hundred or so yards to their left, sails billowing and white water curling from its bow.

'We've got the wind,' Ruby shouts, as they bob up and down in its wake. 'Take the umbrella and open it and hang on at the front. It might help!'

Fei scuttles forwards, springing the black brolly, and tips it to catch the gusting wind. As she does so there's a small but noticeable nudge to their speed.

Small waves ripple at the stern and a moment later thin sunshine spills across the water. Encouraged, Ruby shoves the oar even harder.

After another half hour she pauses, glancing at the reddening skin of her palms. The lines on it show white. The fortune teller said I'd have a long life, she thinks, following her lifeline as it curves around the fleshy base of her thumb. Is that the dodgy bit? Where the fold splits for a fraction? Maybe that was the *Haitun* sinking. The Otherworld. And the first time I saw the thread was right there in Madame Zsa

Zsa's. She said there was love in my life . . . and she was right about that—

Fei whoops loudly and Ruby glances up to see her pointing frantically, sending the boat rocking.

'What is it? Sandbank?'

'No! A river goddess!' Fei calls back. 'A *baiji* . . . !'

A Yangtze dolphin is breaking the surface to their right, swimming at speed. There's a glimpse of a long snout and then it humps its mottled back and dives again with a thrust of the tail.

'That's got to be a good sign!' Fei yells.

The *baiji* surfaces again, closer this time, rolling playfully and then diving right under the boat, before coming up in a mighty leap, clear of the water. It arches its back in the strengthening sun, dives again and then swims powerfully away downstream.

Fei's dancing a jig on the front under the brolly, and Ruby grips the tiller harder, leaning into the weight of the river for all she's worth.

SHANGHAI
1988

'They say they're almost gone now,' the old lady said, walking on briskly through an old alleyway of terraced houses. 'And if they build that dam they're talking about then there will be no more *baiji*. But it lifted my heart that morning, I can tell you.'

At the next corner she paused for breath, glancing back at me.

'I rowed my hands quite raw, young man. Rowed like anything because I felt time was . . . running out. And Fei was amazing, she did even more than me. God only knows how – maybe it was just luck – we avoided every sandbank the other side of Nanking. By late afternoon we were passing the city. Nationalist flags were flying so we just kept going, and I watched the walls go by, in wonderment that I had jumped from them. Felt so sad about Marlais and the rest of

212

them and the poor old *Haitun* too. But we had to keep going. I just knew it.'

She turned and strode down the next alleyway. 'Come on. We're nearly there.'

'How long were you on the river?'

'A day and a half! No food, just river water to drink – you wouldn't do that now! – no sleep, past Nanking and on towards Chenkiang. And at that next dawn it happened— Just a minute, up here I think.'

She turned another corner, onto a busier street. 'Someone told me it's going to be torn down next month, along with all these lovely old houses. Well, that's progress. No use crying about it, I suppose.'

'Tear what down?'

We wheeled round another corner, dodged through the exhaust-belching lorries and found ourselves facing one of those temporary builder's fences. Without a word, and with surprising force, the old lady raised her foot and kicked the panel free. She beckoned me on, then slipped through the gap and was gone. Astonished, I squeezed through, and found her standing in the space beyond, her arms spread wide. 'Welcome, young man. Welcome to White Cloud Temple. Or what's left of it. Come on, we need to be done before my friend arrives.'

The short winter day was ending, but in that fading

light I took in the dilapidated building before me: a once glorious temple, the roof now broken and sagging, one ceremonial dolphin perched precariously at one end – the other one long gone. Tiles lay broken on the weed-strewn courtyard. To one side, under the tangle of trees and undergrowth, gravestones crouched. And there was the crumbling well, its mouth full of shadow – all of it just as I had pictured from my companion's storytelling.

'It all happened here,' she whispered urgently. 'You see: it's real! And this is where I'll tell you the end of my story.'

As we passed the well I felt shivers race over my skin.

'You'll find, as you get older, that endings come faster. Time seems to speed up.'

第二十一章

IN THE MUD

Night darkens the river.

Hunger drags at Ruby's stomach, and their progress slows with the current as the river widens even further. There's not a hint of the thread visible, and even that little sensation at the base of her finger has gone. Like the fish has slipped the hook and all she's got now is water. Maybe we're going to be too late, she thinks. Maybe the vampire's touch has done its work already . . .

She edges to the very tip of the prow, straining her eyes into the dark. How wide the river looks – how colossal the sky. She gazes up. The Milky Way – the Heavenly River – is faint against the stronger light of the moon, but it's still there. On the *Haitun*, Charlie had laughed at her complaint that the electricity of Shanghai was blotting it out. But he had held her hand as he did so – and the space between their hands had felt like nothing.

How can that closeness be gone? she thinks. How can our hands be pulled apart for ever? Just have to get back to the cross scratched in the ground if I don't see the thread again. We're meant to be together—

Her hand is suddenly jerked really hard towards the southern bank, as if someone's trying to pull her little finger clear out of its socket. The sensation lasts for a full two seconds, and then it eases. She gazes at her finger, hoping to glimpse the thread but seeing nothing – and then her whole arm is snatched to one side, as if someone's trying to pull her right off the boat, and she falls, grabbing the side of the sampan, rocking it violently.

'What the hell are you doing?' Fei squeals from the stern. 'You nearly had me in!'

'I can feel it! We've got to go ashore here!'

Her little finger aches like anything. Charlie must be close for it to pull like that. If only she could see the thread . . .

'Quick, Fei! Stop it! Stop the boat! I can feel the thread!'

She's barely got the words out when there's another – even harder – jerk at her hand, rolling her to the edge.

'Can't just stop!' Fei shouts back. 'I'll do my best to get to the side.'

Ruby glances up towards the bank. The land rears to a bluff, a cluster of trees lining the crest of it. From somewhere beyond that, a thin plume of grey smoke is rising. Suddenly there's an orange flash, and a few seconds after, a low rumble comes rolling back across the water.

There's a bigger splash as Fei digs deep and heaves them broadside to the current. Immediately water curls against the side of the boat, and starts to spill across the deck to where Ruby is lying. Desperately she plunges her hands into the Yangtze, scooping backwards, trying to help them faster towards shore.

Water's flowing all around her now, swamping the matting.

'It's all right!' Fei shouts. 'We'll make it.'

Ruby lifts her head again, gauging the distance to the bank. Still too far to swim for me, she thinks – and way too far for Fei.

Boom! There's another thunderous roar beyond the crest of the ridge. And now even the sensation of the thread has gone, her hands numb as the sampan ploughs deeper into the river.

'Keep rowing for Heaven's sake!'

It's darker under the bluff, colder – but Fei grunts

and heaves and they're out of the grip of the main current at last, and moving into the shallows.

'Nearly there!' Fei yells, and a moment later a long sigh comes from the underside of the sampan as they wallow onto a mud bank.

'Push it as far as you can!' Ruby shouts, crouching on the bow. 'I'll jump!'

She takes a deep breath, wraps the mooring rope around her wrist and then throws herself into the gloom. Her feet smack the exposed mud ahead, legs sinking straight to mid-calf – but momentum carries her forward, and she drags herself on hands and knees until she feels the ground solidify beneath.

'Abandon ship!' Fei shouts.

Panting, Ruby turns and hauls the rope, but the boat is well and truly stuck now and won't budge, settling on the submerged mud. No way to refloat it, she thinks. Whatever happens we'll need another way home.

Fei comes splashing through the water, brandishing the furled umbrella in one hand.

'I rescued our brolly at least,' she huffs, as the thunder booms again overhead. 'What the hell do you think that is?'

'I don't know,' Ruby says. 'But I felt the thread tug like mad out there on the river.'

'Can you feel it now?'

'No. It's stopped.'

Ruby glances up towards the ridge as yet another huge detonation blasts the night, then looks back to the river, calculating distances. We must have drifted a good few hundred yards, she thinks, so the tugging on the line must have happened about there. And that means whatever's making that terrifying noise, is coming from where the thread was pulling me.

A track twists away up the darkened hillside, soon lost amongst the deeper shadows of the pine trees. Fei is looking anxiously at the smoke just visible back upriver, the umbrella clutched in both hands.

Another thunderous bang sends a shake through the soft ground beneath their feet, and the orange light flickers again.

'I'll climb the ridge and see what I can see,' Ruby says, her mouth dry. 'You wait here until I give you a whistle. It's Dad's fault you got kidnapped in the first place and I don't want—'

Fei presses a muddy finger firmly to Ruby's lips, a new strength in her eyes. 'Remember our oath we took when we became Outlaws? If one dies, we all die? We mixed our blood and everything, Ruby. You always think you know better than me, but I was the one who rowed us this far. I'm coming too. End of story.'

Ruby holds out her hand palm down, the invitation for the gang's old handshake ritual, and Fei solemnly lays hers on top.

'Only two of us left,' she whispers.

'For now. Let's go.'

The track climbs into the pines, quickly getting steeper and steeper, sandy earth and old needles loose underfoot. Soon Ruby is panting hard, grabbing for branches to stop herself slipping back to the shore below. Faint light filters through the canopy – and, from somewhere away to the right, comes a new sound as they get higher: heavy, slow, rasping breaths, like some giant beast is lurking in wait. Ruby stops, cocking her head, imagining some monstrous spirit ahead, snuffling, pawing the ground.

'Keep together!' Fei calls, scurrying to close the gap behind.

Ruby waits a breath, but then pushes on restlessly towards the ridge, climbing fast until she brushes through the trees at the top. Open ground slopes away before her, gently descending for about fifty yards or so and then dropping abruptly. Away to her right, clouds of smoke are coming up from the cut, a sulphurous tang hanging in the air, the breathing louder . . .

And then a shriek comes up from the cutting and

she realises what it is. A whistle! A train whistle!

She's been so wrapped up in thoughts of the Otherworld that the normal everyday explanation has taken a while to come. Of course it's a train – and not just *any* train by the sounds of it.

Fei scrambles to join her, dropping on hands and knees.

'Bloody hell, Ruby. I think we should get out of here—'

There's another mighty detonation. It shakes the soft ground again, and a jet of flame shoots into the air. Quickly Ruby scrambles forward over the rough ground, crouching as she approaches the lip of the drop – and sees what she's expecting to see.

The Shanghai Warlord's brute of a train lies there. It's a terrifying sight, as terrifying as the night she and Charlie saw it on the Nanking line – somehow worse now seen in its entirety from above, the heavy armour plating and bristling weaponry reflecting chunks of moonlight. Mid-train, its enormous cannon juts a forty-five-degree angle, pointing inland at some unseen target. Beyond that are more armoured carriages and smaller gun turrets – and bolted to the far end of the train like an afterthought are two scruffy wooden goods wagons.

'Rub—'

The shrill call is cut short, and Ruby spins round to see two men in uniform grabbing Fei, one of them jabbing a pistol to her head.

'Communist spy,' the other barks, his eyes locking on to Ruby. 'Stay where you are or your little friend dies now. Hands up.'

Every half minute or so the big gun adjusts its angle with a whining of machinery, and then bangs another shell into the night as their captors frogmarch them along the top of the cutting towards the armoured train. Distantly you can see flame now, maybe ten miles away, or more. The Warlord's men hurry them until they're level with the snorting black loco, then nudge them down a steep path to the rail bed.

'I said you should wait, Fei. I'm sorry.'

'It's better to be together—'

'Silence!' one of the two soldiers snaps, stubbing the nose of his rifle into Ruby's back. 'Get a move on.'

Despair threatens to take away what little energy she's got left, and yet . . . and yet . . . is it just desperation, or can she feel the pulling from the thread again? When she raises her hand she can't see it, but the sensation is quite distinct again, drawing her forward.

'Put your hands on your head,' the soldier grunts. 'Both of you.'

'You could say *please*,' Fei pipes, but does as she's told, casting Ruby a quick glance. 'Blood brothers and sisters whatever . . . '

The men take them the length of the massive train, through curling clouds of steam and smoke snorting from the loco. A tall soldier appears in the gloom, levelling his weapon at them, then lowering it when he recognises the guards.

'What have you got?'

'Found these two skulking round, spying on the train,' their first captor grunts.

'Sling them in the last carriage. We'll sort it out back in Shanghai,' the taller man mutters, almost uninterested. 'We're almost done here. Hurry.'

'You heard the Captain. Move it.'

At a forced jog she and Fei are pushed to the end of the train. As their feet scrunch the gravel and sleepers at the far end of the boxcars the pull on Ruby's finger is so definite that she can't help but bring her hand down from her Fedora: the tiniest glimmer of red is ringing the base of the little finger where the mud from the river bank is drying. She lifts it higher into the swirl of steam and moonlight, and – yes – it *is* there, very weak, a pale red ring.

'Oi, Little Miss Hat. Put your hands back on your head. And move it,' the guard snorts, hammering on the closed door of the wagon.

'Open up! Prisoners!'

With a squeal the door moves on its rail, and Ruby feels herself being lifted suddenly from her feet and hurled into the darkened interior. She lands in a heap, winded by the impact, the Fedora falling from her head. A second later she hears Fei thump down next to her.

Trying to get a breath, Ruby looks up, and finds herself face to face with a young Chinese woman who is looking at her in astonishment.

And there's someone else in the gloom beside the young woman: a slim figure draped in a tattered blanket, half lit by the thinnest strips of moonlight falling across his immobile form. A very familiar figure . . .

His face is much thinner than she remembers, his glasses gone, skin as white as bone. His eyes are closed, strangely peaceful.

'Charlie?'

She whispers his name, afraid she's wrong, that it's just someone who looks like him. Or even worse, that it *is* Charlie, but that they're too late. Tom looked like that, his features at peace after he gave up the struggle that hot day in Hankow.

'Charlie!' Fei squeals from behind her. 'CHARLIE!'

Everything else forgotten, Ruby crawls to him and throws her arms around him, and as the armoured train lurches into motion its whistle shrieks long and loud in triumph.

第二十二章

NIGHT TRAIN TO SHANGHAI

Charlie's hand feels horribly cold – but it's not quite the unearthly chill Ruby remembers when she touched Tom the morning after he died. That day had been another scorching one, but he had felt *so* bizarrely cold she had been unable to let go, until Mother pulled her hand gently away.

This is different. There's still *something* vital under her fingers.

Bending closer, she feels the very slight rise and fall of his chest, and as she calls his name again she sees his eyes flicker behind their lids.

'He's alive,' she shouts, but Fei is already beside her, throwing her arms too around her brother.

'Charlie, it's me, Fei! Open your eyes.'

'I wouldn't waste your breath on that traitor,' a voice drawls behind them. 'If he's not dead now he will be by tomorrow.'

Ruby turns slowly and sees a thickset soldier standing in the semi-darkness levelling his bayonet at her. His eyes widen slightly when he sees her face. 'Oh. So what are you, foreigner? A Russian Red? A Yankee spy?'

The train is rocking harder as it gathers pace, but Ruby braces herself and stands. 'I'm not a Communist,' she shouts in her best street Chinese. 'I'm Ruby Harkner. My father is Victor Harkner of the Maritime Customs Service and I claim extra-territoriality and I demand—'

'Shut your mouth,' the man snaps. 'You're under arrest. You will all be tried in the morning. And that will be that.'

'No. You shut *your* mouth! I claim extra-territoriality and I demand you release us – and my friend. He's ill. Look at him! He needs a blasted doctor, you stupid man.'

'Shout until you're blue in the face for all I care, foreigner. Nobody's getting out of here until we reach Shanghai. That's orders.'

Ruby eyeballs him for a long moment. Behind him now she sees another figure leaning against the boxcar wall, a bald soldier with his pistol drawn. His face is stern, but there's the faintest hint of a smile at the corner of his mouth.

'Be good girls, both of you. The other people in here are already sentenced. But if you're good, who knows—'

Fei has been bending over her brother but she stands now, joining Ruby. 'My brother needs a hospital, proper care.'

'He'll need more than a doctor by tomorrow evening,' the bald guard grunts.

'He's just a boy,' Ruby splutters.

The first soldier shakes his head. 'Old enough to know what he was doing. Save your breath. One Ball Lu might need to ask you a question or two as well.'

Fei groans. 'One Ball Lu?'

'He's ruling the roost since Moonface disappeared. Helping the Warlord.'

Ruby turns away. No point wasting more effort arguing. And she just needs to hold Charlie, to warm him up, to be close after all these long, difficult miles from the Gorges to here.

What must *he* have been through? And how ill is he now? Is he dying?

She puts a hand on his chest, and feels the gentle trembling under her palm.

'Charlie? Charlie! Can you hear me?'

'Poor boy,' the young woman says quietly, a wary

eye on their guards. 'He's been like that since they pulled us out of the American hospital. The other guy with us didn't make it.'

The night cold is reaching into the wagon. 'He's not a Communist,' Ruby says quietly.

The woman sighs. 'Doesn't matter. They've made up their minds. At least I did my best for China. Here, take this.' She shakes herself out of her padded jacket, smiles, and hands it to Ruby.

'I couldn't take it.'

'You're wet through,' the woman mutters.

Ruby bites her lip. 'Maybe just for a moment or two. Thank you. What's your name?'

'I'm calling myself Little Jade,' the woman mutters.

'Thank you.'

Ruby pulls the coat over her shoulders, glad of the extra layer – and then finds Charlie's hand again. She cups it in both of hers, willing it to get warmer, squeezing it.

What would Jin do? Generate some *ch'i*. Energy is warmth, movement, life . . . She breathes as deeply and slowly as she can, trying to calm her racing mind, gathering the *ch'i* in her belly. Fei comes to sit close on the other side, anxiously gazing at her brother's mask of a face.

'Warm him up,' Ruby whispers. 'Sit really close.

Really feel the warmth and send it to him.'

She closes her eyes, willing the energy to build. The train is rattling along, a cold breeze knifing through the gaps in the boards. But after thirty or more deliberate breaths Ruby starts to feel it – a warm, soft pulse of *ch'i* in her abdomen. She makes the in-breaths longer, allowing the sensation to build, and as soon as it feels like there's enough, she sends it through her chest, down her arms and hands, into Charlie's palm.

Does his hand respond, just a tiny bit?

'Keep warming him,' she whispers again to Fei. 'We need to keep him alive until Shanghai.'

'And then what?'

'Just do it.'

She focuses for all she's worth.

Don't get tight, Jin's voice whispers in her head. *Keep open. Be soft. Softer.*

Another wave of warmth rises from her abdomen, and she sends it towards Charlie. And this time his hand surely does respond, giving a little squeeze back – no more than a tremor, but a definite response.

'Wake up!'

She leans closer – and then plants a quick kiss on his marble cheek.

Behind her, the bald guard laughs – but she ignores it and rubs Charlie's hand really vigorously. And, as the train rattles over a set of points, his eyelids flicker, blink twice – and then open properly.

At first he doesn't seem to recognise her – but then as his eyes widen and focus, they find hers. His dry lips move, but no sound comes out.

'I'm here, Charlie. What did you say?'

He mouths something again. It's not her name, or Fei's . . .

'Shhh. Easy. Don't rush.'

She bends the shell of her ear right towards his mouth, feels his feeble breath and hears him whisper a single word:

'Almanac.'

第二十三章

OUTLAWS OF THE MARSH

As night deepens, so does the cold in the boxcar. Charlie's eyes have fluttered shut again, but with Fei pressed on one side, and Ruby tight on the other, his colour seems to have improved just a little bit. And he doesn't feel quite as deathly cold.

Not quite.

'Ruby?' Fei whispers over the clicking of the rails. 'Is he dying?'

'No,' Ruby murmurs, trying to sound sure of it, but unable to meet Fei's eyes. In her head she sees again the *jiang shi* vampires jerking their way across that nightmare landscape of broken graves and jutting bones.

'But he looks so awful, Ruby. And vampires, well, that's really bad magic.'

'Jin said we should get back to the temple and

use the Almanac. There must be a healing spell in it for Charlie.'

'So we'll get away from these morons somehow and look up the spell—'

'Exactly. So don't worry. It'll be OK.'

Somehow, she thinks.

Somehow escape from an armoured, moving train and a squad of the Warlord's troops. Somehow get back to the city, find the Almanac. Somehow do the spell. I can't tell Fei that the book disappeared. Not yet. She'd lose hope. And I need her to believe it's all going to be fine.

She closes her eyes, trying to shut everything else out.

Andrei *must* have stolen the book, that's the only explanation, she thinks. He'll have hawked it for a few coppers cash and bought some noodles. If he could shoot Jin – either out of some stupid revenge or for the reward – then he wouldn't have thought twice about taking the Almanac. And now it could be anywhere.

She wracks her brains for another solution. Amah knows the *sifu* at the other temple, the one the other side of their flat in the Mansions. But the day the wind chimes in the kitchen shook like mad – like they'd been gripped by an invisible hand – Amah had said the only spirits *that sifu* knew about came from a bottle. So he's probably useless. Maybe Madame Zsa Zsa could help. She said all those things that seem to be coming true – about long journeys and love – but as Yu Lan said in that pompous way of his, she's a foreign fortune teller. She probably doesn't know about bad Chinese magic.

Ruby puffs out her cheeks, tries to shake the tension from her body, and then presses closer to Charlie as the rails click and the engine pounds on towards Shanghai.

Slowly night blurs to dawn in the gaps in the boxcar's walls.

A whistle blast startles Ruby from half sleep to find Little Jade nudging her, pointing. The shaven-headed soldier is offering her a grubby water canteen, urging her to take a drink.

Blinking, she takes the bottle. '*Xie xie,*' she mutters.

The man nods, motions that she should share it with Fei.

'I want to give my sick friend some too,' Ruby says.

'Go on then.'

Ruby nudges Fei awake.

'Have a drink. And let's try and give Charlie some,' Ruby whispers. 'It might help.'

Fei nods groggily, and together they ease Charlie

into a half sitting position. He feels so horribly thin now – as if he really is wasting away. He mumbles in his sleep, or whatever it is, words lost against the clatter of noise in the carriage. But Fei is closer and looks up encouragingly. 'He said your name, Ruby.'

'I'm here, Charlie. We're both here!'

Steadying herself, she trickles the liquid onto Charlie's cracked lips. Instinctively he sips at it, and she pours a bit more. And then he lifts his hand, and guides the canteen back to his mouth and takes a big gulp.

The train lurches, spilling more down his chin, but now his eyes open properly, searching for Fei. He reaches out an exhausted hand and takes hold of hers. 'Hi, sis. I'm glad to see you. I . . . promised Dad I'd look after you . . .'

'And now I'm looking after you,' Fei says, tears choking her voice.

Charlie smiles faintly, then looks back to Ruby.

'Where . . . where are we?'

'Going home,' Ruby whispers, trying to make her voice sound calm. But the relief and excitement at seeing him wake up, together with the shake of the wagon, sets her words trembling. 'Everything's going to be fine.'

'I think . . . I might . . . be dying.'

'No,' she counters fiercely. 'No, you're not. I won't let you.'

Charlie nods, and then his eyes close again and he slumps back on the blanket, Fei gripping one hand and Ruby the other. Those last words of his repeat in Ruby's head as the rails click their rhythm beneath.

What if they're true?

Then nothing else really matters.

Every snort of the loco brings them another hundred yards closer to Shanghai and home. And that's good. But it's also a hundred yards closer to whatever fate holds beyond the marshalling yards of the North Station. Even the two guards seem to be getting more and more tense as the miles roll away, stowing their meagre rations and brushing the dust from their uniforms. The chubby guard then checks his rifle, the bald one pressing his ear to the crack of the door.

Almost as if *they're* expecting some kind of trouble.

One positive thing, as the first slivers of sunlight filter into the wagon Charlie opens his eyes again. He glances at his sister, then back at Ruby.

'I'm feeling a bit better,' he says slowly. 'Still so weak though.'

He pushes down with his hands decisively, and manages to get half upright before he staggers. Ruby and Fei both rush to support him as the train sways.

'Sit down, you!' Chubby growls.

'I just want . . . to know . . . where we are.'

The man snorts. 'Passing Soochow. Nearly time for justice.' He glances at Ruby and Fei. 'Firing squad probably.'

'Let them go,' Charlie mutters. 'Ruby is a foreigner and you don't want trouble from the Council. And my little sister knows nothing about anything. Let them go.'

The effort has taken its toll: his legs tremble and then buckle, and Ruby catches him, easing his body back down onto the blanket.

'Save it for the magistrate. Even kids can spy.'

Fei lifts her jaw defiantly. 'Me and Ruby have been to hell and back! Literally! So you two birdbrains don't scare me.'

'Shut it, pipsqueak—'

'My brother is innocent!'

'Then why did he have a red scarf?' the soldier man spits back. And with that he snaps the bolt of his rifle back into place and takes aim at Charlie's chest. 'We could shoot him now. Nobody would care. Or know.'

Ruby stares into the man's eyes, then right into the smooth bore of the barrel. Deliberately she moves in front of Charlie, spreading her arms wide.

'You don't scare me,' she says slowly. 'I am not afraid. Not of you. Not of *anything*.'

She turns and looks back at Charlie, who – somehow, wonderfully – manages a weak smile back at her. Just a hint of the old smile that used to suddenly brighten his face.

'Shanghai Ruby,' he whispers.

The soldiers, Fei, the sickness that has Charlie in its grip, all fall away as Ruby reaches out for him, pulled towards him – and she plants another kiss, lightly, but squarely, on his mouth. She feels his dry lips, the thin line where blood has crusted, and he wraps his arms around her, drawing her closer. Closer, then perfectly still. Not a kiss like the actors and actresses in the picture house, just a tender moment of connection and defiance. She feels warmth spread through her for the two or three seconds it lasts – and then Charlie coughs.

As she leans back she sees the smile still on his face – and it looks as if something has relaxed in him.

'Sorry,' she finds herself saying.

'No,' Charlie says. 'Don't be . . . sorry about something like that.'

Behind her, the guards are chuckling, making crude remarks, but she ignores them. Who cares if there's an audience?

She looks back into Charlie's eyes.

'I thought we'd lost you at the Gorges,' she whispers. 'It was awful!'

Charlie shakes his head. 'I can't remember it really . . .'

'But I kept seeing the thread and Jin said I'd be able to see it as long as you were alive and it would take me to you. And I was so worried, but I kept going and going . . .'

Charlie smiles, but seems too weak to answer again.

'It was nice – at Full Moon Bridge. But I couldn't say what I wanted to say.'

He nods. 'Me too.'

'Get some rest now. We'll keep watch.'

Those few words – and the feeling of the kiss still on her lips – boost Ruby's energy. She feels it expanding in her abdomen, deepening, warming. She keeps hold of Charlie's hand, and feels the *ch'i* enfolding him, giving him – at least for now – the strength he needs. For whatever is coming.

And when at last she looks back at Fei, Charlie's younger sister is smiling – despite everything. 'Ohhh,' she whispers. 'You'll *have* to get married now. Blimey.'

Ruby's concentration on Charlie is so complete that it's Fei who registers the sound of shooting first.

She nudges Ruby sharply in the ribs.

'Listen!'

Ruby looks up to see both guards standing, pressed to the door and peering through the slits in the wood. Over the rails she can hear the sharp retort of gunfire now.

'What do you think it is?' Fei whispers.

'Could be comrades,' Jade hisses back, a wary eye on the two soldiers. 'Doesn't sound like much though.'

Ruby gets to her feet.

'Sit back down,' the shaven-headed guard shouts. 'Nobody move—'

A violent shuddering passes the length of the carriages, wheels shrieking on the rails as the train brakes hard. Everything in the wagon lurches and Ruby loses her balance, tumbling towards the far wall and slamming into it. When she turns she sees the chubby guard sprawled helplessly on the floor, the other gripping the door handle in an attempt to keep his feet. Fei is holding tight to Charlie, trying to protect him as another spasm wracks the train.

The bald guard swears blackly.

'Get the damn door open and have a look,' his companion grunts. 'Didn't expect trouble this far out!' He staggers to his feet, aiming his gun at Charlie. 'Not one false move, got it?'

'He can hardly stand, you idiot,' Ruby snaps,

hurrying to Charlie's side.

There's more shooting from somewhere ahead, and voices raised in what sounds like anger.

The shaven-headed soldier pulls back the bolt and opens the boxcar door to reveal a chunk of bright autumnal sunshine and fresh air. No more shooting, but the confused shouting ahead is louder now. 'Can't see anything. A bit of smoke over Chapei maybe. Nantao too by the looks of it. I'll check. You watch this lot.'

He jumps down and slides the door shut, and the gloom deepens again in the wagon.

'What's going on, Ruby?' Charlie whispers.

'Don't know. We've stopped.'

Her head has been full of images of brave rebels blowing the track. Or a full-blooded uprising stopping the advance of the armoured train. Instead, her spirits drop as she hears laughter from the front of the train. The chunky guard looks less tense, and, curiosity getting the better of him, goes to slide the door to have a look. As he does so the train gives a sudden shunt forwards and the handle slips from his grip, sending the door squealing fully open on its rail to reveal a wide expanse of marsh below them, acres and acres of reeds tumbling in sun and wind. The train is evidently high on an embankment, and in the very distance you can just make out the sprawling mass of what must be Shanghai. The marshes are familiar to Ruby at once: she and the gang used to come this far out sometimes, telling themselves how brave they were to venture into the unknown. Now it feels no more than a stone's throw from home.

The guard is struggling with the door – it seems to have wedged open and try as he might he can't budge it. He puts down his rifle and heaves again with both hands. At that precise moment there's a whistle and the loco jolts forward, throwing him off-balance and pirouetting on one leg like a chubby, novice ballerina.

Sunlight falls on the tatty black umbrella, and it fires an image in Ruby's mind of the dream fox banging so powerfully on the headman's door. She hears the blow resounding, the urgency of the voice that told her to act NOW. She feels the *ch'i* in her belly surge, and then without a single extra thought sweeps the brolly from the straw, hurling herself across the carriage, charging the off-balance guard with a deep roar.

The soldier fumbles for his rifle, but he's too slow – and full force Ruby cracks the bamboo-spined brolly down on his wrist. The gun falls from his hand and she kicks it on the volley straight through the open door and out of sight.

'Foreign devil!'

He makes a grab for her, but she swings the umbrella in a half circle and catches him full on the nose. Nothing at all like the elegant movements Jin did in White Cloud, but her desperation does the trick and he staggers back towards the opening, clutching his face as blood spouts from his nose.

'Chaaarge!'

There's a scream from behind, and Fei flashes past, tackling the man round his middle. Her momentum propels both of them through the doorway, her fists pummelling away as they topple down the bank and into the watery reeds below in an almighty splash.

Ruby rushes to the door. The soldier has already come up for air, and he grabs Fei by the scruff of the neck, spluttering swear words and forcing her head underwater.

In one running bound Ruby leaps clear of the train, the track, the embankment – the umbrella still gripped tight – and hits the water next to the struggle. The guard looks round in surprise, hands still clamped on Fei's submerged neck, and Ruby rams the hard point of the brolly into his chest. Her fingers must snag the catch, because suddenly the umbrella blooms open – and either the *ch'i* moves just right, or a huge gust of wind catches it, or something – because the brolly rips from her hands with incredible force and lifts the guard

243

off his feet sending him flying backwards. He falls into a ditch at the bottom of the bank, the umbrella sailing on through the air to where it bangs against the side of the wagon.

Fei comes up spluttering, fists raised. 'Where is he?'

'I got him. We need to get Charlie out of the wagon.'

She looks round urgently. Has anyone seen the fight? Surely they must . . .

There's more shouting from the front of the train, and turning towards it she sees now what has caused the hold-up. Four – no five – hefty, black water buffalo are blocking the rails, twitching tails angrily, a couple of soldiers trying to shoo them off the track.

They haven't seen us yet, Ruby thinks. But the bald guard must be back any moment?

She looks to the boxcar and sees Little Jade already helping Charlie down from the door, stumbling across the rail bed and then on down the bank.

'This way,' Ruby shouts as loud as she dare. 'Into the reeds.'

The young woman has hold of Charlie under one arm and Fei rushes to grab the other, and together they all squelch into the marshland.

A cry goes up behind – the heavyset guard staggering up from the ditch. 'Stop! Prisoners escaping!'

But he has no weapon, Ruby thinks – and we're already a good twenty paces away. Another shout rings out from the tracks above, but already the reeds are closing around them.

Two gunshots ring out in quick succession. You can clearly hear the whistle of the bullets ripping through the air just to their left. This is it, Ruby thinks. All or nothing now. She batters the rushes down, making as easy a path as she can for her friends to follow. There's more confused shouting from the embankment and a moment later the staccato bark of a machine gun opens up. Just a foot or so from her head a reed is snipped clean in two by a bullet, seed dust puffing into the air.

'Bloody hell,' Fei gasps. 'They'll cut us to bits.'

Ruby glances back. Charlie's face is drawn, but he's still upright, still moving his legs as best he can. Over his shoulder the train is already no more than a dark blur, almost obliterated by the reeds.

'They'll expect us to run straight,' she grunts, 'let's go sideways. Try not to move the reeds too much and give our position away.'

But as the machine gun rattles she realises the wind is helping to cover their tracks. Blowing in squalls it's swaying the reeds wildly around them. The fire from behind is continuous now, maybe two, even three guns opening up – but it's all guesswork. You can hear the bullets straying further and further away.

'Slow down,' Little Jade whispers. 'Keep low. We'll work back parallel to the track for a bit.'

Water and mud churn at her feet as Ruby leads the way bent double, a sliver of hope growing now. When she pauses for the others, Charlie reaches out.

'I need to rest – a moment,' he gasps.

'Just for a moment.'

She helps him to the ground on a drier patch, and the four of them look at each other, panting hard.

More furious shouting drifts across the marsh, the voices ranging up and down the track, some seemingly very close, some hundreds of yards away.

'Maybe they're going to give up,' Fei whispers. 'We can't be worth that much bother for them—'

Another long burst of gunfire sounds, hundreds of rounds being emptied into the reeds. There's something methodical and determined about it this time.

'Coming this way,' Jade hisses. 'Get down,' and as one they flatten themselves into the mud. You can hear the sound of the reeds being chopped as the hail of metal comes closer . . .

Closer.

Ruby's hand reaches for Charlie's and finds it. She squeezes his cold fingers, eyes trying to find his gaze, but he's looking the other way now.

Maybe this is it, she thinks, maybe we're going to die here in the fields. So close to home.

The chopping sound is right on them now and she closes her eyes tight. The reeds whip and snap – and she feels Charlie's grip suddenly tighten as the bullets pass just over them.

'Everyone OK?' Fei splutters. 'I've swallowed half a swamp. Ugh.'

Charlie's grip loosens, and Ruby looks at him in alarm, half expecting to see his face bloodied by a stray bullet.

But instead he's grinning at her. The deathly pallor is still there, but his whole face is lifted. The old smile coming back despite everything – just like it used to be.

'Look at us,' he whispers. 'Outlaws, Ruby. The Outlaws of the Marsh, at last! You're Hu San Niang! Even if you used an umbrella and not a sword—'

Ruby hugs him hard as a cough wracks his chest.

Charlie groans. 'Ooof. Careful, Ruby . . .'

The wind gusts again, shivering the reeds around them. And moments later they hear the steady sigh of the armoured train's loco as it moves away into the morning.

'We did it!' Fei squeaks. 'We showed them. Outlaws for ever! You were amazing, Ruby. Amazing!'

Ruby feels a smile lifting her own face, cracking the drying mud. But Jade is holding a finger to her lips. 'Keep it down, you lot. They may well have left soldiers to hunt us in the reeds. I've seen that happen. And listen!'

In place of the rattle of the machine gun there's a distant popping sound now, not from the direction of the train, but from miles and miles away, towards Shanghai. Sporadic gunfire caught on the wind.

'What do you think it is?' Fei whispers.

The woman pulls a face. 'Might be the next uprising against the Warlord in the Chinese City. But my comrades haven't got more than twenty guns between them yet . . . it'll be a bloodbath.'

'Oh God,' Fei whispers. 'What about Dad?'

'We need to get there,' Charlie says. 'Right now.'

Jade shakes her head. 'Won't be easy. The Green Hand will be shooting anyone they suspect on sight. And first hint of trouble you can bet the foreigners will close all the barricades to the International Settlement.'

'We're going,' Charlie murmurs. 'Aren't we, Ruby?'

Ruby nods. But how, she thinks, if the city is locked tight, will we make it back to White Cloud and even begin the hunt for the Almanac?

第二十四章

FAINT SHADOW

Each and every step now is hard won from the marshland.

But even the thousand mile journey begins with a single step, Ruby thinks. And now there can be no more than fifteen miles to go at most!

Glancing back at Charlie though, that resolve falters. He doesn't look like he can manage even half of *one* of those miles . . .

The loco's noise fades, and when they stop to listen again for any remaining soldiers Ruby realises the distant gunfire has stopped too. Is that good, or bad? Maybe it will mean the barriers open quickly, an easier path to the temple and maybe even the Almanac. But it might also mean any insurrection has been crushed – and Charlie and Fei's father rounded up already.

And what about Dad?

Fei taps her on the shoulder. 'Charlie's got to rest.'

'I know. I'll scout ahead a little way . . .'

She raises herself up on tiptoes, peering through the downy fronds of the reeds. No shots ringing out, no shouting, no one in sight. To the right there's a raised levee, part of the vast network of waterways and flood defences that make up the low-lying area between Shanghai and Soochow. She scurries forward, and, hoping that every soldier *did* leave with the train, clambers cautiously to the top of the bank.

About half a mile away a hamlet sits on a patch of raised land: a few orange-tiled roofs amongst the trees, washing billowing white. Beyond the houses a black sail cuts a chunk from the bright sky – must be one of the canals that criss-cross the countryside here. She turns, checking again for pursuers. In the distance the armoured train is no more than a tiny black caterpillar now crawling along the edge of the watery land. Once again the steady *pop pop pop* of gunshots comes from the direction of Shanghai.

She hurries back to the others, crashing through the stalks.

'There's a village,' she says. 'Let's try and get help there.'

Little Jade looks at her. 'To do what?'

'To get home of course!'

'To Shanghai? The Warlord's men have our descriptions and they'll give those out to the Green Hand too. You can hear the shooting's started again. It'll be a massacre.'

'I don't care,' Charlie whispers. 'We have to get back. Help Dad . . .'

Ruby helps him to his feet, proud of his courage. He's dragging energy from goodness knows where and still thinking about others more than himself. He must remember that the Almanac is lost?

Little Jade looks from one to another, then ties her hair back decisively. 'Well, you're brave kids,' she says. 'But I'm heading for Soochow and North. I want to see my mother cooking and my little brothers playing in the yard again. Just a normal day, or a few more even. Good luck to you. Keep the coat, foreigner. And don't say I didn't warn you if it all ends in a mess. *Zai jian.*'

Ruby leads Charlie and Fei along the bottom of the bank, keeping to the cover of the reeds and aiming for the village as best she can. Charlie's moving under his own steam, waving Fei's support away, but really it looks like no more than willpower shifting his feet now.

Ruby hesitates and gazes into his face. 'How are you feeling, Charlie?'

'OK,' he mutters back weakly. 'But we've got to find that Almanac.'

'Why?' she whispers, voice trembling.

'You know why.'

'What do you mean, *find the Almanac*,' Fei hisses.

'Nothing, sis. Don't worry—'

'You mean it's *lost*? Now what will we do!'

'We'll find it,' Ruby says. 'Jin said he'd help if he could and—'

There's a sudden noise ahead – heavy footfall in the fringe of the marsh – and as one they stop dead. Maybe there *are* still soldiers out hunting . . . Ruby waves them all to crouch, and taking a cautious step forward parts the reeds . . .

. . . and almost bumps noses with an enormous black snout. A moment later she finds herself face to face with a fierce-looking water buffalo. The animal snorts and snuffles – but stands its ground.

'Put your hands up or I'll shoot!' a voice screeches above them, and she looks up to see a boy of eight or nine perched on top of the animal waving a stick frantically in their direction.

'I'll shoot you all!' he yells.

'Keep your voice down,' Ruby snaps, tipping back her hat.

The boy's eyes widen. 'What's a foreigner doing

crawling around in the mud?' he says. 'Are you one of those stupid riders who chase the torn paper? My daddy hates them. They trample the crops and—'

'I'm nothing to do with them! We need help to get out of here and back to the city as soon as possible.'

The boy scratches his head. 'Daddy said not to trust strangers any more.'

'Is that Soochow Creek beyond your village?' Ruby asks.

'That's what you lot call it.' The boy puffs out his chest. 'We call it the Woosung. Our family has worked the river since the Grand Canal was built. When China was great.'

'Well, China's . . . going to be great again,' Charlie says breathlessly, patting the buffalo on the flank. 'And what makes it great is that we are – all of us – brothers and sisters. And brothers and sisters – help each other. So be a good lad and take us to your village. I need to hurry . . .'

Ruby reaches out for Charlie's hand and gives it a squeeze. The cold is radiating from it.

The boy's father has a face like old, polished wood. His eyes flick from Charlie to Fei to Ruby, giving each a long intense gaze. They're covered in slime from the crawl through the marshes, their clothes ragged from the journey. We must look a real state, Ruby thinks, trying to smile at the man and get him on side as he gives her longer scrutiny than the others.

'What were you doing out there?' he asks gruffly, turning back to Charlie.

'We lost our way,' Charlie says weakly. 'I need to get to the city. I'm not very well.'

'I can see that, son. But don't think you can fool me just because I'm old. I saw the gun train. Those soldiers weren't hunting ducks, I can tell you that. So I'm guessing they were shooting at you lot.'

His eyes fall back on Ruby.

'And what's a foreigner doing with these . . . fugitives? I should turn you all in for reward. Save us a lot of bother from the Warlord.'

'Please don't,' Ruby says quietly. 'Just tell us the quickest way into Shanghai.'

'The quickest way is the railway,' the man says. 'And the next quickest is one of those damn automobiles.' He screws up his eyes, looking at Fei and Charlie again. 'Are you two Communists?'

'We're just kids,' Fei says. 'And we want to get home.'

Charlie gives a little groan then, and slumps against his sister, steadying himself. The sun is golden, but it does nothing to lift his colour. Even his shadow looks fainter on the ground than mine, Ruby thinks. Can anyone else see that? As if it's fading. Must be the vampire touch doing its work.

'Please,' Ruby urges again. 'We don't have long.'

The man looks at Charlie again, then nods curtly.

'My brother and I will take you this evening. We have an urgent delivery for the docks. But if anyone finds you we'll say you stowed away – and we had no idea. Got it? Country's going to the dogs, but we can still be decent . . . We'll wait for dark and we'll just have to take our chances with the foxes.'

'Foxes?' Fei echoes.

'If I were you, I'd worry more about the Warlord's men and the Green Hand,' the man says, as another salvo of gunfire echoes across the landscape.

第二十五章

SHOP SHUT

Squeezed between a cargo of clay bricks, and covered by a heavy oilcloth, it's almost cosy on the old man's boat. Moving again, their stomachs full of chicken broth, Ruby feels just a little hope returning. Shanghai is so close – and they're all still alive and in one piece after everything they've been through. Charlie is drifting in and out of sleep, and he's still deathly cold to the touch, but when he opens his eyes he's still present – he even manages a half smile as the boat rocks steadily out onto the main channel. He curls tighter under the blanket they've been given, and then closes his eyes again. Ruby listens to the night around them: just the sound of the barge creaking, a feathering of water on the prow, occasionally the rumble of a voice from the man or his brother on the back.

Fei's face is just a dim oval in the darkness as she looks at Ruby. 'What did you mean about the Almanac being lost?'

'It . . . it disappeared from the temple.'

'Why didn't you tell me sooner?'

'I didn't want to worry you.'

'I'm a big girl now, Ruby. I've been to hell and back!'

'I know. I'm sorry.'

'So what happened to the book?'

'I think Andrei stole it.'

'That scumbag. Charlie's going to die if we don't do the ritual. Isn't he?'

Ruby shakes her head. 'When we get to the city you go and find Amah. Ask her about the local *sifu* and get him to come to the temple—'

'Oh, but he's hopeless!'

'It's better than nothing. I'll take Charlie to White Cloud, but I'll go past Uchiyama's bookshop. Maybe he can find us another copy. Maybe Andrei even flogged it back to him!'

'No way. I'm staying with Charlie.'

'Fei!' Charlie's voice comes from under the blanket. 'Do what Ruby says. We need to try everything. And if one of us gets caught, maybe the other gets away.'

'But—'

'But nothing. Find Auntie. Please, sis. Help Dad if I don't make it.'

'Don't say that,' Fei groans. 'You're going to make it.'

The night drags by painfully slowly.

An owl hoots.

The oar splashes behind them, loud in the stillness. No wind for the sail, Ruby thinks, her spirits dropping with the temperature. She snuggles down into the padded jacket, one hand still holding Charlie's tight.

'Rubbyyy . . .' Fei's voice snakes to her again.

'What is it?'

'When you and Charlie get married, will you have a foreign wedding? Or a Chinese one?'

'I can't think about anything that far off right now.'

'You'll get married,' Fei insists. 'That's why you saw the thread. So what's the answer? It's good to think of something nice. We'll shove the bad thoughts away with good ones, right?'

With our thoughts we make the world, Ruby thinks. Didn't Jin say that once?

Fei nudges her. 'Well?'

She pushes her tongue into the wall of her cheek, considering. Not for one moment can she imagine a

British wedding and all the nonsense that goes with it. Just the noise and colour and firecrackers she's seen so often in Nantao.

'Chinese, of course.'

'Good. So, I'm going to think about that instead of worrying about everything else. I'm going to imagine *every* little detail. All the food, all the fireworks. Clothes. Everything.'

She snuggles closer to Ruby.

'It'll be beautiful. We'll all be there. Dad and Auntie. And Charlie will be fine . . . we'll have mooncakes!'

Fei falls silent and Ruby listens to water lap, and oar stroke. To Charlie's regular breathing, and the cries of water birds as they're disturbed by the passing boat . . .

An hour or more later she has joined the others in fitful sleep, and dreams . . . no sign of the thread this time, but she's high in the air again, on the edge of her usual vision of the river – and this time she can feel the controls of an aeroplane shaking in her hands. She's flying the Fox by herself, banking high over the gleaming snake of the river, either at dawn or dusk . . .

. . . and in front of her, spread out in all its vibrant chaos, is the great city of Shanghai. She swoops low over the buildings, wings vibrating, past trams rattling, cars racing, rickshaws thumping along the neon streets past advertisements six storeys high for make-up and cigarettes and a new sensation at the cinema, flying towards Riverside Mansions. She barrel-rolls over the white wedding cake of a building, and then back up over the factories and the billboards, and all the bells of the city are ringing, and all the ships on the river are sounding their hooters in joy and—

'Rubyyyy!' Fei's shaking her shoulder. 'Wake up! We're here.'

The tarpaulin has been pulled back, and in thin light, over the boatman's shoulder, loom the vague shapes of big buildings.

She staggers to her feet, legs numb, fizzing with pins and needles.

'Hurry,' the man whispers. 'We're near Fukien Road on the International side. A Municipal Police patrol just went past and I think there's a curfew. Better scram into the shadows as fast as you can.'

'Thank you,' Ruby says as she's pulled by the man's strong grip to the jetty. 'Thank you so much.'

In the distance she can make out the skeletal arches of the Garden Bridge, a slow dawn lightening the Huangpu River beyond. She turns back to see Charlie reaching out to steady himself as the man sets him down on the darkened quayside.

'Still OK?' she whispers. '*Ni hao ma?*'

'*Hao,*' Charlie nods – half awake, half still in a world of dreams. Or deeper.

'Keep low,' the boatman says. 'You could be shot on sight.'

Ruby pulls the Fedora from her head. 'They won't shoot a foreigner.'

'I wouldn't bet on it,' the man says. 'Municipal Police not. But the Green Hand are another matter. And you never met us, got it?!'

Without another word he turns and jumps back on board the barge.

Fei hugs Charlie long and hard, then looks back to Ruby, tears shining in the gloom. 'I'll do my best,' she says, lifting her chin. 'I'll come to White Cloud with the *sifu*. Or Auntie at least. It'll be all right.'

'Follow the Creek. We'll go straight up Fukien to Uchiyama's. *Zai jian.*'

A torch is flashing a few hundred yards further up the road. Ruby points, gives Fei a shove of encouragement, and then guides Charlie across the street and into the thicker shadows. His feet drag, like he's walking in his sleep: even though his eyes are open, his focus seems to be somewhere far, far in the distance.

'Where's Fei gone?' he murmurs.

'To find Amah. Remember?'

He nods vaguely.

'We've got to try Uchiyama's, Charlie. And then get to White Cloud. If you can't make it I'll find a rickshaw or something.'

His lips are moving, but she can't make out the words.

'Say it again.'

'Far to go . . .' he whispers.

'Not far to go at all. We're nearly there.'

Carefully she steers him down Fukien Road, their footsteps loud on the deserted street. Normally at this hour there would be early traders and night soil carts – the first trams rattling in the distance. But everything is quiet now. Must be a curfew like the boatman said. How long ago it seems since she and Charlie – and Straw – passed along here on the way to the North Station. Charlie had been full of determination and energy and fight that day, she thinks, but now look at him . . . At least Uchiyama's is close. He's always helpful, even if we have to wake him up he won't mind.

Charlie groans as she hurries them on. 'Where are we now?'

'Fukien Road.'

'No,' he mutters. 'I can see the hill again. I can see bones . . .'

A chill rushes through her. 'No, Charlie. You're dreaming. We're in Shanghai.'

Charlie nods, but he looks confused, dazed. She rubs his cold hands vigorously in hers. 'Keep awake! Keep awake, we're nearly at Uchiyama's!'

Oh God, she thinks as she shepherds him down the road. I was too late for Tom, but I'm not going to let Charlie go . . .

It's far too early for even the Japanese bookseller to have his shop open. She's expected that – but all the shutters are bolted on the ground floor and that's really unusual. Even the boxes of cheap books have disappeared from either side of the door – and when she sees the sign pinned there her heart sinks even deeper.

CLOSED UNTIL FURTHER NOTICE. BY ORDER.

What does that mean? It's not a Municipal Council notice. There's a smudged Chinese seal on it.

Ruby bites her lip, then raps hard on the shutter. In the silence the sound is thunder, echoing away towards the heart of the Settlement where a few neon signs are blinking lazily in the gathering dawn.

No reply. She hammers again, then looks up at the windows above where Uchiyama lives. No sign of life at all. She lifts her hand to drum again, still squinting

263

at the seal – then lets her hand fall. There's not going to be an answer . . . the smudged characters say *Lu, Green Hand.*

God only knows where poor Uchiyama is now – but he's not going to be opening the shop any time soon.

'Come on, Charlie,' she mutters, tucking one arm under his and propelling him back into motion. 'Never mind. We'll get you to White Cloud.' Just being there – where it all started – might help. Jin might appear! Maybe even stupid Doctor Sprick could do something? But that's just clutching at straws . . .

And what seems to be the trouble with your friend, Miss Harkner?

He was attacked by hopping vampires. His ch'i *is being drained . . .*

He'll just think it's my nerves like Mother.

Charlie is stumbling badly. If only there were some rickshaw men around. Normally you have to fight them off as they tout for the first business of the day. But even they clear the streets when there's a curfew.

She rushes them on across the junction at Nanking Road. There's still – bizarrely – not a soul to be seen, and the only normal thing as she glances away towards the Wing On department store and New World Theatre is neon, shining pale blue and green in the morning air.

Maybe we're not back in the real city, she thinks, panic rising again as she hurries them on down Fukien. Maybe we're in some kind of Otherworld Shanghai and—

The boom of a car door slamming snaps her attention back. Reflexes firing she pulls Charlie into a doorway, hugging the shadows pooled there. Three men have got out of a long-nosed, black car. It's carelessly parked right across the street ahead, as if they're not expecting anyone else to try and pass. And looming above it is a familiar building.

Ruby groans at her stupidity. She's been so locked up in worry for Charlie that she's brought them straight towards the Green Hand's headquarters. A driver and another man are lounging against the bonnet of the luxury car and don't look like they're going anywhere in a hurry.

Maybe we should head back to Nanking Road, she thinks, take the long way round for White Cloud via the river.

But looking back, she sees another car has materialised out of the grey dawn behind. It's slewed across the junction with Nanking Road, a gaggle of Green Hand men fanning out on the empty thoroughfare, stretching, laughing. Like they own the place.

'Ruby. I'm cold,' Charlie murmurs. 'I'm really c-c-cold.'

She pulls him tighter.

Green Hand might shoot you on sight, the boatman said. He's right. Normal law doesn't apply on days like these. We need to get hunting for the Almanac – or a decent *sifu* – and now we're stuck here. Maybe the men will move off somewhere else in a few minutes.

But as if in answer she hears another car approaching from Nanking Road. It sweeps past, then slews to a stop beside the Green Hand building. A moment later two Chinese men, faces bloodied, are bundled from the back seat and into the building. And from somewhere a few streets away – it's hard to tell where – there are four gunshots, loud and ugly in the otherwise still morning.

She glances down into the shadow of the sunken doorway, and almost cries out loud.

The thread is visible again. Very, very pale, but it's there, and now it doesn't loop away like so many times before, but is just wrapped tightly around and around her hand, binding it to Charlie's, like a skein of red wool knotting them together. She gazes at it, feeling the thread holding them. We must be meant to be together like Jin said. So Charlie can't die now, we can't be rounded up and shot. There's still a chance.

'We'll wait five more minutes, Charlie,' she whispers, 'and then we're going to make a run for it. OK?'

'I . . . I'll try . . .'

Far away then she hears a clock striking. She counts the bells – four, five, six, seven. Seven o'clock. As the last chime dies away a beam of sunlight slants down into the doorway and hits her hands, swiping away the glimpse of the thread . . .

. . . and in that moment she hears a faint noise, like a distant, muffled engine being stirred into life. It takes a moment for her to place it – train loco? aeroplane? a ship out on the river? And then she realises it's just the steady sound of the city starting up again as the curfew ends. You can feel it all around. Towards the river, towards the French Concession, the Chinese City, a blur of engines and voices and movement. The perpetual background hum of home.

A car horn toots nearby, making her jump, and she turns to see the car at the junction with Nanking Road edging to one side. A few seconds later the first rickshaws appear, then a pedestrian, another, another. Not the usual morning rush at all, but it's something. The returning figures and hint of normality give her more hope – if it can just get busy enough we won't stick out on the empty street, she thinks. Maybe we can just slip past the gangsters and back to the temple.

But as the minutes drag by, the rickshaws and occasional pedestrian remain no more than a trickle.

And to Ruby's dismay she sees that each and every passer-by is being stopped and checked by the Green Hand men.

第二十六章

SWIMMING WITH FISHES

Distantly that same bell strikes half past.

Half a precious hour wasted! Even if I can fight, Ruby thinks – or run – Charlie can't do either. And if I break cover and try and find a rickshaw we might be separated for good. For ever. Oh God . . .

But as the clock's chime fades she hears something else: some kind of distant drumming, and a faint crashing of cymbals, possibly somewhere far away up Nanking Road.

She listens harder. Of all the sounds she's heard in the city over the years she can't work out what it could be. But whatever is making the racket, it's definitely coming closer, and at speed – this side of the Recreation Ground already. Looking back to the junction with Nanking Road she can see more people gathering, the Green Hand men dispersing,

269

mingling with a thin crowd.

The noise swells – and now she can make out Chinese instruments playing, two-stringed fiddles sawing – and voices joining them, dozens, maybe hundreds of voices chanting, singing along.

A protest? Striking workers? It sounds too joyful for that. The Green Hand have given up checking the papers of everyone gathering at the crossroads, but still their sharp eyes are raking the gathering throng. Still not enough cover on Fukien Road . . .

The sound swells and suddenly marching figures appear, striking down the middle of Nanking Road waving huge banners in the air. First a handful, then more – and more – a steady flow of protestors. Two drummers thunder past and then a cheer goes up as a huge dancing dragon bursts into view, weaving red and gold through the marchers and onlookers – even around the bemused gangsters standing on the corner – chasing a pearl waved tantalisingly in front of its clacking mouth. Everyone's eyes are on it . . .

It's a chance. Perhaps the only chance. Quickly Ruby hustles Charlie back into the sunlight and full exposure of Fukien Road.

'Come on, Charlie. Walk!'

She hurries them towards the commotion, bracing for shouts from behind – or even a bullet in the back.

Ahead a banner catches the wind and she sees the slogan billow: FAMINE RELIEF SOCIETY! PEACE NOW!

Are those footsteps running after them? Someone's yelling . . .

'Come on, Charlie. Faster, for God's sake!'

She daren't look, just propels him as fast as she can, one arm under his, eyes fixed ahead. The dragon is still jinking around at the crossroads, encouraging the protestors as it dips and swoops around them – and in the confusion Ruby bundles Charlie into the watching crowd.

Someone's definitely shouting angrily behind, coming closer at speed.

She pushes them both further into the chaos of banners and musicians and marchers, and they're immediately caught up in the protest's flow and movement. A swishing noise whisks overhead and Ruby glances up to see a shoal of paper fish kites swimming above, shimmying pale blue and pea green and pink, the sunlight working down between them as if down through clear water. Smiling faces beam at her from the puppeteers beneath.

'How do you like our fishes?' a voice cries, swirling his salmon close to her face. 'Hooray for the Yangtze! River of life!'

'Have a go, foreigner!' another voice yells. Someone grabs at her arm.

'I can't, I—'

Before she knows it a stout pole has been thrust into her hands, a trout waving rainbow colours from its tip. Unsupported, Charlie stumbles to the tarmac beside her on hands and knees.

'Charlie! Get up!'

'Don't worry, Missee,' a young man shouts in Pidgin. 'We help.' Together with another marcher he lifts Charlie effortlessly from the ground.

'Look at this poor boy!' he yells. 'Weak with hunger! It's time everyone ate decently. Feed the nation!'

Around them the cry is repeated and spreads through the protest. 'Feed – the – nation! Feed – the – nation!'

Charlie is hoisted high, putting out his arms to steady himself amidst the leaping sky fish.

Ruby looks back at the young man. The bright smile under his own Fedora hat encourages her. 'We're in trouble. I need to go to the Bund. To the French Concession. Can you carry him for me?'

'No problem,' the man grins. 'Let's go!'

The procession sweeps down Nanking Road at pace, away from the searching gangsters, and to blend in Ruby waves her fish vigorously. Drums and cymbals crash ahead of them, and somewhere behind a jazz band is pulsing away, saxophones and trumpets clashing against the traditional music. Looking back she sees huge papier-mâché apples, squashes, red peppers. And beyond those, big, perfectly ripe peaches, floating like orangey-pink clouds in the sunlight. She thinks again of the overripe peaches that lured Jin to them all those long weeks ago. Maybe it's a sign? Maybe he's still around like he said, watching over us.

She waves her fish even harder, willing the protest faster. Some of the marchers like her young helper are in Western suits, some in padded Chinese jackets and skullcaps. A few women look like rental dancers stepped straight from the nightclubs, striding along in their split, silk cheongsams . . . but however they're dressed, all are lifting their voices together, chanting for a better time, a better country. The energy of it all is uplifting, the river approaching glittering with morning light. Glancing up she sees Charlie blinking in confusion.

'Hold on, Charlie!' she shouts. 'We're nearly at the Bund.'

Swiftly they dash past the Garden Bridge, around the corner of the Riverside Gardens. Out on the river warships are piled nose to tail and a big liner – the *Franconia* by the looks of it – is pulled up midstream, surrounded by the usual scrum of junks and sampans. In a moment it's swept from sight.

The protest advances another hundred yards – and then shudders to a halt. All the fish concertina together, bumping around Charlie, and he groans loudly.

'Are you all right?' she shouts. He turns his head vaguely towards her, but can't seem to summon the energy for a reply.

She nudges the young man next to her. 'What's happening?'

'Might be trouble ahead,' he grunts. 'Some workers tried to storm police stations and the barracks in the old city last night. So there was a curfew. But we've been planning this demonstration for weeks and weeks so we thought we'd go ahead.'

'Are you Communists?' Ruby whispers.

The man laughs. 'I'm not an anything-ist. I'm a student. I just want to study.'

The procession jolts back into forward motion. 'I think your friend needs a doctor,' he adds, glancing up at Charlie.

'I know,' Ruby pants, looking up anxiously. 'Can you ask your friends to put him down when we get to the War Memorial?'

'Not sure how far we'll get!' the student grunts,

lifting his sunburst carp to the strengthening breeze. 'But let's see.'

Ruby's spirits lift again as they approach the French Concession – the temple is so close now. And maybe Jin will reappear and maybe—

Again the protest shudders to a standstill. Now the music and drumming have stopped too, replaced by jeers and whistling. Instantly the mood of the crowd shifts to something edgier. Ruby steps up onto the kerb, planting one foot on a bollard and raising her self above the heads of the marchers in front. No clear sight of what is causing the blockage, just the banners and fish and the dragon, still weaving red and gold knots. But beyond, lit up by the sun she can just see the top of Riverside Mansions now. For a moment she considers making a bolt for the safety of home. But even if she can think of it as *home*, there's not likely to be any safety there. She remembers the visit of the growling gangster, Dad's hand on his own pistol, the body of agent Woods loaded into an ambulance . . .

'Told you,' the student says. 'They've closed the barrier to the Chinese City – and they're even stopping us from going on into the French area. It could get ugly.'

'Then we need to go,' Ruby says, glancing up at

Charlie. 'We can't wait another minute. Can you put him down please?'

The men lower Charlie to the ground. He stands swaying, shaking his head like a boxer struggling up from the canvas. 'I had a weird dream,' he mutters. 'Fish. Ghost fish . . . they . . . were trying to eat me.'

Ruby looks around quickly to get her bearings: Canton Road. It'll have to do – they'll have to break cover and make a dash for White Cloud. The procession jerks forward again a few steps and the student crouches down beside Charlie, looking back anxiously at Ruby.

'Perhaps I should help you? St Luke's Hospital is not far.'

'No, thank you,' Ruby says firmly. 'We'll be OK.'

She shakes Charlie briskly by the shoulder as the fish move on a few strides. 'Charlie! Charlie! Wake up! We're going to White Cloud.'

'White Cloud?' Charlie says, his voice almost lost in the clamour from the crowd.

'To the cross we made. Remember?'

'Cross? We're nowhere.'

It looks as though he's going to drop again. She bites her lip, then steps forward and gives his cheek a gentle slap. Another, a bit harder. Another.

'Charlie! We're going! Wake up!'

His skin is so pale now that you can see the pink where her fingers have hit.

'I'm sorry,' she mumbles, but the slaps at least seem to have done something. Charlie opens his eyes that bit wider, and when she grabs his hand and pulls him from the procession he follows, somewhat unsteady, but walking – just.

The sounds of the protest fall away as they head up Canton Road. At the next intersection two Municipal Policemen are standing in the middle of the street, hands resting on holstered pistols. They eye Ruby curiously, and she slows her pace, suddenly aware of how weird she must look in the Chinese jacket and hat.

One of them tips his head back, peering down his long beak of a nose. She tries to return the gaze, to force a smile.

'Where are you off to?' the other one says, thumbs jammed in his cartridge belt. 'Should you be out without your parents?'

'Going to the doctor. In Prosperity Road.'

'For your houseboy?' he says, nodding at Charlie.

'Yes,' she snaps, hurrying past.

'Be careful. They might not have cleared the mess up that way,' the second one calls.

She ignores them, focusing all her effort on keeping

momentum to Charlie's dragging feet. If he falls she wonders if she'll ever get him up again. She can feel the policemen's eyes on the back of her . . .

Nearly there though.

Thirty paces further on Charlie groans, and then drops onto all fours.

'You've got to keep going,' she whispers. 'Please. I can't carry you.'

A couple of Westerners are eyeing them from across the road, two ladies bundled in fur coats. They look awfully familiar – maybe some of Mother's gossipy friends? She tries to keep the brim of her hat down so they don't spot her. But now a rickshaw man is turning a big U in the road and coming alongside, spotting a possible fare, calling out loudly.

'You go where, Missee?'

'Not far,' she answers, glancing across the road. One of the women is pointing at her, the other standing with her mouth open.

'We can't pay,' Ruby whispers urgently in Chinese. 'But we're in big trouble. I need to get my friend to Prosperity Road fast.'

The man looks up and down the road, undecided. He glances down at Ruby's soft-soled shoes, then at his own wrecked straw sandals. 'I'll take you for those,' he says.

'Deal!' Ruby shouts, already heaving Charlie into the rickshaw seat. The man helps, then grabs the shafts of his cart – and as soon as Ruby's feet are off the ground he hares away up Canton Road. Glancing back, Ruby sees one of the women waving frantically and calling, but her voice is lost in the rattle of the rickshaw wheels.

'Detour,' the man shouts. 'Kiangse Road's shut. So we'll take the long way round Honan and back into Prosperity. OK?'

'OK. But quick as you can.'

'Getting colder night-time,' the puller says, beaming back at her. 'Plenty cold. No coat.'

'You can have my coat too!' Ruby shouts in Chinese. 'Just hurry.'

The promise of a coat puts real speed into the man's legs and they hurtle past blocked off Kiangse Road as fast as she's ever seen a rickshaw go. But not so fast that she doesn't catch a glimpse of a huddle of men in black suits, a body being lifted towards a waiting cart. Trouble, just like always, just like Jin said . . . In a flash it's gone, and the rickshaw is cornering fast, narrowly dodging an oncoming trolley car, and away down Honan Road.

'Where to?' the man pants.

'Anywhere on Prosperity Road. The side of the old

temple if you can. Why's Kiangse Road shut?'

'Green Hand,' the man shouts, his face contorted with the effort.

What if the temple is still being watched? Maybe the tunnel from White Cloud to Moonface's old base is still being used by One Ball?

Charlie slumps against her. And as the rickshaw man brings them to a juddering stop, Ruby sees with horror that he's virtually out cold.

She pulls the shoes from her feet and hurls them at the rickshaw puller, then shrugs herself out of the coat and lets it drop to the sunny pavement. Charlie sways, his shadow swaying with him. But it looks *really* pale, far paler than her own stamped beside it.

'We're there. Just a few more steps.'

She takes his arm again and they stumble together round the corner to the temple gate – and then Charlie lets out a soft groan and crumples to a heap. His lips are blue, his teeth chattering crazily . . .

I'll have to lift him. Focus all my *ch'i*, Ruby thinks, and, blocking everything else out of her mind, takes a deep breath and heaves his limp body from the pavement.

Whether the illness has lightened him, or whether her desperation and *ch'i* strengthen her, she manages it, and with Charlie sagging in her arms she kicks open the loose board in the gates, and staggers through the gap into the sanctuary of White Cloud.

'We're here, Charlie. We did it!'

And now what?

She eyes the courtyard. Maybe there are still Green Hand here? Or Andrei lurking with the gun?

But she can see nobody, hear nobody, just feel Charlie weighing heavier in her arms by the second. The sounds of the distant protest, the background buzz of the city fall away, and she hurries forward through the weeds, her gaze on the ground ahead.

There's the cross! Still just visible, two faint lines scratched in the dirt. She walks deliberately over it, her legs threatening to buckle, and manages the three steps onto the veranda before her strength falters, and she drops to her knees, sending Charlie sprawling onto the boards of the main hall.

'Don't leave me!' she shouts. 'Wake up!'

Charlie's white face and blue lips are really shocking to look at when she rolls him onto his back. She stares at him for a second, then pulls herself away to the old hiding place. Maybe the Almanac will just have reappeared? Maybe it was there all along and Charlie just didn't look far enough into the recess before hiding from the gangsters?

Or Jin will have magicked it there?

Her hand gropes frantically behind the bit of panelling – but, sickeningly, inevitably, there's nothing there. Nothing but dust and mould.

That's it then. All is lost. Charlie is going to die.

'Where are you, Jin?' she cries out. 'You said you'd help! Where *are* you?!'

She drops to her knees, hears Charlie groan again – and is about to put her hands together in half remembered Sunday school prayer, when she hears the step behind her squeak loudly.

She braces for the worst, expecting to hear the safety catch being released on a gun. Or the rough voice of a Green Hand thug.

But instead she hears a boy's voice. 'Looking for something?'

Spinning round she sees a chubby figure silhouetted against the bright courtyard beyond.

Yu Lan. The first of the gang to falter when the going got tough, and run for the safety of home.

Not a threat, but not much help either. The rich merchant's son is gazing down at her in amazement, his skullcap crammed on his unruly hair.

Her shoulders sag.

'What do you want?' she snaps. 'You ran out on us—'

'I've been *looking* for you,' Yu Lan says impatiently.

'Every day! Well, almost every day. Where on earth have you *been*?'

Ruby looks around, despair replaced by suspicion now. Maybe Yu Lan's in it with the Russian boy. Or he's tipped off the gangsters? What did Charlie say? – *his sort always take care of themselves . . .*

'Where's Andrei? Are you on his side?'

'Of course not.' Yu Lan shakes his head, hurt. 'I saw it all. I was hiding in the bamboo and I saw it all happen. And I got scared and I ran off . . .'

'A fat load of use you are,' Ruby shouts. 'And now Charlie's dying and I don't know what to do. We need the Almanac. Charlie's been injured by vampires and we need a spell, but Jin can't help because he ran out of energy—'

Yu Lan holds up his hand. Unbelievably a smile is playing on his lips. For a moment she thinks he's about to make fun of her and she gets to her feet, hackles rising. But Yu shakes his head. '*I've* got the Almanac, Ruby! I took it to read at home and then I thought I'd keep it safe—'

'Where is it now?'

'Still in my room. In a chest.'

Ruby throws her arms in the air. 'Then go and get it, dummy! As fast as you can. And bring some ink and some brushes. I don't know. And some incense!'

Yu Lan is nodding, already backing away towards the steps. 'Hopping vampires?'

'As fast as you can,' Ruby says. 'Move it!'

Yu takes one more look at Charlie, and then rustles away across the courtyard as fast as his silk gown will allow.

Ruby sits with Charlie, holding him tight.

And waits.

His breathing is very light now, just a slight trembling of his chest.

'Charlie? Charlie, can you hear me? I love you, Charlie,' she whispers, tears welling in the corner of her eyes. 'Did you hear me——?'

Suddenly a gun fires, a single booming shot towards the river, and she jumps.

What now?

Of course. It's just the midday cannon from near the Customs Depot. Twelve o'clock already! Where on earth has that Yu got to?

He was the last to join the Outlaws, and none of them was ever sure how reliable he was. But all her hopes are pinned on him now. She leans close to Charlie, her cheek near his mouth, trying to feel the warmth of his breath.

Still there just.

The wind sweeps the bamboo – that familiar restless sound she's heard so many times before. She looks away at the graves under the trees, wonders again about Jin, willing him to materialise – then focuses back on Charlie, grabbing both his hands, crying properly now, the tears making channels in the dried mud on her cheeks.

Behind her the sound of the gate squeaking open is too quiet for her to hear . . .

As are the stealthy footsteps in the courtyard.

And it's only the third time the voice behind her calls her name that it registers.

'Ruby!'

She whips round, hoping to see Yu, but instead sees a much taller, familiar figure limping towards her.

'Dad!' she gasps, getting to her feet. His face is dark, anger and relief fighting for control of his features.

'Ruby! My God!'

He hobbles up onto the veranda and looks at her, mouth working hard but unable to say anything else. Then he sinks to his haunches in exhaustion.

'I told you,' he whispers. 'I told you you'd go too bloody far one day.'

第二十七章

STROKE ORDER

Before Ruby can reply, Yu Lan comes panting back through the gateway, a cloth-wrapped bundle tucked under his arm like a rugby ball. He gets halfway across the courtyard before he sees Mister Harkner and jams on his brakes.

Those busybody friends of Mother's must have seen me, Ruby thinks, and told someone. And now Dad's going to get in the way and maybe even stop what I have to do for Charlie.

She gets to her feet, eyes meeting Dad's. 'Don't – don't mess things up again,' she shouts. 'You dropped Fei in it with the Green Hand and you're not going to stop me now. Just push off if you're going to—'

Dad is holding his own palms up. 'Now, just a minute!'

She bites her lip, waits for more – and then she sees

that, astonishingly, Dad's eyes are also bright with tears. All the fire has gone out of him as he takes another half step. 'I know I mucked everything up. But you need to come with me right now.'

'I can't. And if you've got the Green Hand with you then you can go to blazes!'

'Why would I have them with me?'

'Because you're up to your neck with them – you betrayed Charlie and Fei!'

'I had no choice. And I'm certainly not in their good books now, Ruby.'

Dad's eyes fall on Charlie.

'Is he OK?'

'He's ill—'

'Then we should take him straight to hospital.'

'No! It's something *you* don't understand. We have to do a ritual to save him . . .'

'Ruby,' Dad says, 'this is hardly the time for—'

'If you're going to call it all "rot" then you can leave now. Right now!'

Dad takes a step back, defeated. 'God knows what I believe any more. You can have five minutes. Then we're going.'

'Why?' Ruby shouts. 'Why should I do what you say any more? You and Mother don't care about me. Neither of you have since Tom died. That's the truth!'

'Well, *that's* rot,' Dad says firmly. 'You can't really think that?'

'That's what it feels like! And you nearly got Fei killed! And Charlie too!'

'I told you. I didn't have a choice,' Dad murmurs.

Ruby takes a breath. The tears are threatening to come harder, but there's no time for this now. Angrily she wipes at them and turns back to Yu Lan.

'Open the book!'

'What am I looking for?'

'Stuff about *jiang shi* of course,' Ruby says. 'Somewhere near the back. I'm sure there was an entry amongst all the stronger fox spirits there.'

She crouches next to him, her eyes scanning the difficult characters, the charts, strange images.

Dad's shadow falls across the book, and she takes the Almanac from Yu, moving it back into the sunlight at the edge of the veranda.

'I can't see anything.' Yu huffs. 'This bit is all about revenants, ghosts that return, that kind of thing. Can't see *jiang shi*.'

'There!' Ruby shouts, jabbing at the book with her finger.

Towards the bottom of the page is a woodcut of a stiff-limbed vampire, strutting along the margin – and above it an enormously complex ritual character smudged in red. Fifty strokes of the brush or more . . .

Ruby peers at the text stamped below. Some of it she can read – chilling words like '*ch'i* loss' and '*very serious*' and '*death*'. But a lot she can't decipher and she turns the book impatiently back to Yu.

'Well?'

His stubbly finger runs along the lines and he frowns, and reads again.

'OK, OK,' he mutters. 'If he was touched by one we need to draw this character very big across the injury. But we need red for it. And I only brought black ink. I could go and buy some—'

'There's no time,' Ruby says, dragging the book over to Charlie's immobile body. 'We'll use blood. Like when we did the Outlaws' oath.'

'Whose?'

'Mine of course. Dad, give me your knife.'

'Ruby. I'm not—'

'Do it!' she shouts. 'And take Charlie's jacket and shirt off.'

To her amazement Dad does exactly as he's told. Meekly he hands her his little folded pocket knife, and then starts to pull back the blanket. 'Five minutes and then we need to get out of here,' he repeats.

Ruby ignores him. With tongue planted between her teeth she folds out the blade, and without hesitation slices into her left thumb. Instantly blood wells in deep red drops against her pale skin.

'Boy should be in hospital,' Dad mutters. 'And Mother will kill me if she sees what you're doing.'

'I don't care.'

Yu Lan frowns, concentrating. 'It's got to be done just right, the book says. The stroke order and everything. Do you want me to do it?'

'No,' Ruby says. 'I'll do it.'

Dad unbuttons Charlie's shirt to leave his slim chest exposed. Near his faint heartbeat, there's an ugly purple-black bruise on the ribbed, coppery skin. It seems to be spreading across the chest.

'What happened to him?' Dad whispers.

'You wouldn't believe me.'

Ruby looks back at her thumb. Quickly she takes a brush from Yu, licks the point into shape, and then dips it into the bleeding.

She squints at the book again, takes a breath, and then over the wound draws a quivering top line to start the character.

'Don't stop,' Yu reads. 'And make it big enough to cover the whole thing.'

'Let me focus,' she mutters, and moves the tip of the brush across Charlie's torso, leaving the next curled line. Her eyes flicker from the character to the book to her thumb and back again, concentrating as hard as she has ever concentrated in her life, dipping, looking, drawing, over and over, as each line builds the Taoist pattern.

Now a top to bottom line, now two across with a flick on each, now another descender with a hook . . . she squeezes her left thumb against the other fingers to force out more drops of blood.

'What does it mean?' Dad asks, gazing at the maze of lines.

'I don't know. It's to make him better.'

Her head is starting to swim and it's getting harder to focus, lines blurring, her thumb throbbing. Charlie's eyes shift restlessly behind the closed lids – and suddenly his lips twitch.

'That's it,' Yu urges. 'You need to do that line now, Ruby.' He points his finger at Charlie's chest, guiding the next stroke.

Quickly, her hands getting shakier, Ruby forces more blood onto the brush and is just finishing off the curving line at the bottom when Charlie gives a violent cough. The line blobs under her brush, and she waits a second for his chest to calm before finishing the last stroke with a flourish. Charlie coughs hard again and one hand reaches up into the air.

It's not perfect, she thinks, getting to her feet. Not

great calligraphy. But it's working . . . it's working and I . . .

She doesn't feel the fainting fit coming.

Her head suddenly goes as light as the midday sky above, and she drops to the boards of the main hall. The last thing Ruby sees is the negative imprint of the talisman stamped on her fading vision . . .

She wakes to find herself laid out across three chairs in Doctor Sprick's stuffy waiting room. Dad is crouched over her, face knitted with concern.

She struggles up, head groggy. 'What are we doing? Where's Charlie!'

'Just getting you checked out. Iodine for your thumb.' Dad drops his voice conspiratorially. 'And I need to get your mother discharged from St Luke's and onto a boat.'

She feels nothing but panic for a moment, and then a great surge of joy swipes that away and sits her bolt upright as she sees Charlie standing next to Dad.

'You're alive!' she whispers.

He smiles back, face still grey, but a real smile plastered there. And his eyes are awake, alert. 'Yes, I am here. You are fine too. Good.'

'Why are you speaking English?'

Charlie looks abashed, and nods at Mister Harkner,

before adding in rapid Chinese: 'It's all a muddle in my head, but Yu Lan says you drew a talisman,' he blushes, 'on my skin, and the next thing I was waking up . . . And you were lying there and your dad was asking me questions and I felt so awful I just wanted to throw up and cry and lie down all at once . . .'

He hesitates and looks at Mister Harkner again. 'Can we trust him, Ruby?'

'We can now. I thought I'd lost you, Charlie. I thought—'

'Oh do speak English,' Dad says. 'What are you talking about? Something about me, right?'

There's a new note in his voice. Or, rather, an old one – one she hasn't heard for ages, not since before Tom died and there were at least as many good days as bad. Stargazing and throwing pebbles onto the backs of stone elephants. A note of warmth.

Of something like care.

Ruby looks at him. 'It doesn't matter. Everything is OK.' She pushes off the chairs and wraps her arms around Charlie and hugs him hard, and ignores Doctor Sprick when he comes out to call her name and sees her and the slim Chinese boy locked in a tight embrace.

'If only it was,' Dad says gravely after waiting a moment. 'But everything is *decidedly* not OK.'

SHANGHAI
1988

It was getting dark now on the temple veranda. Cold seeped from the building behind me as we sat on the step looking out at the courtyard, and every few seconds shivers went running over my skin.

'There you are. We're almost at the end,' the old lady said, glancing at her watch. 'Maybe my friend can't make it. Gives me time to give you the last few pieces of my story.'

'Please. Please do,' I whispered, spellbound. 'Was it a happy ending, you and Charlie? What about your mother? What about Charlie and Fei's dad and—'

She laughed. 'Strange tales often have strange endings . . .'

'Tell me what happened to you at least, you and Charlie. Did he get better?'

'Very quickly,' the old lady sighs. 'His colour slowly

came back, and he stood up straighter and his voice got stronger, and we talked and talked and talked about everything.'

'And you?'

'My dear boy, I had just fainted. Tiredness and hunger and relief. My father said it was the damnedest thing he'd ever seen. Told Doctor Sprick about how I'd drawn on Charlie's chest and brought him back to life. And Sprick gave Dad a strange look and offered him sleeping pills.' She laughed. 'And then Dad called him a *bloody quack* and marched us out of there!'

'Where?'

'To a hotel on the Bund, Astor House across Garden Bridge. Dad slipped the desk clerk a bribe and we checked in under a false name. And Amah came the next morning and brought Fei back to us. *Almost* a happy ending!'

'What about you and Charlie?'

She puffed out her cheeks. 'Well, that's the bit that still brings back the sadness. I'll sketch it out for you. You can maybe fill in the rest.'

'Tell me.'

She took a deep breath, composing herself. 'Well. Dad said we had to stay under cover, that something grim was being cooked up between the Green Hand and the city's authorities. That his name was mud with just about everybody, and anyone – like Charlie and his family – who were even suspected of Communist links would be for the high jump. So.'

She cleared her throat, gazed into the deep shadow under the trees. 'So here it is, young man, my last chapter if you like. We could call it . . .'

第二十八章

...FAREWELL TO SHANGHAI

Everything looks normal below the windows of Astor House. Or almost normal.

From the fourth floor Ruby can see the usual traffic on the riverfront road, the checkpoint open at Garden Bridge, a clutter of boats on the Huangpu. Anchored midstream like a giant amongst pygmies lies the bulk of the liner *Franconia*. This morning she has felt something like ease and rest for the first time in over a year. Charlie lies safe in the next room, sleeping – not the weird half sleep brought on by the vampires, but a natural, deep, restoring slumber – and Fei is on her way with Amah, under strict instructions to criss-cross the city in case they're followed.

Apart from that it's just a typical day in autumnal Shanghai.

Except Dad says it isn't. 'Notice anything about

the *Franconia*?'

'What?'

'She's not docked at the pier. They're holding her out there in case she's swamped.'

'Who by?'

'People like us. People who need to get out of the city. This place is a powder keg.'

'But we're not going anywhere.'

Dad grimaces at his damaged leg, adjusting it to try and make the prosthetic comfortable. 'Our descriptions are in the hands of the Warlord's men *and* the Green Hand. I've double-crossed One Ball Lu, and he's in cahoots with the French and the Council. We *have* to get out.'

'Out?' Ruby says in alarm. 'What do you mean, out? I thought you just meant Mother. To somewhere quieter for her nerves. *I'm* not going anywhere!'

'Just listen for a moment—'

'But where do you mean? Kiuling? Soochow?'

'Heavens, no. I mean *England*, Ruby,' he says, clumping over to join her at the window. 'I mean *home* home.'

The ground seems to give beneath her feet. 'But *that's* not my home—'

'Have you *any* idea how lucky you are to be alive? Things are going to get much worse here before they get better. Sooner or later Shanghai's going to fall to the Nationalists and the Communists. Or they'll turn on each other and it'll be a bloodbath. And *then* the Japanese will probably have a go. And then? Well, God only knows. We're going back.'

For a long minute Ruby can't speak. She feels the room get smaller, her chest tightening.

'But this is my home!' she splutters again. 'I've never been to stupid old England in my life. I don't feel English or British. I'm . . . Chinese! I'm a Shanghailander!'

Dad holds his hands up.

'But the thing is, old girl, you're *not* Chinese. You're English. And in the end that's all people will see—'

'But—'

'It's not just about you, damn it! It's about your mother and me too – and her nerves have taken far more than they can here. It's time to leave your little brother in peace and restart our lives.'

'But—'

'But what? Out with it.'

Charlie, she thinks. I can't leave, Charlie. Not now. She gives Dad a fierce look.

'I know it will be hard on you. I can see you're keen on that boy—'

'Not "that boy". *Charlie*.'

'OK, *Charlie*. But you'll adjust. We all have to deal with things we don't want in life.' He nods at his leg. 'I wanted to stay at university, for example, to keep studying physics, outer space. Who knows – if the Great War hadn't happened, and my leg – maybe I'd be working with Eddington and his pals now. Calculating the distances to other *galaxies* rather than counting *tofu* consignments on the dock. Light years and nebulae and all that and not messed up in squeeze and looking the other way while some hoodlum smuggles opium under my nose. So *don't* tell me I don't understand that life isn't fair sometimes. And if I hadn't lost my leg I wouldn't have met your mother and you wouldn't be here!'

It's not like Dad to mention the loss of his leg or the war. To talk about himself for that matter.

'I need your mother to be better again,' he says quietly, rubbing the shadowy stubble on his chin. He gets up, comes over and puts a hand on her rigid shoulder.

'And I don't want to risk losing you. Remember that day at the seaside? I tried not to let it show, but it was touch and go you know? You could have drowned—'

'I went to the Gorges and back on my own! I flew in a plane! I can cope if you leave me here.'

'Impossible,' Dad says abruptly. 'You're not even fourteen yet. And that's an end of it.'

'You can't make me,' she says. 'I'll run away again.'

'Over my dead body,' Dad says. 'Who knows, maybe you'll come back here in a few years when you're grown up and everything's settled—'

A sharp rap on the door startles them both. The knock repeats its pattern and Dad's shoulders relax. When he opens the door it's to the Amah's crinkled face, and delighted whoops from Fei.

'We did it, Ruby! Where's Charlie?'

Amah rushes forward on her crippled feet and squeezes Ruby tight.

'Oh, my girl, I've been so worried. So worried.'

'Amah,' Ruby whispers in Chinese. 'What's going on? What's all this about us going to England? Do you know about it?'

'Yes,' Amah stifles a sob. 'I do.'

'When are we going?'

'Tomorrow. The tickets are bought.'

Ruby groans, and then rushes to the connecting door that leads to Charlie.

Sunlight washes the room. Charlie is propped up on pillows, and he greets his sister and aunt with huge hugs, before settling back to listen to Fei and Amah talking nineteen to the dozen about how they dodged their way across town, occasionally asking a question and nodding thoughtfully. Every now and then he looks to Ruby, his eyes bright behind the replacement glasses that Amah has brought from home.

'I got questioned,' Amah says, 'by a Green Hand man. But I just acted dumb and he let me go in the end.'

Charlie leans forward. 'And you say Dad's safe? Where is he?'

'I don't know exactly. Somewhere in Kiangsu. With friends and getting better the last I heard. He sent a message that I should look after you both until he sends for you.'

'When?'

'Very soon.'

And then Fei's bubbling away again, telling Charlie about the aeroplane and the ghost junk and the hungry ghosts and Jin. Amah listens, her eyes widening, her hand going to her mouth in shock, then laughing, then looking shocked again. Ruby's glad to see her again, to hear Fei laughing away and bouncing on the end of the bed – but really she just longs to have Charlie to herself. Time is ticking away. And as if to confirm it the noonday gun bangs and shakes the glass in the window frame.

302

'I'm taking you two to my place,' Amah says. 'It'll be safe enough in broad daylight with the streets busy. We'll use the backstairs and nobody will bother us there.'

'But I need to talk to Charlie,' Ruby says. 'Please, Amah. In private.'

'Oooooh!' Fei whistles. 'Did you know, Auntie? Charlie and Ruby are in love.'

Amah looks from Ruby to Charlie and back again, and then nods solemnly.

'In that case, niece, let's give them a little privacy, shall we?'

The door closes and Ruby sits on the side of the bed. She takes his hand and feels relief again at its warmth, how it responds in hers. But it's hard to say what she's got to say.

He looks into her eyes. 'What is it, Ruby?'

It takes Charlie a full minute to digest the news. Then he clears his throat – but when he speaks, it's not what she wants to hear.

'You have to go, Ruby. No arguments.'

'Noooo!'

'You have to. Your dad's right. This place could blow at any minute and we're all marked now. And if *my* dad sends a message, we'll have to drop everything and go heaven knows where.'

'I'll come with you then.'

'This is going to be about the Chinese and nobody else. And besides, I want you to go somewhere really safe.'

'Then you could come with us. You and Fei and even Amah and—'

'You know that's impossible.'

She stares away at the window, blinking tears.

'But what about . . . what about you and me? You saw the thread. We're *meant* to be together.'

'Not now,' he says quietly.

'But you saw it!' Ruby says, squeezing his hand.

He nods, and looks down at their knotted fingers – and they sit like that in silence for a moment.

'If you love me, Ruby, then you'll go. Understand—?'

Dad comes in briskly without knocking, hesitates, and takes a deep breath.

'You'll have to go, young man. Savvy? Rickshaw waiting. You two say your goodbyes – I'm sorry, but it can't be helped.'

Ruby looks back at Charlie, ignoring Dad.

'When are you going?' Charlie asks.

'Tomorrow at noon.'

'Come and see me before you go,' he says swiftly in Chinese, getting off the bed. His old energy is returning, bunching in his shoulders. 'Meet me at

White Cloud later if you can.'

Ruby nods, but she's fighting hard to control the tears, and turns back to the window so Charlie can't see. Out on the grey-brown water she sees again the beastly *Franconia*, steaming up clouds from her black funnels, moving slowly towards the transatlantic pier.

It's the most depressing sight she's ever seen.

'Plenty fast,' Dad's saying again. 'A friend in Customs told me they've been searching hotels. I'm sorry again for what happened.'

Charlie's listening intently, studying Mister Harkner's face. He nods and then holds out his hand and shakes Dad's firmly.

'I am ready.'

He turns to Ruby and says slowly in English, 'Goodbye, Ruby,' and then adds in hushed Chinese, 'until this evening. *Zai jian.*'

第二十九章

SKY FLOWERS

She argues with Dad for another hour after Fei and Amah and Charlie have slipped away through the back entrance to Astor House. The promise of seeing Charlie again has softened *this* parting. But when the *Franconia* sails from the pier it will be as good as heading for outer space.

Stubbornly she retreats into her own thoughts, gazing at her hand. How far can a red thread stretch? How long can it bind us? she thinks. Thousands of miles? A year? Ten years until I'm grown up?

Dad's on the phone now, talking urgently. From his side of the conversation she gathers that Mother is to be discharged from St Luke's and taken straight to the ship where she will wait for them.

She thinks about arguing again, but Dad hangs up, and as if reading her mind, silently picks up the day's

306

paper to show her a photograph of a neat row of bodies lined up on a street corner. He taps the paper once.

A GRISLY SIGHT, the headline reads. DEAD TRAITORS IN THE CHINESE CITY.

Underneath she sees the name of One Ball Lu and his sharp face in an inset photo gazing out at the camera.

'Did you hear about poor old Uchiyama?' Dad says, whisking the paper away. 'He's sold his last book apparently. Dumped in the Creek they say. We need to keep low and get the blazes out of here.'

The sun edges low over the city and Ruby pretends to have given up the fight. Dad has taken up station by the door, within reach of the telephone. He's hooked the chain and listens intently to footsteps come and go in the corridor.

As light fades the phone trills again.

'Yes? I see . . . are you sure? But they said tomorrow . . . Where? . . . And who are you?'

He looks at Ruby, takes a sharp breath. 'Very well.' Then clicks the mouthpiece back to the wall, twisting his mouth up.

'What is it?'

'The *Franconia*'s going early. Ten o'clock this evening. Everyone's got the wind up after that business night before last.'

Ruby gets to her feet, alarm surging through her. 'No. I'm not going. Not until I've seen Charlie again.'

But it's as if Dad doesn't hear. He goes to the window – peering out at the liner in the brooding dusk, pondering. 'But I'm not sure. She *is* on the pier now, but that was a voice I don't know. It may be a trap to lure me out . . . Chinese.'

He leans his forehead against the glass, lost in a calculation, his guard down for a second. Ruby looks to him, to the door and back again – and then she dashes to the door, grabbing her Fedora for luck, and ripping the chain back. Trying to push on his bad leg Dad stumbles, and before he can reach her she's out of the door, into the corridor, running like crazy.

'No!' Dad bellows. 'For God's sake—'

'I'll meet you at the boat!' she shouts. 'I'll meet you at the pier at nine! I promise.'

She's not even sure she means it. But at least it might reassure him. 'I'll see you there!' she shouts again.

Or maybe I'll just disappear with Charlie and Fei, she thinks as she runs. Maybe upriver somewhere to a quiet place like Full Moon Bridge.

Somewhere in China.

'Rubyyyyy . . .'

But she's already hurtling the stairs three at a time, down and down, and out through the hushed lobby.

The streets are still busy, and if anyone is watching the hotel I can just outrun them, she thinks. Her feet feel clumpy back in stiff Western shoes, but the strength is back in her legs, and she runs and she runs.

In the gathering gloom green sparks strike from the tramlines.

Across the river whistles are sounding a shift change. Rickshaws whirr past her as she weaves through the crowd, Chinese mingling with French and German and Arabic and other more exotic languages she can't place. She runs on: past the great clubs on the Bund, the bang and crash of jazz coming from one, a string quartet floating from another, the neon signs overhead welcoming the night. Intoxicating smells of food mingle with smoke and the whiff of the river as she runs for the temple. The world she loves . . .

I can't go, she thinks. I can't.

And she sprints every single stride to White Cloud.

Breathing hard, she pauses in the temple gateway and lets her eyes roam the courtyard one more time.

One *last* time?

Shut up, she thinks. Just focus. Any danger? Dad

meant all those warnings . . . And where's Charlie? Where *is* he?

She moves forward, senses on full alert as she edges towards the main hall. A crackle of explosions from behind sends her spinning, fearing the worst. Strange-coloured shadows race around her, as if the trees are grabbing for her with their twisted branches – and then with relief she sees that it's just fireworks away towards the river. Flowers of violet, crimson, lemon yellow, followed by resounding booms a fraction later.

The *Franconia* must be leaving tonight then, she thinks. They do that when one of the big liners is about to go. A colourful send-off for the passengers on board – a last glimpse of China.

Her gaze follows the drift of smoke and light . . .

. . . and then she hears her name being whispered.

Charlie is standing there, out of breath, the fireworks blooming reflections in his glasses.

'I thought you weren't here!'

'It's been tricky,' Charlie says. 'I heard the *Franconia*'s leaving early and got a friend of a friend to phone your dad. There's Green Hand everywhere.' He looks round, biting his lip.

'I'm not going,' Ruby says. 'I'm staying.' Another firework bursts overhead but she doesn't look up. 'I want to stay with you.'

Charlie looks at her intently.

'I love you, Ruby. Do you love me?'

She nods.

'Say it.'

She takes a breath and whispers the three Chinese words back. '*Wo ai ni.*'

'Then, I mean what I said. If you love me I want you to be safe and get on the boat. Fei and I are leaving tomorrow for Shantung. And the people who are taking us *won't* take you.'

'Why?'

'You know why. I know you're different from the rest, but they won't. And I've got to look after Fei and find my dad.'

Ruby looks around at the darkened temple, struggling to breathe.

'Then I'll come back, Charlie. I'll come back as soon as I can and find you. Wherever you are. I promise.'

Charlie nods, looks awkwardly away. It's all so stupid, Ruby thinks, shaking away the tears. We should just be able to be together . . .

She grabs Charlie's face with both hands and then plants a kiss on his mouth again, longer than on the train – like she's seen them do in the picture house. And he responds and kisses her back for a brief, glorious moment.

That was make-believe on the silver screen.

But this, this is real.

One last huge rocket thumps up over the Huangpu and bursts, and then slowly dies away to nothing.

Sounds and images seem muffled, distant – strangely dreamlike – as they make their way back towards the Bund. Charlie is alert though, on edge, his head twitching this way and that, pulling her into the buildings when a car sweeps past. The whiff of the fireworks still lingers towards the river as the crowds thicken around them.

'I mean it,' she says breaking the silence at last, trying to find the right words. 'I'll come back and find you. The fortune teller said I'd have a long and happy life. I'm going to live for years and years and come back and find you! And if I die I'll come back and haunt you!'

A smile flickers across his face. 'I believe you! But I don't even know where I'll be by this time tomorrow.'

Ruby glances down. Even in the intensity of this moment there's no sign of the thread. As if there would be. It feels now like the world is losing its magic, the strange and supernatural. Just coal smoke and backfiring cars and trams – no foxes, no ghosts, no Jin . . .

'You'd better hurry,' Charlie says, urging her on towards the pier. 'I'll be waiting for you. Promise. Even if I meet some amazing girl, I'll wait.'

A deep hooter sounds from not more than a hundred yards away. It has to be the *Franconia* – its drawn-out note sounding the end of her Shanghai life. She tries to slow her footsteps.

'At least you're going to be safe, Ruby—'

Charlie suddenly stops in his tracks, eyes widening through the round glasses.

'Green Hand!' he hisses. 'They're checking the queue. And there's more over there!'

Ruby follows his line of sight and there – yes – the typical Shanghai gangsters, scrutinising the last of the passengers heading for the boarding ramp. And then her heart beats even harder: standing next to them is the tall figure of One Ball Lu, his eyes roving the dockside, face contorted in a scowl.

I can't let Charlie be caught, Ruby thinks. He and Fei have got to get away even if Dad or I get stopped.

She turns and gives Charlie another quick kiss on the cheek, the brightest smile she can manage.

'I'll be fine! You run, Charlie.'

'No—'

But already she's striding forward, pulling the Fedora from her head, feeling a surge of energy as she moves towards the queue, the gangsters, the boarding ramp. And then – a little way off, crouching behind a huge stack of suitcases – she spots Dad.

He sees her almost at the same moment, and leaps forward from the shadow, frantically pointing at One Ball Lu and his men. In his haste he knocks a case over, and the sound attracts one of the gangsters who spins round. He slaps One Ball on the shoulder, and then whips out his pistol, levelling it at Dad.

Ruby rushes forward. Vaguely she hears Charlie screaming her name, as the other henchman raises his weapon and points it at her.

The first thug is walking towards Dad, aiming right for his chest as passers-by edge away. At that range he can't miss . . . And One Ball Lu is laughing, tipping his head back as if he's just seen the funniest act ever at The Great World.

'Hey! One Ball! Want to know what happened to Moonface!' Ruby bellows. The gangster boss turns towards her, raises his eyebrows – and laughs even harder.

But then his laughter stops abruptly.

A horn is blaring frantically away to Ruby's left – and every head turns in its direction to see a pale green van hammering out of the mouth of Nanking Road. It goes careering across the junction – and then on, towards the boarding ramp and straight at Ruby. She can just make out the driver behind the dusty windscreen, waving frantically with one hand. Mouth wide, feet glued to the pavement, Ruby watches as – clearly out of control – the van's front wheel strikes the kerb, throwing it sideways at the last moment and away from her, towards One Ball and his henchmen. As one they dive for cover: one man over the mound of suitcases, and One Ball and the other straight over the quayside into the river. The lorry slams into the pile of baggage, slowing, until finally it hits a lamp post and comes to a rest on the very edge of the Bund, one wheel spinning over the black water below.

There's a stunned silence on the side of the dock.

Wild splashing and shouts from the river.

The van driver staggers from his cab, holding out his hands in apology.

'I don't know what happened,' he stutters. 'Nothing worked properly.'

Ruby looks back to Dad to see him kick the prone gangster hard and then grab his weapon and hurl it into the shadows. A little way off police whistles are blowing and she races over to Dad, grabs his hand, and propels him limping up the gangplank.

Dad flashes a paper at the bewildered official at the open doorway of the *Franconia*.

315

'Green Hand won't board the boat,' Dad pants. 'We've done it. My God. We could all have been killed.'

But Ruby isn't listening. She's gazing back down to the quay to where the policemen have reached the scene, fanning out to take control of the mess. Already the van is being rolled back from the brink, and its green livery suddenly shines under a streetlamp.

And in that bright sodium light, on the side of the Liska Bakery van, Ruby sees the big cartoon fox illuminated. Just as she expected to see. By a trick of the shifting light his tail seems to move.

And then, a split second before the companionway door bangs shut, the fox winks at her.

Once.

Twice . . .

. . . and then with a clang her view of the great world of Shanghai is gone.

SHANGHAI
1988

It was so dark now I could hardly see the old lady sitting on the veranda beside me. A stiffening breeze caught the corrugated sheets of iron along one of the temple walls and banged them.

Somewhere a clock was chiming. I glanced at my watch. Ten o'clock.

'Maybe your friend isn't coming?'

'We'll give it another minute, then I've got to go.' The old lady got to her feet, took a couple of steps into the murk. I sensed a presence behind me, the hairs on the back of my neck rippling. I was . . . well and truly *spooked*. Something seemed to brush my shoulder and electricity shot through me. I spun round.

The lady laughed. 'You see? We are *all* susceptible.'

I edged away from the temple, leaving the crumbling statues and dragons to their shadows, struggling to hold on to my composure. 'It must be strange to be here after so long. Is this the first time you've been back?'

She looked at me, and smiled the saddest smile I think I've ever seen.

An intuition seized me: 'No. You came back before now, didn't you?'

'Indeed I did, young man. I knew you were the right person to listen to me.'

'When?'

'I was here for a good few years in the 1930s,' she said. 'I keep my promises.'

She cleared her throat and beckoned me towards the darkened graves.

'All the way down the Huangpu I watched from the *Franconia*, hoping, longing for a last glimpse of Charlie waving. Maybe at Garden Bridge, maybe further out. But I knew he had to run and hide. And I kept looking at my hand, and thinking maybe the thread would be there again. But nothing came. Dad and I stood at the rail silently, and he seemed to know just how hard the pain was, because he did something he didn't normally do. He put his arm round me. And I did something awful, young man. I shook his arm off. But he waited a moment and then put it back. And then I felt someone else and Mother was there. She didn't say anything for a long time, just stood staring at the lights of the city sliding away – and I knew she was saying goodbye to Tom. We were never close, her and me, but we found a way to be that was good enough.'

She paused, one hand stroking the other as she walked through the undergrowth.

'I refused to go inside and mingle with the other passengers. I just wanted to feel my anger, my pain! About five miles out the *Franconia* was starting to roll. I wanted to cry but no tears would come. I looked down at the black waters, and I saw the thread one last time. Like a shooting star, a red shooting star zipping across the surface of the water. Then gone . . .'

'And then?'

She pulled a lighter from her pocket, sparked a little flame, moving from one stone marker to the next. Very faintly the black and white photographs of the long dead appeared, blurred by time and condensation behind their glass.

Another world.

'Long story short: thirty days at sea. Me sulking and writing everything down I could remember, and composing letters to Charlie in my head. Then boarding school for five years. Then a horrid six months in a finishing school, from which I ran away twice and finally got expelled for letting off fireworks on the tennis court . . . All the time I kept my eyes peeled for stories from China, read with horror about the massacre of Communists and workers in early 1927, watched with more horror a newsreel of the bombing of Shanghai in 1932 – and hoped that Charlie and Fei were safe somewhere.

'No ghosts. No red thread.

'But in my dreams I saw it. Saw the red line twisting across the globe to Charlie. And there were foxes *everywhere*! Everywhere I went. The lane that led to my boarding school was called Vixen Drove, Dad and Mother moved into a new house next to a pub called the Fox and Hounds. Everywhere I turned images reminded me of the tobacco packet and the pictures in the consulate and Lao Jin.

'I sent letters to Shanghai with Amah's old address, the Tangs' place, but got nothing back. In '34 I applied for a job as a teacher in Shanghai and, against my parents' will, set sail for this place again.'

'And . . . ?'

'The city was weary from conflict, the build-up of tension with Japan. But I threw myself into teaching and spent days off walking our old haunts, asking people if they knew the whereabouts of the family. Nobody knew anything. Or if they did, they weren't talking. And then I was walking past the Mansions one autumn day, and was looking up at the bullet-ridden Shanghai Dairy sign – and I suddenly knew he, Charlie – was very close by. And then I heard my name.'

She parted some undergrowth and flashed the lighter again.

'And it was him?'

'Yes! There he was, smiling at me, taller and filled out, hair grown a bit. But the same shoulder lift, the same smile. He'd been back three days in the city – just three days! – and had been hanging around the old haunts, and we had found each other. Can you imagine what I felt?'

I could. All my skin was tingling.

'And we left the city next day. He was still on the run, and we went far up the Yangtze and found a quiet place where the civil war had passed and we lived a good life for a few years in a small town. Had a quiet Chinese wedding. Very happy.'

'Full Moon Bridge?'

'That would be too neat,' she laughed. 'Just a quiet place. And I wrote articles for a newspaper back home about it. And Charlie taught in the local school. Ten happy years, and we dodged the invasion of Shanghai and famines and floods and the terrible things that went on.'

She stopped and I felt her body tense.

'And?'

'History caught us up. More fighting. Charlie died. And I went home to England.'

She sparked the lighter briskly.

'Ah! Here it is! Look!'

Expecting now to see Charlie's grave I was taken aback for a moment to see no name – just a faded face staring back at me. Not how I'd imagined the young Tang boy – but an older face, wise, curious, one eyebrow cocked. Lively eyes. Mrs Harkner took my hand in her aging fingers and guided it to the worn inscription.

GONE BACK TO THE MOUNTAIN the characters read.

'You see, Lao Jin's message to us! It was real!' she said. 'All real!'

She straightened, eyes gleaming triumphantly. 'And look at me now, young man. You could say I'm just a pale revenant – come back for one last look.'

There was a creak from the flimsy gate, and turning I saw a small hunched figure edge through the gap.

'You could tell my story one day if you like!' Mrs Harkner said. 'Ah! Here she is.'

An old Chinese lady waved, greeted my companion with a hug, then turned her face towards me, chin raised.

'Who's this?' she said in croaky Chinese.

'A lost soul!' Mrs Harkner said. 'Young man, I'd like you to meet Tang Fei.'

I shook the elderly woman's hand, and her eyes sparked. 'So has Ruby been telling you her tall stories?'

I longed to ask her a question or two – a hundred! – but Mrs Harkner was already leading them both away.

'You saw it yourself, Fei. Now, come on. It's late! But please do look me up when you're back in England, young man.'

The elderly Chinese woman gave me a look then. A strange look, as if asking me her own question with her eyes. She looked from me to Ruby's departing figure to the darkened hall and back again.

As if to say, well, what will you believe?

AND THEN...

I went home and started to sort my life.

Dealt with my grief about my dad bit by bit (I never saw him again, but that one glimpse I'd had now felt reassuring somehow), and found myself a job, someone to love. The usual story.

But I couldn't get Shanghai Ruby and her strange adventures out of my mind. Those three nights of storytelling had filled my head with ghostly Gorges and spirits and foxes.

With a bit of distance and back in 'normal' life I started to rationalise Ruby's story a little. Some of it, I thought, must have happened just the way she said. After all, children growing up in Shanghai did often lead extraordinary lives. And ghosts – well people do see them, I knew that much from my own experience of seeing Dad's apparition. But the

324

wilder shores of Ruby's tales seemed now more like the product of an overworked, overstressed child's imagination, growing up in violent and superstitious times. Maybe her young mind had enlarged things – and then the older one muddled them, or slowly embroidered them in each retelling.

Or maybe even she was suffering from dementia of some kind?

But I didn't believe that last thought. She had seemed so sharp, so *present*. And I just couldn't shake off the sensation of that last hour or so in the darkening courtyard. The urgency of her voice, the look in old Tang Fei's eyes at the end. The gravestone. It had *felt* real as she told it to me.

By then I was working as a researcher on film and TV, getting used to digging out obscure facts from forgotten corners. So I decided to do some research of my own.

I could find no trace of a Ruby Harkner with directory enquiries, and with nothing in the books about foreigners in China in the 1920s and 30s – and with no internet to trawl then and other matters pressing – I gave up.

But a few years later, a friend – the librarian at a Chinese research institute in Cambridge – sent me a newly published book on the history of Westerners in

Shanghai. I flipped straight to the index and ran my finger down the entries for H.

And there she was. *Harkner, Ruby pp 242, 253–4 n4*

Fingers shaking, I flicked to the pages.

The first entry made a glancing reference to *the colourful and vivid eyewitness reporting from foreign journalists like Ruby Harkner* . . . And the second to a newspaper report, filed by *R Tang-Harkner* for the Manchester *Guardian* in 1944, of life near Ichang as the second world war rumbled to a close.

Not much – but there was still the footnote to that.

And as I read the tiny print at the bottom of the page I felt the goosebumps rise all over me.

Ruby Harkner, it read, *was a sometime journalist who lived on the Yangtze between 1934 and 1944. After China she got a pilot's licence, became a teacher, travelled extensively and then lived a quiet retirement in Kent. She never revisited China, never talked about what she had seen there, and died in Canterbury in 1987.*

1987.

The shivers rippled harder through me.

But it was definitely 1988 that I was in Shanghai. I knew from the date of Dad's death. Maybe the author of the book had got her dates wrong.

But even as I sat down to write her an email to

check, I knew neither she – nor I – were mistaken.

And look at me now, the old lady had said. *I'm just a pale revenant – come back for one last look.*

She hadn't been making a play on words.

She had been telling the truth.

And so am I.

Q AND A WITH JULIAN SEDGWICK

**1. I love the atmosphere of 1920's Shanghai and all
the detail about Chinese culture. How did you find
out everything you needed to know?**

I feel that I've been researching this book for about
thirty years – or more! My fascination with Chinese
culture started early in life – we were lucky when I was
young that there were great TV adaptations of Chinese
classic stories: from the magic and supernatural
elements of 'Monkey' to the heroic swordplay and
martial arts of 'The Water Margin'. Some of that
makes it through into *Ghosts of Shanghai*. Then at
university I studied Chinese, and a few fragments come
from that. But it was working as a researcher on a
couple of films set in Shanghai that I really developed
a love of the city's colourful past – particularly the
1920s and 1930s when Shanghai was the most exciting,

glamorous (and dangerous!) place you could hope to visit on the face of the earth.

But there was still a lot of work to do: I read a stack of books about the period, from exciting diaries of river boat captains on the Yangtze, to very dry academic books about the housing and economy. Sometimes an entire book yielded just one fact that made it into the story. I also spent a lot of time gazing at maps and street plans from the period (some of them huge!) and imagining myself as Ruby running along those streets and alleyways.

By the end of work there were forty or fifty books in my research pile. And I was lucky to find a long Russian documentary of the city filmed in 1926 that was invaluable. Then all I had to do was work out which facts were ESSENTIAL to telling the story . . . (See below!)

2. What was the most exciting thing you discovered? And how did you choose the locations?

The most thrilling discovery (early on) was to read how freely *some* Western children lived amongst all the colour and danger of the city: a gift for a children's book. And when I found the gem of a fact that coffins used to move in the soft, silty earth under Shanghai, I knew I had discovered a key image for the whole story: restlessness.

For the specific locations, I gazed at hundreds of photos from the period – and let my mind drift. The ones I wanted to explore more became key places for the story. From the very start I knew I needed Ruby and her gang to have a lair – a special place they considered their own private world. The image of the tumble-down temple was in my head from day one, and I knew it would frame the very first and last scenes.

3. In the beginning of *Return to the City of Ghosts* there is a young man, a student of Chinese, who listens intently to Ruby's extraordinary story. Is that young man real? I wondered if he might be you!

He's sort of me – and sort of not me. He is me *emotionally* – I did see my dad's ghost about a year after he died, and I had a difficult start to early adult life. But although I studied Chinese at university like the young man, I never went to the country as a student. After a year and a half of Chinese I had a bit of a breakdown and had to start again, studying something less demanding (Philosophy!). It's fun to explore different versions of yourself when you write.

4. Do you believe in the Supernatural. In Shanghai Ruby's own words: 'Do you believe in ghosts, young man?'

I don't know. The more we learn about the world the more we find out what we don't yet know. Although I have seen and heard a few things that might be described as ghosts, I reckon there's always an explanation – often in the mind of the person who sees and hears them. Or a weird physical cause. That said, after talking about the book, people often come and tell me incredible stories that make my skin bump all over like Ruby's. I'll keep an open mind. It's more fun for one thing.

5. Ruby is a great character. She is fierce, brave and cares about her friends. What do you think is the most difficult thing about writing characters from the opposite sex?

This might sound like a strange answer but when I'm writing well I don't see or notice myself at all. I hear the character talking and thinking, and I trust that. (And I'm lucky to have always had very close female friends, and in my work as a therapist have listened to a lot of women discuss their younger selves!) Of course there are dangers to writing about other lives of any kind: not just gender, but cultural, historical etc.

The interesting thing about *Ghosts of Shanghai* is that early versions of the series featured a boy protagonist – and I just couldn't make them work. As soon as I made my central character a girl, the book started to fly. In the end, the story determines who your hero or heroine is.

6. Do you hide any secrets in your books that only a few people will find?
Loads! Just for the fun of it. I hide friends as themselves or as slightly changed versions of themselves, my own experiences, important names and numbers, and references to places I've been. They're not vital to the plot, but when a friend reads about an experience we shared, or a place we visited, I hope that gives them a special added bit of fun.

7. What was the hardest scene to write in *Ghosts of Shanghai*?
The first chapter! There was so much I had to do – and wanted to do – to set the scene. It took about three years to work out exactly what information about Shanghai and China in 1926 I needed to give in order to set up Ruby's world and adventure. I had about a hundred facts I was desperate to share, but had to whittle them down and then make sure that

they didn't overshadow my central character. There must be at least twenty versions of the opening in folders in my study . . .

8. Both *The Mysterium* and the *Ghosts of Shanghai* trilogies are full of alternative worlds, outsiders and people who feel they don't fit. I'm curious – where does your interest in the 'Other' come from?

That's a very good question. I have *always* looked to other cultures and people leading non-typical lives for inspiration: all the way from circus performers to Zen Buddhist monks. At first I think this was partly to do with escape – aged 11 and 12 I was having a very disturbing and difficult time at school. By looking to people and places that were totally different to my own life I could find a good place to live in my imagination – and imagine having those skills that would make me stronger back in the 'Real Blasted World' (as Ruby's dad calls it).

Gradually I realised that it's really important to look at people and cultures and times that are different from our own experience: it's fascinating for one thing, and it makes our lives 'bigger'. And it helps us see how our own world could be different, or better. (Or worse!)

All my central characters feel somewhat like misfits. Most people feel that at one time or other in their lives, and I think it's important – and hopefully useful – to weave stories about people finding their place in the world.

ACKNOWLEDGEMENTS

Heartfelt thanks first to Jon Appleton for guiding Ruby throughout her journey. His insight and patience have made each book in the trilogy far better than it would have been. And to Sarah Lambert and Ruth Girmatsion at Hodder Children's Books for seeing that young Ruby did get to make it to a decent old age and complete her story! My gratitude also to the rest of the staff at HCB, and in particular to Michelle Brackenborough for giving my heroine such elegant covers. And for the *Ghosts of Shanghai* trailer, thanks to Prosper Unger-Hamilton for superb animation and Alice Sedgwick for being Ruby's voice.

I want to also say *xie xie* to all those teachers and friends whose conversations about Old Shanghai and China over the years helped to shape these 'strange tales': in particular Charlotte Ashby, Phil Agland,

Lindi Harman and Yoshio Kanamaru. Thanks to John Moffett at the Needham Research Institute who makes a ghostly appearance of sorts towards the end of the story, and to Emily McMullen and Alison Binney who gave me invaluable help and real-world inspiration.

Deep gratitude as ever to my special agent Kirsty McLachlan for guidance and reassurance.

And to all the librarians, booksellers and teachers who have supported the series and associated events. It is much appreciated and you know who you are. A very special nod though to Kate Goujon for being top-notch road crew for many of those visits.

Finally – and most importantly – love and thanks to my wife, Isabel, and to my wonderful sons, Joe and Will, who are a consistent fount of common sense, rock-solid support and good humour. I couldn't have done any of this without you.